STERLING

A CAROLINA REAPERS NOVEL

SAMANTHA WHISKEY

Crimson Covenant

A Modern-Day Fairytale Romance:

The Crown

The Throne

NOW AVAILABLE IN AUDIOBOOK!

Grinder
Enforcer
Winger
Rookie

Let the Seattle Sharks spice up your morning commute!

To the readers who stay up late

STERLING

"**G**ood to have you back, Sterling," Paul, one of the jacked security guards at the player entrance to Reaper Arena said as I made my way to the door. It had been a long year, but I was finally home.

"It's good to be back," I replied. "How are the kids?"

"Are you talking about my middle schoolers? Or that group of juvenile pranksters you like to call teammates?" He cocked his head to the side.

"That's them," I said, flashing a grin. With a wave, I disappeared into the arena.

God, I'd missed this place. Not that Bangor hadn't been awesome, but I was a Reaper through and through.

Before that expansion draft, I'd taken it for granted—being a part of a team I loved. Never again. I might not be able to control my future in its entirety, but as of last night, I had a five-year contract to play where I belonged, right here in Charleston, South Carolina.

"So the prodigal son returns," came a voice I knew all too well. Canon, one of the best forwards on the team, pushed off the wall across from the entrance to the locker room.

"I'm not sure I'd say prodigal," I responded with a shrug. "But I'm back."

An uncharacteristic smile broke across the guy's face, and he grabbed me into a quick hug with a less than subtle back slap before quickly releasing me.

I guess marriage could soften even the hardest of hard asses.

"Hey," a guy called out as he stuck his head through the locker room door. "Why the hell didn't I get a hug when I signed?"

The kid couldn't have been older than twenty-two, maybe twenty-three. He still had that slick shine that came standard with most rookie contracts and an undeserved ego.

"Because I don't fucking like you, Olson," Cannon snapped, folding his arms across his chest.

"For the last time, it's Thornton," the kid fired back.

"Still don't give a fuck." Cannon lifted his eyebrows.

A bigger player pushed Thornton out of the way, his familiar face lighting up as he saw me. "I thought I heard your voice out here!" Briggs pulled me into a hug, half-dressed for the ice. If we weren't careful, the atmosphere would slip into mushy territory. Not that I gave a shit. My heart was full, and my feet were so light I couldn't imagine anything bringing me down today—I was home.

"Signed last night," I said after the back slaps. "How many Reapers are here?" Gathering before preseason for a few pickup games was one of the things I'd missed in Maine.

Hell, I'd missed all my friends here, including Briggs, and I hadn't even known him as well as the others before I'd been caught up in the expansion draft.

"Enough to have some fun this afternoon," he answered. "Where's your gear?"

"In the car." I motioned behind me. "I have to sign one last thing with Silas, and then I'll grab it." There was a part of me that expected this deal to fall through at any moment. "What were you doing out here in the hall, anyway?" I asked Cannon. "Waiting for my smiling face?"

He snorted. "Hardly."

In what could only be fortuitous timing, the elevator doors opened down the hallway, and a tiny, waifish blonde stepped out, her eyes locking onto Cannon with a magnetism the two had always shared.

"Ahh, I see now." I grinned. "Hey, Persephone!"

"Jansen!" She waved, her smile lighting up the space and even bringing one to Cannon's face. The guy might have been a tatted-up giant, but damn if he wasn't wrapped around his wife's little finger.

After yet another hug welcoming me home, and a low growl that told me to keep my hands far, *far* above her waist, I stepped back, feeling better than ever.

"Are you headed up to Silas's office?" she asked as Cannon tucked her against his side.

"Yep." I nodded.

"Good. We just finished a meeting about the foundation, so I know he's up there waiting. Have you moved back into the village yet? Did you get your old house? Want to come over

3

for dinner this week?" She fired off each question before I had answered the previous one, which only made me smile. Persephone didn't just run the Reapers' charitable foundation, she was pretty much charity incarnate, always looking to put people at ease.

Cannon chuckled and pressed a kiss to the top of her head.

"I'm moving back tomorrow if the truck gets here with all my stuff on time, and no," I finished softly scratching the back of my neck. Another aspect I'd missed about the Reapers was the housing development just outside Charleston that the team owned. Most of the players lived there, contributing to the family atmosphere that I hadn't found in Maine. "Unfortunately, there were a couple of last-minute trades, and whoever signed his contract right before me got my old house."

Persephone's face fell. "Oh. Well, that's okay. You're still on the street, right?"

I nodded. "Right next door, actually. And yes, I'd love to come over for dinner." My phone buzzed in my back pocket, and I quickly turned off the alarm. "That's my five-minute warning. I'll catch you guys out there." I said my goodbyes and strode for the elevator. Asher Silas—the owner of the Reapers—had infinite patience for his players with the exception to a few small pet peeves. Being late was one of them.

I stepped into the elevator and hit the fifth floor. Silas's office was at the highest level of the arena, far above the coaches and admin. Even the escalators that carried fans up to their seats couldn't reach his domain.

"Hold the elevator, please!" Just as the elevator doors were closing, a slender hand reached through.

I stabbed the *door open* button and retreated to the back of the small space to make room for the woman who hurried in, her face hidden behind a veil of black hair. "Thank you," she said quickly, turning to the panel, but halting her finger just above the fifth floor. "Oh, you're going up, too, I see." Her shoulders rose and fell quickly, and her posture was ramrod straight.

"Sure am." I leaned back against the furthest wall and crossed one ankle over the other as the doors shut. A light, acoustic version of *Tonight* by Smashing Pumpkins drifted through the speakers as the doors closed and we began our ascent.

The markers above the door lit up with each floor we passed, and I kept my eyes glued to the little illuminated numbers and off the figure of the woman just ahead of me. Not that I hadn't immediately noticed a delicately curved waist that led to an incredible pair of hips under a navy blue sheath-style dress, but I liked to think that noticing was above *staring.*

She adjusted the file folders in her arms, and I was *noticing* again as we passed the third floor. I tried to drag my attention back to the numbers, but those hips led to an ass that made my mouth water, and then mile-long legs that ended in the sexiest high heels I'd ever seen. The blue pumps—at least that's what I thought they were called—had red soles and must have given her petite frame a five-inch boost.

How the fuck did women *walk* in those things?

The file she'd braced on her hip slipped, sending papers fluttering to the floor as the number four lit up, and I immediately dropped down to help her.

"Oh, that's not necessary," she said, her voice light and breathless, but her trembling fingers told me it most definitely was.

"I don't mi—"

She turned slightly, and her hair fell away as our eyes met.

Holy fucking shitballs of fire. The world stopped at the sight of those crystal blue eyes. Crystal wasn't even the right term. I'd only seen that color once—back a couple of years ago when I'd volunteered to help Axel with his summer camp back in Sweden. Her eyes were the exact color of the glacier he'd made me hike to.

Thank God the captain of the Reapers didn't take no for an answer, otherwise I never would have known what to call that shade of blue she was rocking, but there it was. She had bright, glacier-blue eyes...and the world. Fucking. Stopped.

She gasped, as though she'd felt the earth shift too, like I wasn't the only one experiencing whatever connection this was between us. Fuck me, she was breathtakingly beautiful, her features as dainty as she was. All except those eyes. Those were huge and so damned gorgeous I only noticed something was really wrong when they disappeared.

The elevator had gone black.

She cried out, the sound breaking something deep in my chest, and I instinctively reached for her, grasping her small shoulders to keep her from tumbling over on those impossibly high heels that I could no longer see.

I would have laughed if I couldn't feel the panic tensing her muscles into bricks. The world hadn't stopped, but the elevator had. *Talk about some fucking timing.*

"It's okay," I said softly. "The backup should—" The lights came back on, but only a fraction as bright as usual. "There we go."

Her shoulders began to quiver, and her eyes widened, staring at me in abject horror.

"I'm sure it's nothing," I assured her like I fucking knew.

She nodded slowly, her entire body shaking.

"Why don't we sit you down?" I suggested.

She nodded again, and I tightened my grip slightly, taking her weight so she could lower herself to the floor without falling straight on her ass. "S-s-sorry. I don't do small spaces," she whispered. "Are we stuck?"

Claustrophobic. This had to be her worst nightmare. "I'm sure it's just a hiccup," I said, keeping my voice as soothing as possible. "I'm Jansen, by the way." Hell, I couldn't remember the last time I'd introduced myself by my first name, but there it was.

She blinked rapidly, swallowing before she took a steadying breath. "Sterling?" she guessed.

"That's me." I slipped my cell from my back pocket, before crouching in front of her. "I'm guessing you must work for the Reapers seeing that you're headed up to Silas's little treehouse."

A smile tugged at her lips. "Treehouse?"

"His office is on the highest floor, accessible by only two elevators, one of which only he has the key to, so I feel pretty safe about calling it a treehouse." I grinned, hoping it would put her at ease.

"I never. Thought of it. That way." Her breaths were coming faster.

Shit, she was going to hyperventilate.

7

"How about I call and see what's going on?" I said as I quickly scrolled through my contacts and hit the button for Langley's phone. The Reapers' publicist—who was also Axel's wife—was always chained to the damn thing, so I knew she'd pick up.

"Hello? Shit," she muttered, followed by the sound of something shuffling.

"Langley, it's Sterling."

"Hey! Look, I'm glad you're back, but we just had a power outage—"

"Right, and I'm stuck in the elevator with…" I looked at the blue-eyed woman and lifted my brows.

"London," she answered.

"London," I repeated, loving the way her name curled around my tongue.

"Well. Shit. Hold on."

There was another shuffling sound like she'd covered the mouthpiece, and her words became muffled.

London closed her eyes and started to focus on her breathing. In through her nose and out through her mouth. She might be terrified, but I had to give her all the credit in the world for managing what she could.

"Okay, Sterling, you there?" Langley asked through the phone.

"Yep, if you consider *here* somewhere between the fourth and fifth floor."

"Okay, the building manager says the power is coming back right—"

The lights flared to life, brightening to their full level. "Now," I finished Langley's sentence, breathing in a sigh of relief.

"Thank God," London whispered, scurrying toward the panel of buttons and pressing the fifth floor.

Nothing happened.

Fuck.

London stabbed the buttons for every single floor, but we weren't budging. "This is not happening!" she shouted, pushing them all again.

"Right, so we're still stuck," I said to Langley, my chest clenching at how trapped London had to be feeling.

"Awesome. Okay. I'm on it. We'll get you out of there as quickly as possible. The south elevator, yes?"

"That's the one." I hung up with Langley and slid my phone back into my pocket. "They're sending someone to help."

London leaned back against the wall, then slid down it, slumping in defeat. "We're stuck in here." She stared at the closed doors, her eyes unfocused and her breathing shallow.

"What can I do to help you?" I leaned back, letting my ass hit the floor and bracing my elbows on my raised knees.

"Um. Talk to me, I guess?"

"I can do that." *Happily.*

She blinked those glacier-blue eyes at me and sucked in a breath. "I'm not crazy."

"I would *never* even think of using that word," I assured her.

"I just have a small—" She winced. "Okay, a *large* problem with claustrophobia. I fucking hate elevators."

9

"So distract you?" I offered.

"Distraction is good." She tucked her hair behind her ears and nodded. "Incredibly long story short, I got myself locked in a *really* small tornado shelter as a kid during a game of hide and seek. The bad news? I was alone, and it took my brother almost twenty-four hours to find me."

My stomach plummeted. "And there's good news?" I asked incredulously.

The corners of her mouth tweaked upward. "I won the game."

I laughed, the sound filling our little corner of the world and earning me a full, but shaky smile out of London. "Well done, but I can definitely see how that would lead to some claustrophobia."

"It's something I've been working on ever since," she admitted, dropping her forehead to her raised knees and breathing deeply. "Tell me something you're scared of."

"Hmm." I moved so I sat beside her, our shoulders touching so her body would register that she wasn't alone. Normally I would have given her some sarcastic answer, but this wasn't exactly a normal situation. "I'm not scared of too much, honestly. Except maybe disappointing my mom. She gave up everything to raise me and did it on her own."

She lifted her head, clearly surprised. "Really?"

"If you knew my mother, you wouldn't look so surprised. She's pretty much a cat five hurricane when she's pissed. Stubborn as hell, too. And it's not like she had any help from my father since he'd hidden the fact that he was already married when he knocked her up." That was the lightest version of events I was willing to divulge to a near stranger.

The truth was that my sperm donor of a father was a Grade-A asshole…and one of the best goalies the world had ever seen. Sergei Zolotov was a legend, not only here in the NHL, but in Russia, where he was born, and probably still lived with his perfect wife and two of his perfect kids. The third kid, who was no more than three months older than I was, currently played for Las Vegas. We'd crossed paths exactly seventeen times, and only on the ice. He'd never once gotten a shot past my glove and never would. Fuck him.

I had never once uttered the Zolotov name out loud, and thought about that family the least amount possible. My parentage might be one of the best-kept secrets in the NHL, but for all intents and purposes, I was a Sterling, just like my mother and grandparents. The other half of the family tree could rot off for all I cared.

London looked at me like she was reevaluating, her black, delicate brows knitting.

"What?" I asked, my voice coming out all scratchy. Shit, the woman even smelled incredible. She wore just the right amount of perfume, and I wanted to slide my nose along the slender line of her neck and breathe in.

"You're just…" She shook her head. "Not how I pictured you." She nibbled on her lower lip.

"You've pictured me?" I kept my eyes locked on hers, instead of staring at that plump bit of flesh she tortured with her teeth. There had to be a halo waiting for me somewhere. I couldn't remember the last time I'd been attracted to a woman and not made a move, not that this was exactly a move-making situation here.

"No!" She did that adorable blinking thing again, and her cheeks flushed with color. "I mean, I'm the new game day

11

coordinator for the Reapers, so when the news came down yesterday that you'd signed, I looked you up, of course." She swallowed like there was more to the story than she was willing to share.

"Right. You have me at a disadvantage there," I teased. "If I'd known you were signed to the Reapers, I definitely would have looked you up." A grin spread across my face.

She snorted and rolled her eyes, but hey, she was breathing slower now. "Do you flirt with every woman you meet?"

"Only the ones I'm stuck in elevators with." That was a lie. I'd done more than my fair share of flirting and fucking when I'd joined the NHL, but I'd slowed that second part down in the last year. Nameless hookups after random games were getting old. "And in my defense, you did say I could distract you." My grin widened.

She rolled her eyes again. "Why is it men think that sex is the answer to every question?"

My dick twitched at the word *sex*, but I ignored the horny fucker. "Not every question. Just the right ones."

Her gaze flickered to my mouth before she huffed and looked away. "Not in my experience."

"Then you're answering the *wrong* questions," I teased.

She swallowed, her breathing picking up again as she stared at the opposite walls. "What is. Taking them so. Long?"

"At least look at me if you're going to complain about being stuck with me," I joked, hoping my tone carried through even as worry settled in my gut like a stone. She'd done better while focused on me and not our surroundings, and it wasn't like I could guarantee when we'd get out of here.

"It's not you I'm complaining about," she blurted, her eyes locking on mine. Now that rosy little blush was creeping down her neck. "There are very few women in the world who would complain about being in a confined space with Jansen Sterling."

"True. It's usually me kicking them out of the confined space that leads to the complaints," I teased.

She scoffed, her eyes dancing, losing a little of the panic. "You kick your girlfriends out? Nice."

"Hey." I grabbed at my heart like she'd wounded me. "I've never kicked a girlfriend out in my life. Scout's honor."

Her eyes narrowed in mischief. "Because you've never had a girlfriend?"

I laughed again. "I guess you really did look me up."

"Please. As if I care who the players sleep with. I know the important stuff." She fidgeted with her bracelet, keeping her hands busy.

"And what's the important stuff?" I challenged, hearing movement above us and keeping it to myself. Who the hell knew how long it would take them to get us out. Drawing her attention back to the fact that we were stuck in a small box wasn't going to help her out.

"Your stats, of course," she fired back. "You're Jansen Sterling. Twenty-six years old. Six-foot-three inches tall. You have a ninety-three percent save average, which has only gotten better with your year in Bangor. You have endorsements from Bauer and Gatorade and prefer your charity work to be done with the Big Brother program. You were the second most popular player in Bangor when it came to meet and greet requests, and you generally agreed to them all. Am I missing anything?" She cocked her head to the side and lifted a single brow.

"I think I'm in love with you." I grinned.

"Oh, please. Every staff member on this team can rattle off player stats." She shook her head, but now that flush had crept to her collarbone.

Not under pressure like this, they can't. I kept that shit to myself. "Tell me you don't have a boyfriend."

It slipped out.

Smooth, jackass. Very smooth.

Her mouth dropped open for a few seconds before she snapped it shut. "No. I don't. Not that it's any of your business."

I was about to fucking make it my business because this woman here was the total package. She wasn't just gorgeous, she was smart, sharp-tongued, and was holding her own under circumstances that would test people who *didn't* have claustrophobia. If I knew all that about her in the few minutes we'd been stuck here together, I couldn't wait to learn more.

"No boyfriend. Excellent. How exactly does a guy go about getting a date with you?" I asked. Holding back had never been in my nature, and I wasn't about to start now.

Her eyes narrowed slightly as she studied me carefully. "Guys like you don't date girls like me."

"On that, we can agree."

"Seriously?" Her voice rose.

"Seriously. You're way out of my league." I leaned toward her slightly but didn't invade her space.

Her lips parted and stayed that way as she stared at me in disbelief.

"I'm serious. How do I get you on a date?" My voice lowered.

"Well…asking is usually the first step," she whispered, tilting her head up.

My chest clenched as I lowered—

A screeching, metal-on-metal sound made both our heads snap toward the door. The tip of a crowbar appeared, and the doors opened a few inches. "Are you guys okay?" a voice called in.

Silas.

"We're okay," I answered for us both.

"Hold tight for a second," he instructed in that no-nonsense voice of his. "Get a good grip," he said, but it didn't sound like he was talking to us.

Multiple pairs of hands appeared at the edges of the elevator doors, and I helped London to her feet.

"One, two, three!" Silas counted out, and the doors opened to the sound of a collective grunt, giving us about three-and-a-half feet of daylight at my collarbone. It was just as I'd suspected—we weren't quite at the fifth floor, but it was far better than I'd feared.

Silas crouched down, his shirtsleeves rolled to his elbows, but still wearing the vest of his three-piece suit. "Damn. Jansen, London, you guys ready to get out of there?"

"She goes first," I stated, just in case anyone debated.

She shot me a thankful look, then gathered up her files and headed for the door only to look up at the opening that was well above her head and curse.

"Can I lift you out?" I asked, already moving behind her.

"Please." There was a slight crack in her voice as she tossed her files up through the doorway.

Work apparently came first with this woman. *Noted*.

Silas reached in for her, and for the first time since I'd signed with the Reapers my rookie year, I noticed just how fit the guy was. *Good, he'll be able to lift her.*

"Give me your hands, London," Silas ordered.

She lifted her arms, and I gripped her hips, noticing everything *except* the way her motion lifted the hemline of her dress. Nope, I kept my eyes locked on Silas like the good guy I was trying desperately to be.

Then I lifted London straight up. She weighed next to nothing, and the heat of her skin blazed through that dress, warming my hands in the few seconds it took Silas to get a good grip on her.

"I've got you," he promised, so I knew he did.

Silas didn't break promises.

He pulled her out of the elevator, and then Axel helped me out and into the hallway of Silas's private suite of offices.

I gained my feet as London leaned back against the wall, sucking in lungfuls of air as if the reality of it took this long to hit her in full.

"The others are on their way up," I heard Silas say to some of the others who had helped pry open the doors.

16

"We didn't all fit in the first load," Cannon said, rolling his shoulders back. "Only your elevator was broken."

"Thank you," I replied.

Sawyer, the other Reaper goalie, clapped my shoulder as I nodded at him, walking straight toward London. I needed to make sure she was really okay.

The private elevator dinged, and three other Reapers walked into the hallway. The first two were rookies I barely recognized but the third—

My stomach dropped all five floors to the fucking basement.

"No fucking way," Cannon muttered, coming to my side. He was the only one in this hallway who knew, and that was only because he'd been there that night.

"London?" The guy's eyes frantically searched the hallway.

"Maxim!" she cried, wrapping her arms around herself and walking straight into his goddamn arms like she'd been there a thousand times.

He pulled her in and held her tight, his eyes closing in... relief? Yep, that was relief as he ushered her into one of the many conference rooms that looked out over Charleston, taking her out of my line of sight.

What the hell was he to her? What the hell was he doing *here*?

Axel's brow furrowed as he looked over at me. "I'm not sure what you mean."

Guess I'd said that out loud.

Silas turned toward us, putting his hands in his pockets. "I just signed him yesterday. Right before you, in fact," he told me like it wasn't the most explosive shit to ever rock my world. "Paid a pretty penny, too. And yeah, I've heard he's an asshole to work with, but we needed some strength on that left wing since Lukas retired last season."

That. Fucking. Prick. Was. On. My. Team. He was in my arena, with his hands all over *my* girl. The logic in me retreated from the argument that she wasn't exactly mine.

"No." I shook my head.

"Oh, shit," Cannon muttered next to me. "Let's get you out of here."

Every muscle in my body vibrated with barely restrained violence. "You signed him."

"Was that Maxim Zolotov?" Axel asked, glancing between me and where my stare was currently burning holes in the conference room doorway.

"Yep," Cannon answered.

"Anyone want to clue me in here?" Silas asked.

"Holy shit," Sawyer muttered. "You move just like him, especially glove-side. How didn't I see that?"

"I am nothing like him!" I snapped.

Sawyer's hands shot up like he was under arrest.

"Someone tell me what the fuck is going on!" Silas demanded.

The hallway fell silent, but even the quiet couldn't help my thoughts wrap around this dumpster fire. He'd already consumed the family I'd been given by biology, and now the fucker was moving in on the family I'd chosen? *No. No. No.*

"I think you signed his brother," Sawyer said slowly.

"Shut up," Cannon barked toward our friend.

"He's not my fucking brother!" I growled. Fuck biology.

Silas tensed, taking in the information at the genius rate the tech guru was known for. "Your birth certificate says unknown," he said softly, moving directly in front of me. "Are you telling me that Sergei Zolotov is your biological father?"

I nodded once and once only because Silas was the only person who could solve this shitstorm of a problem.

"So Maxim Zolotov..." Silas studied me, no doubt choosing his words or lack thereof carefully.

I nodded again.

"Holy shit," someone mumbled as the subject of my worst nightmare walked out of the office with his phone on his ear, his eyes flaring in shock as our eyes locked.

Guess the secret was out now.

"Okay, let's see how we can make this work," Silas started.

I looked him square in the eye. "Let me out of my contract."

All hell broke loose.

19

2

LONDON

No way. There was no way...and yet there he was. Jansen freaking Sterling, sitting in the booth next to my best friend's...well, the love of her life. Despite the two being split up at the moment.

I wasn't sure who I was more shocked to see—Jansen or Hendrix, who had just been traded from his NFL team in North Carolina to Charleston, yet there I was, walking toward both of them.

"You know London?" Sterling asked, his eyes widening.

"He sure does," I said, stopping next to Sterling and tucking my hair behind my ears. "How are you, Hendrix?"

Jansen paled, glancing past me to the bar, where my brother sat with Maxim. "Oh, God, tell me you didn't—"

Did he seriously think just because I'd walked in with Maxim I was *with* him?

"Didn't what, Jansen Sterling?" I cut him off, glaring at him. "Didn't sleep with him? I mean, that's where your thoughts jumped to, right?"

Jansen opened and closed his mouth a few times, but said nothing.

Smart of him.

"Boys." I rolled my eyes. "First, if I decided to sleep with Hollywood over here, that would be my business. Not yours. Second, no, I have not slept with Hendrix, though I can admit he's been naked in my apartment more than a few times." I fashioned Jansen with a smirk. Let him chew on that. If he wanted to ghost me because of Maxim—

"Her roommate," Hendrix hurried to say, drawing me out of my thoughts. "How is sweet little Savannah?" he asked, and my heart softened a bit. The two were perfect for each other, they just really...*really* needed to work out their issues.

"Miserable," I snapped. "How the hell do you think she is with you down here in Charleston?"

"Seems to me she got everything she wanted," Hendrix said.

"Wait a second, Caz is your brother?" Jansen's gaze snapped from Caz to me and back again. "How the hell did I not put that together?"

"Damn, Hollywood!" I exclaimed. "You've been in town all of three seconds and already outed me?"

"Didn't realize you were keeping it a secret." Hendrix cringed.

"Yes, Caspian is my brother, which again," I said, my gaze swinging back to Jansen, "is none of your business." Because if he truly wanted to know any of these details—which I would've freely given him—he wouldn't have ignored my attempts to reach out after the elevator.

"But it's Maxim's?" Jansen retorted as he stood. I had to crane my neck to meet his gaze.

"Seriously?" I lifted my chin. "The next time you want to act all pissy that I show up with Maxim, remind yourself that you could have asked first." I'd given him every opportunity, and he was pushing me away over something I barely understood.

A muscle ticked in Jansen's jaw. "Fine. I will."

Guess what? He didn't.

* * *

"Were you *sitting* on this juicy intel?" Langley Pierce placed her palms on the mahogany that separated us, her dark brown eyes practically glowing.

"No," I said, slightly flabbergasted. "I just figured you knew."

"Axel doesn't really talk about the guys' private business."

It had been a month since everyone had found out about Maxim and Jansen being biological brothers, but we were all still reeling.

I *should've* known.

Maxim Zolotov had been my brother Caspian's best friend for years. And for the past two, I'd seen more than plenty of him since he tagged along with Caspian on breaks versus going home to Minnesota. We'd become friendly, as one does when your brother and his friend are constantly raiding your fridge on visits.

Maxim never *once* mentioned that Jansen fucking Sterling was his brother. Sure, he'd talked about Sterling being an asshole, but not in a brotherly way.

Jansen, the same man whose scent had filled that elevator—all rugged and invigorating with hints of mandarin and sage. God, that memory—being stuck in the elevator with him—both haunted and excited me, if that was possible. The walls had threatened to close in, to suffocate me. I'd been close to choking on my own panic, and I likely would have if he hadn't properly distracted me. Heat flushed over my skin at the memory of his teasing words, his scent, the way electricity had crackled in those small inches between us.

"Interesting," Langley said, glancing at Persephone Price with a secret look I couldn't decipher. The petite blonde looked like a fairytale Barbie, definitely not someone I'd picture as Cannon freaking Price's wife. The guy was ruthless on the ice and grumbly off of it.

Though, to be fair, I wouldn't go anywhere near Langley's Viking of a husband either. These women had serious guts to be able to wrangle those two. Either way, it was only my first month on the job, and while they'd been more than welcoming, we hadn't reached the stage of silent conversations yet.

I really hoped I earned the chance to make it to that level.

Being a game day event coordinator was an all-time high, and doing it for the Reapers? One of the hottest NHL teams to take the ice? Beyond a dream come true, even if my brother had been traded to the team I now worked for. I swear Caspian was more overprotective than our parents, and I had thought graduating college would give me some distance to stand on my own. Him being on the team...well, that was a problem for later. Right now...

"But you have a history with them, right?" Persephone asked from where she leaned against the wall in Langley's office.

"Maxim is Caz's best friend. I've known him for around two years. And Sterling..." Another warm shiver danced over my skin as our heated argument at Scythe last week raced through my mind.

"I only recently met Sterling," I finally answered Langley.

Langley nodded, settling into the leather chair behind her desk. "This could be a great angle," she said, the gears churning behind her eyes. "As you know, this year's main charity organization is Ronald McDonald House. We've been mapping out strategies to ensure we uphold their family-oriented mission statement and how the Reapers can represent that image off the ice. Having brothers on the team and running promo spots to showcase that would go a long way to showing the nation what the Carolina Reapers truly stand for."

"They didn't look like the kind of brothers that knock back beers on Saturdays," Persephone said, gracefully taking a seat in the empty chair next to mine.

I barely held back a laugh. Whenever they were within ten feet of each other, they looked one wrong *blink* away from an eruption. And Sterling wasn't the asshole Maxim had said he was. "That's an understatement."

"Everyone has family drama," Langley said, waving us off. "This is a business. I want us to earn a ton of donations for Ronald McDonald House this season. If highlighting the famous brothers loosens investors' pockets, then it's a win."

I nodded, seeing her point. I couldn't help but admire her— she was practically a legend in the public relations game. And even though I wasn't gunning for her job, I *was* gunning for her approval. And I wasn't the only one. Asher Silas had hired *two* game day event coordinators, and only one of us would be kept on for next season. Sean Cook was straight out of college just like me, but without the familial ties to the industry. Having Langley's approval at the end of this season would go a long way in Silas' eyes, especially when I proved my worth without my brother's name attached to mine. Which I *would* do.

"Do you think you could get them to cooperate for promo spots?" She asked me, and I blinked a few times, wondering if she'd intended the question for Persephone.

"Me?"

Langley laughed. "You know them better than we do," she said, motioning to Persephone.

"Sterling was traded before I got a proper chance to truly know him," Persephone said. "But I know Cannon is so thrilled he's back."

"Can you do it?" Langley asked, and the weight of the question punched me in the chest. The panic was nothing like when I'd been trapped in that elevator, or any other small, confined space. That panic was ice-cold and debilitating. *This* panic? It crackled with an adrenaline-fueled challenge.

Because that's what this was.

A massive, fuck-all of a challenge.

Getting two brothers who *hated* each other to smile pretty for the camera? Locking myself in a closet seemed an easier feat.

"I'll make it happen," I said, hoping like hell I was telling the truth.

Langley and Persephone smiled at me before they shared another silent, secret look.

"Good," Langley said. "Keep me posted on your progress with them."

I nodded and pushed back from my chair, heading toward her door. She'd given me a chance to prove myself as the new employee on the docket, and I sure as hell wasn't about to let her down.

Even if it meant I had to tie the brothers together and yank their asses into submission, I would.

I suppressed another laugh as I headed out of the arena. The idea of willing either of those hulking, delicious men into submission was ridiculous enough to have my head spinning.

I was so screwed.

* * *

"Caz?" I called as I pushed opened the unlocked front door to his brand-new home in Reaper Village. Had to hand it to Silas, the man was a business genius. And herding his players into one easily monitored yet secluded location? Totally brilliant. Not only did it boost morale for the team, it gave them a sense of privacy in a world desperate to expose them. And since my big brother was one of those celebrity athletes subject to stalkers, overzealous puck bunnies, and blood-thirsty paparazzi, I was super grateful for it.

"Back here!" Caspian hollered, and I walked down the hallway, dodging unpacked boxes until I ended up in the kitchen.

26

The space was all clean white cabinets, stainless steel appliances, and a giant marble island in the middle.

The same marble island that Maxim Zolotov leaned against.

"What are you doing here, sis?" Caz asked as he unloaded groceries into his bare fridge. "And why didn't you bring those scone things with you?"

I huffed out a laugh, sitting my purse on the clean island. "One, I've barely settled into my apartment, let alone have time to bake for you." I shook my head. I loved my brother and often went out of my way to make his favorite treat—maple cinnamon scones—but I was here in a business capacity. "And two," I said, motioning to his glorious kitchen. "You have all the tools necessary to make them yourself now."

He glared at me in faux shock before returning his groceries.

"You didn't answer the first question," Maxim said, his strong arms folded over his chest as he looked down at me. He had that tiny lilt of an accent to his words, something I'd grown used to over the two years I'd known him.

I looked up at him, narrowing my gaze. "Whenever you talked about Sterling before, you said he was a selfish, playboy of an asshole. Why didn't you ever mention that he happened to be your brother?" Not that he owed me any explanation, he was my *brother's* best friend, not mine. We were friendly, sure, but not on a level where I deserved to know every detail of his life. But…why hide a brother?

"Did you ask him the same thing?" he asked, the hard line of his jaw popping just a fraction.

Oh, there was a nerve there. Well, I'd guessed that but *seeing* it was totally different. Not that Maxim didn't always look… intimidating. He did. The NHL shape—all muscles and

27

strength and dominance—didn't help, but there was something in his eyes. A kind of guarded anger that threatened to spill out any second. And mentioning Sterling as his brother? You'd think I'd called him an awful skater or something.

"I haven't spoken to Sterling yet," I said, not at all deterred by his sharp tone. I'd been around him and Caz long enough to hear more than my fair share of bro-vent sessions. "He's next on my list," I said. If I was being honest, I was delaying speaking to Jansen. Not only because of his reaction at Scythe, but because of the way he'd snuck into my thoughts on more than one occasion.

The idea of seeing him again? Catching that scent, staring into those crushing-blue eyes, peeking those whorls of black ink that teased above the collar of any shirt he wore? Warm shivers danced down my spine. I wanted to know where those tattoos led beneath the fabric—

"You put me first?" Maxim grinned. "I always knew you had a crush on me."

I rolled my eyes. His teasing was another thing I was used to. Sure, I knew the man's hockey stats, but that didn't mean I had a thing for him. "Funny," I said. "You're always mooching off my brother," I teased right back. "You were easy to find."

He smirked. "I'd be easy for *you*."

"Good," I fired back. "I need you to be easy."

"The fuck you say?" Caz snapped as he shut the fridge and spun around. He cocked a brow at his friend, but there was no real threat in his tone. He knew Maxim liked to mess with me. I think it was like a rite of passage to pick on your best friend's little sister.

"For my *work!*" I snapped at my brother, then looked to Maxim.

Maxim laughed, shaking his head.

"Seriously, Maxim," I said, softening my tone and totally ignoring my grumbling brother. He was the definition of cock-block, not that I had any interest in Maxim. Just, my brother being who he was, not many guys had the balls to pursue me. And even if they somehow made it past Caspian's wicked intimidating grill-sessions, they often couldn't stand the heat of the life. Which was fine. I'd had one relationship, and that was just about enough as far as I was concerned.

"Would it be possible for you to play nice with Sterling?" I asked. "Langley wants to do some family promos to highlight our sponsorship with the Ronald McDonald House this season. It would be super beneficial for the organization, the team, and our image."

All teasing left Maxim's eyes as he shrugged. "I'm a professional," he said. "I don't let anything stand in the way of the game. If it's good for the team, I'm in."

"Great," I said, sighing a little. One down—

"Don't expect Sterling to be as mature as me," he said.

I furrowed my brow. "Why didn't you ever mention him? Why is it such a secret—"

"Not much of a secret anymore," he cut me off. "Now that you and Langley want to parade us around—"

"Not what we're doing," I interrupted him and fashioned him with a glare for good measure. "This was me *asking*. I'm not threatening your contract if you don't comply."

He tipped his chin up.

So that was a plead-the-fifth on the brother questions. Got it.

"Okay," I said, blowing out a breath as I grabbed my purse. "This has been *super* fun." I glanced to Caz, who was in the middle of building a sandwich four slices of bread high, before returning to focus on Maxim. "Maxim, thank you for being a professional. I'll text you the details as soon as I know them." I spun on my heels, my heart hiccuping a little at the thought of my next obstacle—Sterling. A huge obstacle, since he'd done everything to avoid me since he'd seen me being *friendly* with Maxim.

"You can text me any time," Maxim called as I walked toward the front door, and I rolled my eyes.

I settled into my car, butterflies flapping in my stomach. Somehow I knew convincing Sterling to do anything with Maxim beyond throw punches would be ten times harder than it had been with Maxim. But the challenge sparked something in my blood…

Or it could be that I hadn't been able to *stop* thinking about Sterling since the night in the elevator. I quite possibly hated him for that reason alone—the last thing I needed right now was a distraction, but holy hockey Gods, Jansen Sterling was *the* distraction. All carved muscles, crushing blue eyes, and a smirk that promised pleasure. And he'd been so…sweet in the elevator. Not mocking my fear, but helping to disarm it. That alone would be enough to have me intrigued, but add to it his pure, primal vibe at *Scythe*? It was a terribly irresistible combination.

Getting him to agree to the promo spots might be impossible, but I couldn't deny how much I *wanted* to be the one to get him to agree.

I just had to hope like hell he'd listen.

3

STERLING

*T*he locker room hummed with the kind of palpable excitement that only existed during preseason. There was always an energy before a game, but it changed depending on our record and where we were in the season. If we were doing well and headed toward playoffs, it was a fierce, almost cocky atmosphere. If we were playing like shit, there was always a bitter tang of desperation in the air. But preseason? That shit was magic. Anything was possible.

We had yet to find out who we were as a team or whether our individual talents might be swallowed up by massive egos or welded together in a united purpose.

For the last few weeks, we'd been practicing, and it wasn't like I didn't know the lines or couldn't remember how to depend on Nathan or Hudson, but this wasn't the same team I'd left three years ago. There were two new rookies this year alone, and a lot had changed in the year the expansion draft had forced me to Bangor.

One of them, Hudson Porter sat on my left, putting on his gear.

"You're seriously considering retiring after this year?" I asked, pulling on my Under Armour shirt over my head.

Porter strapped on his shoulder pads over bare skin and nodded. "I love this game, but it's about that time. Kills me to admit it, but the bruises last longer. The injuries don't heal as fast, and well, the twins are almost two. I'd like to see them grow up in person as opposed to Facetime, and Elliot is fifteen." He shook his head. "I only have a few years left with her before college. Time is passing."

"Yeah, I guess it is," I said quietly. Hudson was in his mid-thirties, and yeah, it was a reasonable deduction, but still a mindfuck to think about. One day we'd all be too old to play professionally.

"You starting today?" he asked, reaching for his elbow pads.

"Nawh. Sawyer's up today. I'm on tomorrow." There were no bitter feelings about the schedule, either. We were a team with two excellent goalies, and that was all that needed to be said about that.

You're weak glove side. You don't anticipate or react fast enough.

His words sliced through my brain, intruding on the real estate I'd worked my ass off to take back from him. My father had seen me play a total of one time, and that was all he'd had to say when he'd ambushed after the game two years ago. Luckily, Cannon had been at my side, which had only served to remind me that blood didn't make family.

But as much as I'd wished I could say that little encounter hadn't affected me, it had. I'd spent the last two years honing my weak spots, focusing glove side.

With perfect timing, Maxim sailed through the door, bobbing his head to something in his ear pods, then took the seat directly across the room. As if it wasn't bad enough that I had to stare at a locker with a Zolotov jersey hanging from it, the fucker looked just like our father. Same cheekbones and chin, same arrogant stare that came out of the same dark blue eyes that we happened to share.

Genetics were a bitch.

"You okay?" Briggs took his seat next to me, brushing his hair out of his eyes.

"What's not to be okay about?" I brushed off what I could. Silas had refused to let me out of my contract, and to be honest, I didn't want to go. I wanted *him* to get the fuck out of my locker room, but that wasn't happening either.

"That's how you're going to play this?" Briggs glanced between Maxim and me, then stretched back for his gear.

I shrugged and grabbed my chest protector.

The door swung open, and Brogan "The Demon" Grant stalked through, wearing his typical, perpetual scowl as he walked straight to his spot.

"Glad to see he's still a ray of sunshine." I scoffed and slipped my pads over my head. Guy was fast, mean, and accurate as hell with his shot. He also kept to himself. Now whether that was by his choice or a result of his sparkling personality, I'd never know.

"He got arrested in a bar brawl last night," Briggs said under his breath, earning a quick look from both Hudson and myself. "It's all over that gossip site. They got pics of Silas bailing him out."

"Well, he earned that *Demon* nickname back in L.A. for a reason," I muttered. We all knew what it was—he had the temper from hell.

"I'm just saying that I've seen her around the arena, and she's fine as fuck," one of the rookies said from across the room.

Go figure it was the kid sitting next to Maxim, and yes, apparently I now defined twenty-two-year-olds as kids, even though I was only a few years older.

"You're just lucky Caz is in the bathroom," Maxim said with a scoff. "He'd beat your ass for talking about his sister like that."

London. I nearly groaned at just the mention of her name. It had been almost a month since we'd been trapped in that elevator, and I'd avoided her like the fucking plague ever since. Had she known Maxim was my brother all that time? Had she sat there, listening to me say my mother had raised me on my own, knowing exactly *why*?

Was she with him?

That question sliced me open like a damned scalpel. Those eyes had been in my dreams almost every night since. Her voice was in my head. Her curves were branded on my fucking palms from helping her out of that elevator. Her number had also shown up on my phone about a dozen times in the last week. All were filed under *unanswered*.

She was the Reapers' newest game day coordinator. The only reason she had to be calling me was about Maxim, and fuck if I was talking about him with her.

He asked first. That's what she'd said that night at the bar when she'd shown up with her brother and the guy I shared some genes with. Shit still grated on me.

"You think Foster doesn't know his sister is hot?"

"As if you had a chance anyway," the kid out of Boston—McKittrick—said, shaking his head at the other one. Shit, I really needed to learn names.

"I would be all over that if Foster didn't keep her all locked up." The rookie grabbed his jersey—Greene—and put it on.

"Want to bet on it?" Maxim shook his head, yanking his pads on.

My fists curled. There was zero fucking chance he'd just said what I thought I heard.

"Sterling," Briggs muttered in warning.

"I'm up for a little wager," Greene said with a cocky smirk that sent me over the edge.

"You're fucking kidding me, right?" I said across the room, nailing them both with a glare.

Greene raised his eyebrows.

McKittrick winced and scooted a little farther down the bench, putting space between him and Greene.

"I'm sorry, were you in this conversation?" Maxim cocked his head to the side and looked me over like an insect that needed to be squashed.

"You can't just bet on a woman. This isn't some shitty teenage movie." I stood.

So did Maxim.

"Don't ever try and tell me what I can or cannot do, especially when it comes to London," he hissed through bared teeth.

35

"Guys," Hudson rose, rolling his shoulders back. He was known for throwing more than his share of punches on the ice.

"Relax. He's just pissed that I have a history with the woman he apparently…" He arched an eyebrow. "What? Developed a crush on in the elevator?"

My chest tightened, and my muscles coiled. His words were too close to the truth for comfort.

"That's it, isn't it?" Maxim grinned like the asshole he was. "You can't really blame London for preferring me, can you? After all, our own father chose me, and as for your mother—"

"Asshole!" I launched across the room and slammed my fist into his face with a satisfying crack.

His head snapped to the side for a second before he snarled and launched himself at me, throwing a punch of his own as he took me to the ground.

The first one connected with my mouth, and the coppery taste of blood splashed over my tongue before the pain of it even registered.

My chest protector made me bulky and slow, but I deflected his second punch and rolled, getting him beneath me as I sent a series of jabs into his ribs.

"Fucking hell!" a voice shouted to my right. Briggs?

"Sterling!" That was Axel.

"What the fuck?" Not sure who that was.

Maxim landed another punch, and fire exploded in my cheek, but I got him right in the fucking mouth before I felt hands tearing me off him and pulling me up. He hit me one last time, but it barely grazed my jaw as I was lifted away.

Maxim scrambled to his feet and came at me, but Foster and Axel had him by the arms before he could take a step.

Demon and Briggs had me by the biceps and shoulders. I wasn't going anywhere, even if I tried.

"Bastard." Maxim lunged forward, but Foster and Axel held firm.

"Max!" Foster snapped.

Briggs sucked in a breath, but I just grinned. "If the best you've got is throwing around medieval legal terms—"

"What the fuck just happened?" Coach McPherson stormed in from his office, putting himself between me and Maxim.

Maxim and I locked eyes, each daring to rat the other out, and both keeping our mouths shut.

"I'd say the cause is pretty obvious, Coach," Briggs remarked.

Coach's head swung both directions, studying both Maxim and me repeatedly before he cursed. "We have a game in less than an hour."

"That's pretty obvious, too, Coach." I said, earning me narrow-eyed glare from Coach.

"Guess Bangor didn't teach you any manners while you were up north, did they, Sterling? And to think, I actually missed you." He shook his head, and his jaw flexed before turning back to Maxim. "And is this really how you want to make a name for yourself, Zolotov? Coming into my house and starting shit? Because I've coached Sterling for a couple

37

years, so I'm pretty well acquainted with what it takes to prick his temper."

Maxim sneered but didn't correct Coach.

Huh.

"I threw the first punch, Coach," I admitted. "This one is on me."

"I got the last one in," Maxim retorted.

"Both of you shut the hell up," Coach snapped. "You're both out for this game."

My stomach hit the floor.

"You're fucking kidding me!" Maxim snarled.

"I'm not." Coach shook his head. "I'm not taking either of you out on the ice. Not like this. Get dressed. I'll see you both upstairs *after* the game."

Shit.

* * *

WE WON, according to the television screen in Persephone's office, where I'd watched the entire thing play out. It was close, five to four, and I knew it wouldn't have been if I'd kept my shit together in the locker room.

Sawyer was exhausted.

The planned lines were fucked without Maxim.

The sinking pit of a feeling growing in my stomach was some well-deserved shame.

A knock on the doorframe made me turn. Persephone stood in the doorway, offering me a kind smile. "You've been summoned to the headmaster's office," she said with a cringe, handing me a fresh ice pack for my busted lip.

"Silas?" I guessed, coming to my feet.

She shook her head and scrunched her nose. "Langley."

I sighed but nodded, following Cannon's wife to the Reapers' publicity office. Five minutes later, I sat across the small conference table from Maxim, who was glaring daggers at me as we waited for Langley.

"You hit like a girl," he growled, leaning forward.

"Nice ice pack." I motioned toward his cheek, where he held an identical compress to mine.

"Both of you shut the hell up," Coach growled, taking the seat at the foot of the table as the door shut. "I have no problem knocking your heads together."

"Now that everyone's here," Langley, the head of the Reapers' publicity staff, sang as she sank into the chair at the head of the small table.

London lowered herself into the chair between Langley and Maxim.

Our eyes met and held for a moment that was just long enough to stutter my heartbeat and steal the breath from my lungs.

Her suit was tailored to perfection and just as black as her hair, which only seemed to make her eyes stand out even more. Those strawberry lips parted, and she leaned in slightly.

"I don't know what happened in the locker room," Langley launched in, drumming her fingertips on the table. "And I honestly just don't care. But I do know that it can't happen again." Her lips pursed as she looked at Coach. "Sorry, did I just steal your thunder?"

"Feel free," he motioned her onward. "I plan to take it out of their asses during practice this week, so the floor is all yours."

"I can't even begin to tell you what a fucking nightmare you two have the potential to be if you don't pull your shit together," she leveled a stare on both Maxim and me. "And I'm not just talking about the scoreboard. That's not my department." A tiny smile tugged at her lips. "But I bet my husband is going to have plenty to say to you about that one, too."

Maxim sighed, letting his head fall back slightly.

At least I knew Axel…and Coach. Maxim was the outsider here.

"But if you think we're going to pull off any kind of family-centered promotion like we have planned…" She shook her head. "Just look at you!" She threw out her hands, pointing to each of us. "Black eyes and busted lips. How the hell are we supposed to bring in a photographer? Of all the unprofessional, immature antics to pull, a locker room brawl is right up there with a—"

"Bar?" I helped her along, knowing she was probably up to her elbows dealing with Brogan's arrest last night.

"Don't fucking start with me, Jansen. Not today. Not when I thought I could count on you to stand up not just for the Reapers—but for the Ronald McDonald House cause."

"Wait. What?" I leaned forward, bracing my elbows on the table."

"I told you he was going to be the problem." Maxim reached across the back of London's chair and rested his arm there.

Fucker.

"Right. Like I'm the problem." I threw my ice pack on the table.

"I'm sorry, what?"

"Put that ice back on your Armani ad face, you idiot." She pushed the ice pack toward me, and I took it, because it was Langley. Because as pissed as I was, she was my family. The Reapers were my family, not the smirking jackass across the table with his arm around my girl's chair.

Not. Your. Girl.

"It was only one Armani ad," I grumbled, wincing at the pressure against my lip.

"The promo shots are scheduled for this week!" she snapped. "And I *never* thought you would be the issue here. Maxim already agreed!"

Something was wrong. There was a loop here, and I wasn't in it. I wasn't even close to it.

London sank backward, and her lip was back between her teeth. "Right, about that—"

"I can't even get these two to behave in the locker room, let alone make it through a game, and you honestly think they're going to do some brotherly promo?" Coach rubbed the bridge of his nose.

"Brotherly *what*?" What the hell was he talking about?

"The photoshoot with you and Maxim? The whole brothers-on-the-same-team aspect of our public relations strategy—" Langley explained.

"I'm sorry." I went rigid and tried to remember that I wasn't just seeing red at the head of public relations, but my captain's wife. "On what planet do you think I'm going stand next to that asshole and declare that he's my brother?"

"You picked a fine time to tell us that, Jansen!"

"He already knew? I'm just hearing this for the first time!" I swiveled in my chair and threw the ice pack into the trash can. "And the last." I rose to my feet.

"The first..." Langley startled, her head swinging toward London.

London scrambled out of her chair and came around the table, gripping the sleeve of my hoodie. "Outside. Now."

"Or?" I challenged.

She looked up at me and swallowed, a flash of fear streaking through those glacier-blue eyes. "Please," she whispered.

I nodded. What the fuck else was I supposed to do when she looked at me like that?

She tugged me out of Langley's office and into the deserted hallway, then closed the door and marched me right into another office.

This one was small. Windowless. She took one, sweeping look and shuddered, yanking me back into the hallway, where she dropped my sleeve so she could pace.

I leaned back against the wall and folded my arms over my chest, doing my damnedest not to notice that the sexy little

42

black heels on her feet were the same height the others had been. *I bet she barely comes up to mid-chest on me when those things aren't on.*

"Are you going to tell me what the hell is going on?"

"I did something." She stopped right in front of me. A single step, maybe two, and she'd be right between my feet. "And you wouldn't pick up your phone, so I just went with it, and…" She sighed, then turned those blue eyes on me. "I need your help."

4

LONDON

"Jansen," I sighed his name as I tried and failed to collect the right words to explain myself to him.

Something deep inside me trembled at evidence of raw power rippling off of him—the slightly swollen cheek, the cracked lip. The way he'd slammed the ice pack down in the office moments ago, the look he'd given Maxim, all pain and rage.

It was absolutely stupid and reckless to even think *ask* this of him. To put myself in the middle of two thrashing beasts...

But I *had* to.

"Jansen," I said, more gently this time. He had *let* me drag him into the hallway, trailing behind me with an eerie sort of silence as I pulled on that muscled arm.

I gazed up and up at him, those dark blue eyes churning with barely leashed hate and pain. My fingers itched for more contact, to trace the hard line of his jaw, to smooth those

44

furrowed lines between his brow. A few blinks, and his emotions were replaced by cool calculation as he finally met my gaze.

"How deep does this issue with Maxim go?" I asked after a few moments of heated silence.

I asked that question instead of what I *needed* to ask him because part of me couldn't bring myself to admit what I'd done—that I'd already booked the brother promos and had tried constantly to speak with him about it for the past month. Granted, with how easily Maxim had agreed to the promos, I didn't think the hate ran this deep. But, after their locker room brawl, and the evidence on his face...God, I don't know what I'd gotten myself into.

The tension practically vibrated off him, his muscles bunched and flexed beneath the tight black Reapers T-shirt he wore.

He parted his lips a few times, then shut them.

I blew out a breath, shaking my head as the adrenaline tried to cool in my blood. "Why would you go after Maxim like that? Your own brother?" *Why did no one know until recently you were brothers? Why is there so much pain there?*

Something ice-cold flash in his gaze—shock and disappointment. "Figures you're worried about Maxim," he grumbled, and my concern quickly shifted to anger.

"I'm worried about *both* of you!" I snapped. And the truth in those words hit me in the chest. It wasn't just because of my job and that their cooperation depended on it—it was because of that look in Sterling's eyes...

It *bothered* me.

Like an itch I couldn't reach. I wanted to soothe that hurt I'd seen flash behind his eyes—not physical echoes from the brawl, but emotional. That pain radiating out of him before he'd had the sense to hide it from me. I *wanted* to know more so I could help him.

"You don't need to worry about me," he said, narrowing his gaze. "I don't start these things. *He* does. Maxim is the problem—"

"He's your brother," I cut him off, exasperated. How could two people bound by blood be so vicious with each other? "Can't you cut each other some slack?"

"You have *no* idea," he said, closing his eyes and taking a deep breath. "No clue."

"Then tell me," I said. "Explain it to me." He had no reason in the world to open up to me. Just because we'd shared a charged moment in an elevator didn't make us connected. But I couldn't help it—I *felt* connected to him. Like those moments together had solidified something in my heart that begged and ached for more.

More of Jansen.

More snarky teases and gentle questions.

More molten looks that turned my insides liquid.

Just more...

And maybe, if he could enlighten me on the situation, then I could talk to Langley and—

"That's none of your business." His words cut into my racing thoughts, and I inwardly recoiled.

But he was right.

It truly wasn't my business. Just because I'd developed this... feeling around him didn't mean he'd done the same for me.

Fine. Fair enough.

"Okay," I said, my stomach twisting as the confession rose on my tongue. "I honestly didn't realize how deep this went, and I'm sorry. But I'm going to put myself out there and *beg* a favor." He tilted his head, so I hurried on. "I've been trying to reach you for weeks to talk this out," I said, my breath shaking. "But you've ghosted me for some reason, and that's okay!" I spoke a little quicker when he looked like he might apologize. "I get it. Kind of. I'm not someone you want to pick up the phone for. But, if you would have, then I would've asked you weeks ago."

"Ask me what?"

He knew what. He had to after what Langley had said. He wanted to hear me *say* it.

"To agree to take part in these promos. The exposure will be so good for the family image we're going for—"

Jansen scoffed, cutting off my words. That anger returned sizzling in my chest. I cooled it, taking a deep breath. Yes, I had tried to contact him for a month. No, I hadn't realized how shitty the situation was. This was on me, not him. But still, he wasn't even hearing me out.

"What's it going to take for you to cooperate?" I popped my hip out, resting my hand there for good measure. If he was about to shut me down, then I wanted to at least appear strong enough to take the blow.

He tracked the move with a hawk-like gaze, the corner of his mouth ticking up into that smirk that drove me crazy.

"Why is it important to you that I get along with him?"

"You know why," I said. "Langley has left me in charge of the pair of you. The promo spots are incredibly important for this season's direction."

Sterling shook his head. "I think you should convince her to drop the idea."

"Give me a good enough reason, and maybe I will." I arched a brow at him, waiting.

He tilted his head. "You'd do that for me?" Was that hope in his eyes? "Or for Maxim?"

"Maxim has already agreed to be a professional. He's willing to set aside whatever this is between you two and do what's best for the team."

A muscle in his jaw flexed, those blue eyes turning hard as gemstones. "You already talked to him about it." It wasn't a question, he knew as much from the meeting prior.

"Yes," I said, the air suddenly tight in my lungs. Why did that feel like a betrayal? That'd I'd gone to Maxim first. "He was at my brother's house," I hurried to add, relieving some of the pain in my chest. "It wasn't hard to talk to him."

"But it's hard to talk to me?" He folded his arms over his massive chest. "You didn't have too hard a time in that elevator." His eyes trailed the length of my body, and warm shivers danced along my skin.

But I saw the deflection for what it was—hide whatever this anger was behind teasing flirts and distracting looks.

"What's it going to take, Jansen?" I asked again.

"What's between you and Maxim?" he fired back.

I furrowed my brow, then shook my head. "That's none of your business," I hurled his own words back in his face.

He flinched as if I'd smacked him, but something clicked in his eyes, some mixture of disappointment and anger.

I blew out a breath. He'd had an attitude ever since Maxim had rushed to help me out of that elevator, and I was so *beyond* done with the bullshit. They had issues, clearly, and I wasn't about to get in the middle of a family squabble. Didn't matter how much I ached to help Sterling through whatever plagued him so badly. Didn't matter that I hadn't been able to *stop* thinking about him since that night in the elevator. I couldn't and *wouldn't* allow these sensations to stand in the way of my work.

"This is *that* important to you?" he asked after a few tense moments of silence.

"It's important to the team—"

"I'm asking if it's important to *you*."

A crackle of fire licked up my spine at the primal tenor in his tone.

"Yes," I breathed the word. "What's it going to take to get you to play nice for the season?" I asked for the final time.

Sterling shifted, something playful returning to his eyes. "I'll agree to work on this issue and play nice if you work on yours."

I scrunched my brows. "What issue?" My voice trembled on the question.

I knew which issue. And just the thought of it, just the mere fact that he'd brought it up had a cold sweat breaking out on the back of my neck.

He took a step toward me, his body towering over mine as he lowered his voice. "You know what. Your fear of confined spaces." His hand twitched at his side almost as if he were going to graze the back of it over mine but then thought better of it. "You told me you hated it. The fear. That it made you feel helpless."

My heart raced in my chest, and I couldn't tell if it was the fact that he was talking about it or if it was just *him*. His scent swirled in my senses, the warmth from his body practically begged me to reach out and span the small distance between us. And those eyes? God, he was looking down at me with such hope and confidence, like he alone had the power to help me walk through this fear of mine and come out stronger on the other side.

"Let me help you," he said. "Like I did that night."

The memories flashed in my mind, an incomprehensible mixture of fear and desire. It churned and ached and throbbed inside me.

"That would only benefit me," I said, shaking my head. "You'd be doing two things for me. What's in it for you?" I asked, my voice breathless. God, I needed to take a step back. To breathe in air that wasn't filled with *him*, but I couldn't physically pull myself away.

"I get to spend time with you," he said. That smirk of his shaped his lips, and heat flashed up the center of me.

"It could take...a while," I said. "I've been to therapy. I've had this issue for years." Ever since that game of hide and seek when I was ten. I shoved that memory down, having zero strength to revisit it right now. "It won't happen overnight."

"You'd be surprised how much I could change in one night." He cocked a brow at me, and I swear my cheeks were on fire. "But I understand," he said with more seriousness. "I don't care how long it takes."

Why? Was it just because he wanted to help me? For real? Or did he actually want to get to know me better? Or was it a combination of both?

The questions stormed through my head, right alongside the idea of spending that much time with him outside the arena. With his attitude toward Maxim—and him being my brother's best friend therefore he constantly popped up around my house—it could get complicated super quick.

"If I agree," I said, heart racing. "But I have a condition."

"Naturally," he said, a full smile on his lips now.

"No Maxim talk," I said, and the smile fell off his lips. "Not unless it's about *you* and him," I clarified. "Because while I'm more than willing to hear that story when you're ready to tell me, I will not become a median between you two. Loyalty is important to me. So is family. I'm not going to be the go-between with whatever is happening between you two."

Something resolved settled into his features, and my stomach plummeted the longer he kept those gorgeous lips sealed. God, why did I have to put a stipulation on it? Why did I have to blow my shot at spending more time with the man who legit drove me bat-shit crazy and deliciously wild at the same time?

Because you don't want to come between them.

Right.

"Fine," he said, and I swear the breath I released was heard even downstairs in the locker room.

"Really?"

The smile was back. "You sound surprised," he said, leaning one muscled arm on the wall next to us. The motion brought him another inch closer to me, and if I wanted—which I *so* didn't—all I'd have to do was reach up on my tiptoes, and our mouths would brush. "And excited," he added.

I kept my feet firmly planted on the floor and fastened him with a glare for good measure. "Oh, yes," I said, rolling my eyes. "I'm so excited to plunge myself headfirst into situations that literally incapacitate my body." A tremble vibrated through my muscles. In truth, my therapist had been gently nudging me in this direction for a while. And the idea of doing it with him by my side? It didn't seem as terrifying as I once thought. Why was that? Was it simply because I'd already been in one such situation with him before and lived to talk about it? Or did it have more to do with the connection I couldn't deny pulsing between us?

"You don't have to worry," he said, his voice low and hushed between us. "I'll take care of you, London." He held my gaze for a few burning moments before he pushed off that wall and walked down the hallway.

Leaving me standing there breathless, aching, and this side of terrified.

* * *

"HE WANTS TO HELP YOU?" Savannah—my best friend and partner in crime—asked a few hours later as I sat across from her at her kitchen table. She also happened to be in the professional athlete career, having grown up with a dad who happened to coach the Raptors' NFL team. She'd gone into contract management, and currently did so for Charleston's MLB team, the Hurricanes. "Like…what? Take you to certain places and talk you through it?"

I shrugged. "I think so?"

It had been a couple weeks since his offer, and I was still mentally battling what would be the best course of action.

Savannah smiled, leaning back in her chair. "Hell, that doesn't sound too bad to me," she said. "If it helps you, then I'm all for it. I mean, you've been wanting to work on it forever. This condition might be the push you need."

"I know," I said, sighing. And how had he realized that from just that small encounter with me? Had it been that obvious? Or could he just understand me on a level I wasn't used to? "And I agreed because I have to get him to stop trying to pummel his brother every other second…"

"But," she asked when I hadn't continued.

"But I don't really know him that well." And I hated the truth in that statement. I'd known Maxim for two years, sure, but he was nothing like Sterling. Maxim was all dark flames where Sterling was a bright, blazing light—almost like a star.

"You want to, though," she said, eying me. "Know him better."

I nodded. I'd never lied to Savannah, and I wasn't about to start now. "I haven't been able to stop thinking about him since that night," I admitted. "Not that I want anything from him. Honestly, the last thing I need is a relationship with someone on my team." I shook my head. "But…friends? I wouldn't mind that."

Savannah looked at me like she might argue. Like she might call me out on what she could likely read in my eyes. That my thoughts toward Sterling were anything but *friendly*. Her phone rang, and she scooped up her cell, rolling her eyes as she answered the call.

"Yes, Maddox?" She had that professional tone she'd adopted since becoming the contracts manager for the Charleston Hurricanes—one of the hottest MLB teams in the nation. She shook her head. "No, absolutely not." She sighed. "Because it's an effort to get *wives* inserted into contracts benefits. I will not draft a loophole where your flavor of the week are allowed to travel on the team bus with you."

I covered my laugh with my hand.

"The answer is no," she said again. "You'll thank me later." She ended the call, and I raised my brows at her.

"Trouble at work?" I teased.

She set down her phone. "Pro-athlete life," she said. "Maddox Porter lives to make my life harder."

"Hudson's brother?" I asked, recognizing the name from one of my players on the Reapers. He was making this season his last before he retired.

"Yes," she said. "I thought Hendrix was a playboy," she said, and I smiled at the way her eyes lit up saying her boyfriend's name. "But Maddox makes Hendrix's history look like a Hallmark movie." She shook her head. "He had the audacity to ask for his contract to include dates on the bus." She rolled her eyes. "Last week, it was for unlimited box seat tickets for home games for anyone he chooses."

I laughed, sipping the tea she'd made when I'd come over. "Sounds like he's bored," I said, and she nodded.

"He's something," she said. "The other players I've drafted contracts for haven't given me nearly as much trouble."

"What a life we live," I said, but there was a smile on my lips. One of the things I loved about our lives were the challenges. The constant go-go mentality, the fast-paced, high stakes that came with working with professional athletes.

"Truth," she said, clinking her mug against mine.

Her phone rang again, but this time her smile was wide and genuine, and it didn't take me a second to figure out who was on the other end.

"Hey, handsome," she answered the phone, and I tried to hide behind my mug. They'd had some rough patches recently, but had *finally* leapt over every hurdle that had been thrown their way. The love that radiated from her now was so bright it was nearly blinding. "I miss you," she said.

Hendrix was at an away game for the Cougars, but they somehow made it all work—away games, paparazzi, her dad being his ex-coach, all of it.

I guess when it comes to real love, nothing seemed impossible.

"I'm glad you checked in," she said, then set the phone on the table between us. I tilted my head at her when she pushed the speaker button.

"Of course, you are," Hendrix said, his tone anything but speakerphone-approved. "You're desperate to hear all the ways I'm going to worship you when I get home."

"Babe," she said, her eyes flying wide.

"First, I'm going to start with that dirty mouth of yours," he continued without a hitch, and *I* flushed. "Second, I'm going to pin your arms above your head so you can't move. Then I'm going to slide my huge—"

"You're on speaker, Hollywood!" I shouted because the mortification of it was too much for me to bear. Savannah was laughing so hard she could barely breathe.

Hendrix cleared his throat on the other end of the line. "Butterfly," he said to Savannah, his tone teasing. "I know you like to play, but I didn't realize we'd upgraded to a three-way phone situation."

Savannah reeled in her laughter, sucking in a sharp breath. "I tried to tell you London was here," she said. "You were too wrapped up in your fantasy to listen."

"Can you blame me?" He laughed. "Hi, London."

"Hi," I said awkwardly.

"Why am I on speaker, Butterfly?" he asked.

"Right," she said. "I wanted to ask you about Jansen Sterling."

"You wanted to ask me about Sterling?"

"Yes," she said. "Is he a good guy? I know you met him a while back. Or is he one of those we should be wary of?"

"We?"

Savannah rolled her eyes at his tone. "Hendrix Malone, you aren't seriously jealous, are you?"

I rolled my eyes. The idea that Savannah would be thinking of anyone other than her lovestruck fiancé was downright comical.

"Never," he said. "But a man has to clarify."

"She's asking for me," I said, my tone shaky. "I have to work with Jansen on a more personal level for my position."

"And you want to know if he's an asshole."

"I suppose I do," I said, flashing a glare at Savannah. She shrugged, returning the look with a silent *"oh, come on, you wanted to know"* in response.

"I haven't known him as long as Roman or Nixon," he said, referring to his quarterback and running back best friends. "But everything he's shown me points to him being a stand-up guy. He's no angel, but none of us were in our rookie days —doesn't matter if it's football or hockey. Just saying."

Savannah shook her head, a smile on her lips.

"You should be good," he continued. "And not that you need the support," he said. "I know you have your brother watching your back. But I've got it too. If he does get out of hand—"

"Thanks, Hendrix," I cut him off, not needing to hear the threat to follow. I'd heard that plenty—too much—from my brother in the past. And while it warmed my heart to know that my best friend's fiancé cared about me enough to say that, I didn't want to make this into a bigger deal than it was.

Because it was just a means to an end, right? He was helping me, and in truth, I *was* helping him. These promo spots weren't just about our direction this season on the Reapers, but highlighting where he was in his career. Which was increasingly climbing to be one of the best goalies the NHL had ever seen. That had to be the real reason behind his sudden bargain, but it was great to hear that Hendrix vouched for him nonetheless.

Savannah scooped up the phone, returning the call to private, and I waved to her as a silent goodbye. I did *not* need to be here for that conversation, having heard more than enough beforehand.

Though, as I drove back to my apartment, I couldn't help but wonder what it would be like to have that kind of relationship. I'd had sex all of one time, and it was nothing to write home about, let alone have an intense, detailed conversation over the phone about. I mean, how would it feel to want someone so bad that they couldn't wait to get home to you? So badly they had to start it up on the phone because they simply couldn't stand to be without you?

A flush raked over my skin as I thought about Sterling and the way he'd haunted my thoughts since that night. How I'd been restless in my big, empty bed, tossing beneath my sheets with his dark blue eyes flashing in my head and his smell lingering in my nose.

We'd barely spent more than an hour of real time together, and I couldn't stop.

What would happen when I saw him outside the arena? In close quarters nonetheless?

My heart raced at the thought, and the logical side of my brain told me to check myself. I was a professional—much like Maxim had said—and I had a job to do. This was the only way I could do my job, so therefore, I had to do it.

It had nothing to do with the way Sterling made me feel inside—like that passion I'd always stated as overrated could be *real* with the right person.

But thinking like that was dangerous, and I wasn't one to walk that line.

No matter how fun it might sound.

5

STERLING

The best part of being a highly visible, professional athlete? I got special admission to *Seven Wonders*, Charleston's brand new amusement park that had only opened a month before.

"How does this thing work?" London asked, glancing down at the lanyard around her neck that held a hard, plastic pass.

"That's your quick pass!" Our bubbly attendant told us as we stood at the shaded VIP entrance. The blonde shot me a coy look as London flipped the little pass over. "It means when you find something you want to *ride*, you can skip the line." She arched an eyebrow with meaning.

Some other year, I might have been tempted. It wasn't in my nature to turn a good thing down, but my dick wasn't interested, and neither was the rest of me.

"You walk right up to the front and tell them you'd like to get *on*." She trailed a finger across her collarbone.

Damn, she wasn't even being subtle about it.

London looked up and caught on quick, clearing her throat and moving a step closer so her shoulder brushed against my elbow. She was in sneakers, and I'd been right. She didn't even reach my collarbone without her heels, and I wasn't even *thinking* about the little scrap of white fabric she deigned to call shorts. They barely covered her ass. I knew because I'd looked.

A lot.

"Is there anything else I can...offer you?" The attendant smiled.

"I think we've got it. Thanks." London's eyes narrowed, and damn if that little display of jealousy didn't go straight to my dick. "Shall we?" she asked me while looking directly at the blonde, then took my wrist and tugged.

I was laughing by the time we cleared the entrance.

"You're lucky I saved you. She was ready to maul you in public," London muttered as we walked through the light crowd that filled the shop-lined street. Above our head, a roller coaster rushed by, carrying shrieking, happy riders.

"Who said I wasn't up for being mauled?" I teased.

London rolled her eyes. "You can do way better than that. Trust me." She pulled her mass of ebony hair into a top knot, leaving her sunscreen-clad shoulders to glisten in the sunlight. They were bare, with the exception of the two little straps of her tank top. "So what are we doing at an amusement park?"

I pulled my baseball cap backward and grinned. It had taken over a week for London to agree to this. "Well, first, I figured crowds probably don't trigger you since you're a game day coordinator for a professional hockey team."

"True," she said with a nod. "But I do appreciate you getting us in for the early hour." She flashed me a smile, and my thoughts evaporated. Beautiful. She was exquisite, really. "So, what's the plan?"

Plan. Right. I cleared my throat. "I thought we'd start with a little light restraint," I nodded toward the entrance to a roller coaster.

Her eyes flared. "Restraint, huh?"

"From what I read, it can cause the same reaction as an enclosed space."

She stopped, so I stopped with her, letting the crowd part around us like a rock in the middle of a rushing creek.

"What?" I asked.

"You read?" She lifted her sunglasses to the top of her head. "About claustrophobia, I mean. I know you read. You went to college. I know because it's in your file. I'm going to stop babbling right now."

Fuck me, she was cute. "Yes, I read, and feel free to babble all you want. I figured we'd just work our way up to what you're uncomfortable with, and at any time you're at your max and can't take anymore, just tell me." I shoved my hands into the pockets of my board shorts to keep from touching her. What the hell was wrong with me? I was never this needy, never had to physically remind myself to keep my hands off a woman.

Then again, I'd never wanted a woman like this before, either.

"So I just tell you that something is too much, and we'll skip it?" She lifted her brows.

"Exactly. Pick a safe word or something. You say honey badger, and I'll know it's a no-go." Seemed relatively easy.

She sputtered. "Safe word? Restraints?" The corner of her lips rose in a smirk. "Sorry to break it to you, but I'm not interested in touring your red room of pain, and *honey badger* is the last thing I'd think of in the middle of sex."

I grinned. "Noted. You prefer your sex honey badger free." Leaning down, I brushed my lips over her ear. "And we'll work up to the leather restraints just to make sure you're comfortable. Fuzzy handcuffs are always the best way to start."

She shivered slightly and stepped away, shaking her head like she needed to clear it. "So, roller coaster it is." Color flushed her cheeks.

"Right this way." I led us through the fast track lane of the ride.

"People are staring," she said softly as we passed the waiting line.

"You're not used to it?" I asked, then caught her flinch. "I mean because of your brother, not...Voldemort."

"Voldemort?" She sputtered a laugh as we reached the little velvet rope.

"He who shall not be named." I shrugged. "I figure you grew up as Caz's sister, so stuff like this has to be pretty normal for you. Passing lines and stuff." I wasn't egotistical enough to think that anyone in line actually recognized me. Hell, the attendant at the front only knew because it was listed on our VIP pass request.

"Honestly, I did my best to give Caz some space, hoping he'd do the same, but he never did." She sighed as the coaster pulled into the dock and the riders shuffled, the new ones taking the place of those who had just finished. "I don't think he ever really got over losing me that day. Not that it was his fault, because it wasn't." She raised her eyebrows at me and said the words emphatically as if I'd ever question her brother's character.

"I don't doubt that he did everything he could to find you," I said softly as the ride attendant checked our passes and let us through. "So, the front car can be scarier, but you might not feel as trapped since there won't be anyone ahead of us."

"Front it is," she said with a nod, straightening her shoulders as we walked into the stall.

These things always made me think of herded cattle, not that I was going to say that to her. She was nervous enough. "You sure you're up for this?"

"It's not like you're sticking me in a closet. I'm good." She bounced up on her toes as the coaster pulled into dock.

"Here we go." We shuffled in as the other parties made their way out, putting our belongings into the pocket in front of us, and then she pulled the shoulder harness down, clicking it into place.

"Am I going to fall out of this thing? It feels loose." She pushed on the bar, her voice pitching upward a little.

"I've got you." I gave it a tug and clicked it tighter, then locked myself in.

The attendant gave his little talk about keeping our arms and legs inside, and then we were off, shooting forward to begin the incline.

Click. Click. Click. The coaster started to journey upward on the track.

"You okay?" I asked, turning my head as much as I could to look at her.

"Um. Yeah. I mean. I think?" Her hands clenched at her thighs.

"You're doing great." I offered mine, brushing it lightly over hers, and she quickly laced our fingers, squeezing tight.

Click. Click. Click.

"What happens when we get to the top?" she asked as the breeze whipped over us, thick with September humidity.

"We fall."

Much to my surprise, she laughed the whole way down.

* * *

FOUR ROLLERCOASTERS, two spinning rides, and something called *The Scrambler* later, we finished up our lunch at a picnic table.

"I never pegged you for a funnel cake guy," she teased as I popped the last bit of sugared dough into my mouth.

"I'll run it off later," I answered after I swallowed. "I'm usually way stricter about my diet during the season, but I swear, I smell one of these, and I'm powerless."

"You like the sweet stuff, huh?" She smirked and took a sip of her lemonade.

"You have no idea." I devoured her with my eyes, unable to help myself. Tendrils of her hair had slipped free during the rides, and her smile was even brighter than when we'd gotten here. I'd grown used to seeing her suited up or in heels at the arena, but seeing her relaxed and...touchable was twisting me into knots. I'd never been so turned on by the scent of coconut sunscreen in my whole damned life.

The straw slipped free from her lips and our eyes locked, the space between us going taut with a feeling that bordered on anticipation. It was like we'd stepped off the ride only to become the ride, steadily *clicking* our way to the top.

But the top of what? I couldn't shake the memory of seeing her in Maxim's arms.

"So, what next?" she asked, her voice sounding a touch breathless.

"Whatever you want," I said the words slowly, and her eyes flared.

She gulped and broke eye contact, fumbling for the map of the park we'd picked up along the way. "Um. Let's try pushing it a little," she offered, her fingers tracing a path near the colorful designation for the picnic area.

"How far would you like to push it, London?" Shit. Even when I wasn't trying to flirt, it came out flirty.

She pointed to a ride. "Journey to the Center of the Earth."

"It's inside."

"So the description says." She folded up the map and stuck it in her back pocket.

Worry spun my stomach. "I'm guessing it's in the dark."

"Yep, read that, too." She stood up from the table. "Let's try. What's the worst that happens? I shut my eyes for all four minutes and seventeen seconds?"

She had a point there. I hated the idea of pushing her, but if she was the one stretching her limits, who was I to argue? "Let's do it."

We cleaned up our trash and started down the path. The park was at its peak and packed with people, but I kept her as close to the edge as possible.

"You're sure about this?" I asked as we found the entrance to the ride.

"Are you going to ask me that every time we try something new?" She paused at the board that described the attraction.

"Yep. Every time."

She shook her head, but there was a slight tilt to her lips. "See, it's a single boat on a track, and it might be dark, but I know it has an end. I can do this." She nodded, and I wasn't sure if she was talking to me or herself.

"Okay," I agreed, taking a breath like I was the one being challenged here. "I just want you to be comfortable."

She turned and looked up at me with the same look she'd given me in the elevator like she was trying to figure me out.

"What?" I asked gently, pushing her sunglasses to the top of her head so I could see her eyes.

"You. You're just so…" She sighed.

I pocketed my Ray-Bans and grinned. "Sexy? Charming? Irresistible?"

She scoffed. "Cocky much?"

You haven't even seen how cocky I can be. I opened my mouth but let the comment go unspoken. "You know what? I'm going to let that one go. Just know that I had the perfect line."

"Then deliver it." She folded her arms under her breasts, lifting the creamy swells to the top of her neckline, and my mouth fucking watered. She might be a tiny little thing, but her breasts weren't. They'd fill my hands perfectly, and my mouth...*knock it off.*

"It's highly inappropriate, and I'd hate to be accused of work-place harassment," I teased.

"Seriously? We're not even close to work and I'm pretty sure I can handle any of your *harassment.*" Her gaze drifted down my chest, lingering where my T-shirt stretched tight across my muscles.

If she'd been anyone else, I would have kissed her right there. I would have crushed her body against mine, picked her up so she could wrap those sun-kissed legs around my waist and take her mouth exactly like I'd fantasized about—hot, hard, and hungry.

But she wasn't anyone else. She was London, and I wasn't even sure she was free to be kissed. I couldn't go another minute without at least knowing.

"Look, I know we promised not to talk about Maxim," I started. Her gaze snapped to mine and her shoulders tensed, but I pushed on. "But I have to know...how close are you?"

Her brow furrowed. "You're right. We promised not to talk about him."

I laced my hands behind my neck and blew out a slow breath. "Then at least just tell me if you're together. Put me out of my fucking misery, please."

"What?" She did that fast blink thing. "Together like..."

"Like dating. Sleeping together. Whatever." *Please say no.*

She laughed. "Are you being serious right now?"

My stomach clenched. "You know what? Forget I asked. Let's go on the ride." It wasn't my business, and if she was sleeping with my—*don't even go there*—whatever, then maybe I didn't want to know. Thinking about his hands on her would fuel my fucking nightmares.

I started down the fast track part of the line, and London raced after me.

"Jansen!" She tugged at the back of my shirt just as we reached the shade of the giant building that housed the ride, and I slowed.

"It's really not my business," I muttered as she moved to keep pace beside me.

"I'm not dating Max. He's my brother's best friend."

"Really?" I studied her just long enough to see the honesty in her eyes, then looked forward so we didn't walk into a steel railing. We were inside the building, and though we were skirting the massive, twisting line, the noise level was exponentially higher.

"Really."

We reached the end of the lane, and there was one other couple ahead of us. I turned slightly, wishing the lighting in here wasn't so dim. "The way he puts his hands on you says something else entirely."

Not to mention he'd made his intentions perfectly fucking clear in the locker room.

She shook her head slowly. "Friends. Seriously. He's just... Maxim. That's why I laughed."

"Huh. Well, okay then." That was a huge relief. It didn't mean the guy wasn't actively trying to get her, but at least she wasn't taken yet. I didn't share. Ever.

"Wait, is that why you didn't call me back?" The couple in front of us moved, and we shuffled forward.

"Maybe." I winced.

"Boys," she muttered as the attendant lifted the rope for us. "Do you have any idea how many of the world's problems could be solved if you just said what was on your mind?"

"In my defense," I said, putting my hand on the small of her back as we walked toward the moving platform where empty boats were readying for launch. "You got out of the elevator and raced right into his arms."

"I would have hugged Caz like that, too," she said as we climbed into the two-person boat. "Doesn't mean I'm dating him."

We took our hard, plastic seats, and the attendant ordered us to put our lap belts on, so we did.

Then it was just us, and another boat maybe fifteen feet ahead that disappeared into the darkness as the platform moved us forward.

"In that moment, I probably would have assumed you were dating Caz, too, since I didn't know he was your brother," I admitted as we dipped off the platform and into the water.

She laughed. "I assure you I'm not dating my brother."

"Thank God for small miracles," I teased.

Her breath caught as we passed through a misty veil and into complete darkness. A voice boomed around us, saying that we'd begun our journey and must now descend.

London's hand clutched mine, and the boat plummeted down an unseen slide, throwing up a splash of water as we landed below.

"Holy shit!" she cursed.

"I didn't know that was coming," I said quickly as the room around us illuminated in red, the voice announcing that we were in some kind of magma tube or whatever.

"I figured," she muttered, her hand tightening on mine like a vise. Girl had a grip, I'd give her that.

"Maybe try the breathing thing?" I suggested as we passed some kind of animatronics for…I didn't even fucking know. The ride didn't have my attention—London did.

She rolled her eyes at me, and I got the point to stop mansplaining. Her breaths were steady and even as we turned the corner, and I had to admit, the dark red lighting of the place was a little unnerving. I couldn't see the boat in front of us or behind us as we drifted from chamber to chamber, listening to the ride tell us the different layers of the earth we were sliding through.

The next drop was easy to see coming, and London even cracked a smile as the water rained down, drenching us both.

We turned into the next chamber, and the voice's tone changed to one of urgency, telling us that everything eventually returned to the surface.

"I'm going to hit you if this thing spits us out of some volcano," London threatened, but there was no anger in her tone.

"Hey, you were the one who wanted to ride it—"

The whole chamber went black, and the boat stopped.

What the fuck? Was this part of the ride?

"Jansen?" London asked, her voice cracking.

"I'm here." I dropped her hand and pulled her against my side, wrapping my arm around her shoulder. Shit, I could feel her breath coming faster. "I'm sure it has to be—"

"Ladies and gentlemen," another voice boomed. "We are experiencing a technical delay. Please remain seated while we work through this unforeseen issue."

"Are you fucking kidding me?" London shouted, her voice reverberating off the walls.

I didn't even know what to say, so I just held her tighter. "We'll be out of here in no time."

"So is your luck bad? Or mine?" she asked, turning her face against my chest.

I rested my chin on the top of her head. "Would it be inappropriate to crack a joke that I get to hold you in the dark?"

She scoffed. Good, my girl was holding on.

"Tell me something." There was unmistakable urgency in her voice and she gripped the fabric of my shorts in one hand

and my shirt in the other. "Anything. Just distract me."

My mind drew a blank for several panicked seconds.

"Okay. My mom didn't want me to play hockey. At least not at first."

"Really?" She burrowed in tighter, and I could tell by the rise and fall of her shoulders that she was nearing hyperventilation.

"Really. I figured out the reason eventually, of course, and I don't blame her. Hell, I fell in love with being a goalie by the time I was seven, and still didn't know who my biological father was. There's just something I love about defending the net, being the last line."

"When did. You figure. It. Out?" Yup. She was panicking. *Shit.*

"I overheard my grandfather telling Mom that she couldn't fight genetics when I made the AAA team. I was thirteen. And I remember that I wasn't pissed at her for keeping it from me. I'd always figured that dads who wanted to be in the picture were, but how blown away I was that she let me play. She was terrified of me becoming exactly like him, but she overcame it because she knew just how much I loved the sport."

"That's. That's. Amazing." She was taking heaving, gulping breaths now.

I pulled back just enough to cradle her face. "Tell me what to do here, London."

"I don't. Know. I don't know." Her face trembled in my hands, and my gut clenched. She'd said the claustrophobia made her feel helpless, but I was right there with her, powerless to take it from her.

"God, I'm so sorry." Someone had to get us the fuck out of here. I couldn't even see her, couldn't read the feeling in her eyes.

"I. Chose." She took a breath and held it. "Distract me."

"I'm trying," I promised.

"Try. Harder." Her face rose to mine and our lips collided.

Soft skin. Hard press. Over before I could blink.

"London—"

"Kiss me, Jansen." She brought her lips to mine again.

I groaned and gave in to exactly what I'd wanted all along. Damn, she tasted like sunshine and sugary lemonade. So fucking sweet. I licked the line of her lips, and she opened for me without hesitation.

My tongue swept inside, stroking over hers.

Mine.

She gasped, clutching my shirt, and kissed me back, sealing her mouth under mine and giving just as good as I gave it. Electricity shot down my spine with every thrust of her silken tongue against mine.

I sank my hands into her hair and took her deeper, exploring every corner of her mouth until I knew it as well as my own. Fuck, I wanted to see her. Wanted to lift my head to read her eyes, her body language, but there was something utterly sensuous about only being able to feel.

Every sip at her lips, every stroke of our tongues felt magnified as if the world only existed in this kiss—this moment.

"Jansen," she moaned against my mouth.

I wanted to hear her scream it, to feel her body clench around me as I brought her to orgasm.

My lips found her chin, her jaw, the impossibly soft skin of her neck as I licked and sucked a path to her collarbone. She cupped the back of my head, arching her neck, and another groaned again, concentrating on the little spots that made her breath catch.

"Holy shit," she whispered. "That feels so good."

"You're so fucking sweet," I replied, returning to her mouth. "I could kiss you forever."

She whimpered, and I did just that, taking her mouth until we were both breathless, both straining at the belts that kept us locked in place. Just this kiss had me hard and hurting, pushing against the fabric of my shorts.

My palms itched to explore the curves of her body, but I wanted to *see*—

The lights came back on, and the ride jolted forward, breaking our kiss.

Her eyes were so bright they were almost luminous as she looked up at me, her tongue drifting across her lower lip. Fuck me, it was swollen from our kiss, and she was only more tempting now that I knew exactly how she tasted.

I rested my forehead against hers, struggling to catch my breath and praying this wasn't the only chance I'd have to kiss her.

The boat hit a ramp, and we were slowly lifted into the lighted tunnel above as the ride came to an end.

She gasped and pulled back quickly, horror filling her eyes. "Ohmigod. Did I just force you—"

"Hell no," I assured her. "I've wanted to kiss you from the second you walked into that elevator." I ducked my head again, but she pulled back.

"You have to promise me that no one will know about this. At least not on the team."

I would have been insulted if not for the panic in her eyes. "I'm not sure I follow." Fuck staying quiet. My heart was pounding, demanding that I crow to the world that I was the lucky asshole who got to kiss London Foster.

"Caz will kill you. I mean it. He'll slaughter you." Her hands slipped to my chest, gripping the fabric of my shirt as we crested the ramp.

Okay, there was something to be said for feeling like I'd just taken advantage of her in a vulnerable state, whether or not she asked me to. I'd probably go after the guy who did that to my baby sister, too…if I had one. But if he kicked my ass, I deserved it.

"Please," she begged softly as we approached the offloading zone, where the amusement park workers waited. "Please, Jansen. Promise me."

"I promise." There wasn't anything I could deny her in that moment, my secrecy included.

She nodded and sighed in relief as our belts were unlatched, and we climbed out of the ride.

That had been the single most incredible kiss of my life. If I had to keep quiet in order to get another taste of London Foster, then I was more than willing. And if Caz found out… well, she was worth that risk, too.

6

LONDON

"*H*ey, London, wait up!" Maxim called to me, and I slowed my pace, whirling around to find him hurrying out of the locker room. He had a white bundle in one hand, his pads already on beneath his Reapers' gear.

"What are you doing?" I hurried to meet him halfway. "You're going to take the ice in twenty!"

He glanced down at his gear then flashed me a severely cocky look that screamed *obviously.* "I wanted to give you this," he said, extending the bundle toward me.

I tilted my head, wondering what in the world could be so important that he'd chase me down the hallway when he should be in the locker room prepping for the game. The arena was already packed with fans, and I'd been heading toward Langley's office to tell her how the pre-game fan meet and greet had gone with Reaper Captain Axel—her husband.

Unrolling the fabric, I raised my brows when I saw the jersey.

A Reapers' jersey with *his* name and number on it.

"They just came in," he said.

"Thank you?" I meant it as a statement, but it sounded more like a question.

"I figured as an official Reaper you needed one," he said, his eyes such a darker blue than Sterling's. How could they have some similarities but be so vastly different? "One that didn't have your brother's name on it," he continued.

"Thanks," I said again. "That's actually really sweet."

I *did* have a plethora of jerseys with Caz's name and number on it, and I tried to wear them in support as often as I could. It was nice of Maxim to notice that I might want to switch it up now that I actually worked for the team.

"Will you get a chance to watch today?" he asked.

The walkie on my hip flared to life, and I quickly answered Langley's call. "Talking to Maxim, be right there," I answered her inquiry as to why I was late. "Maybe," I said to Maxim. "Have a great game." I clipped the walkie on my side and started to turn.

"I'll look for you," Maxim said, flashing me a rare grin. He usually stuck to the dark and brooding giant in the corner for his moods, but after two years of him hanging around my brother, he had started to loosen up.

I flashed him a thumbs up and headed on my way, feeling slightly awkward in my own body. Maxim had slowly opened up over the years of knowing me, but nothing major. We were friendly, sure, but...I couldn't put my finger on why the jersey and his recent attempts to seek me out made me feel twisted up inside. I shook my head as I made my way to

Langley's office, flashing Persephone a grin as I settled into the chair in front of Langley's desk. I was overthinking things, as usual. Maxim was Caspian's best friend—he just wanted to look out for me and go out of his way to be nice to me. Probably at Caspian's request, too.

"What's up with Maxim?" Langley asked, a sigh following the question. "Did he get into another brawl with Sterling?"

I quickly shook my head. "No, nothing like that." I glanced down at the jersey folded neatly in my lap.

Langley followed my gaze, her brows raised. She glanced at Persephone, who took a seat next to me.

"The meet and greet went amazing with Axel," I said, suddenly feeling all kinds of tense.

"I had no doubt it would," Langley said, biting her lower lip. "That man has a way with people."

I tried not to laugh—Axel was a hulk of a Viking who could make mortal men cower.

"So, Maxim?" Persephone nodded toward the jersey. "Are you two…" she let the sentence hang there.

I *did* laugh then. "Together? No!" I shook my head, another laugh stealing through me as I thought about the absurdity of it. Jansen had asked too, and I'd had to explain the same thing to him.

Heat flared in my core at the memory of Jansen's searing kiss on that amusement park ride. I hadn't been able to stop thinking about it since.

"Maxim is Caspian's best friend," I hurried to explain. I held up the jersey in my hand. "This is just him being a friend."

The two shared a skeptical look, and I swallowed my laughs.

It was just a friendly gesture, right? There was no way Maxim—dark and mysterious and could have any girl he wanted—was interested in me. It had never been that way whenever between us.

"Sterling, then?" Langley asked. "We've noticed how his mood did a one-eighty on his attitude toward promos—"

"No," I cut her off, but my heart did a little hiccup. Memories of our kiss raced red-hot through my mind. God, I'd lost myself in him like I'd been starved for that kind of kiss. Consuming, slick, and electrifying. He'd brought my body to life in places I hadn't known existed. With. Just. A. Kiss.

And I'd be lying if I said I didn't want more.

Because I *did*.

But I wasn't about to tell my two superiors that.

"No," I said again because they were staring at me like they couldn't tell if I was lying to them or myself or both.

"Good," Langley said, and Persephone nodded. "Because getting involved with players—let alone *brothers*—is like walking down a spiral staircase in stilettos."

Persephone laughed, shaking her head. "It's a hard road," she added. "And you just started here. Plus with Sean—"

"Aren't you two married to players?" I reminded them but smiled to show I meant no ill-will.

They both laughed, and Langley rolled her eyes. "True," she said. "But neither of our marriages started off as legitimate." I tilted my head, but she hurried on. "It's a long story. Either way, those brothers are already a lit fuse. Put you in the middle…" She mimed an explosion, and if I wasn't so shocked about their assumption that not one brother, but *both* liked me on that level, I might've laughed.

I waved her off. "It's not like that."

The truth.

Because *yes*, I'd basically become a sparkler when Jansen had claimed my mouth to distract me in that amusement park, but that's *all* it was.

A distraction.

He didn't *want* me—he genuinely wanted to help me. And in that moment, I'd needed an epic distraction to stop me from having a fully fleshed panic attack in the very locked and very suffocating ride. He'd provided that distraction, and then some.

"Look," I said when neither of them seemed convinced. "I'm London Foster," I said, and they both raised their brows in a *where are you going with this* way. "I love my brother…most of the time." I laughed. "When he told me he'd made a deal with Asher Silas to play for the Reapers, I considered applying for a position on another team." Langley tilted her head, so I hurried to continue. "I've grown up with the game. I understand it and the celebrity athlete lifestyle. I love it. Love the challenges, the long hours, the enthusiasm of the fans. But, for as long as I can remember, I've been *Caspian Foster's* little sister."

Persephone tipped up her chin, understanding filtering through her eyes. "And you don't want to be known for that anymore," she said, and I nodded.

"Like I said, I love my brother. He's a tad over-protective, but he has his reasons." Reasons that currently had Jansen Sterling trying everything he could to help me work through my fears. "But I want to stand on my own. Prove myself through my own merit and my own hard work. For what *I* bring to the team, not my brother."

"I believe you," Langley said, an easy grin on her face. "And I have no doubt you'll be an asset to this team. But what does any of that have to do with Maxim and Jansen?"

"I don't want to be known as *that NHL star's girlfriend* either."

Langley nodded, and she leaned back in her seat. She propped one red-soled heel on her desk, a canary grin on her face. "That's smart thinking," she said, crossing her an ankle over the other. "But best intentions and all that." She shrugged, then glanced to Persephone.

"Yes," Persephone said. "If anything does happen, you can come to us. We will understand."

I smiled at the pair of them and hoped like hell it was convincing. "I appreciate that," I said, rising from my chair. "I have to get ready for the post-game fan experience."

"Good luck!" Langley called as I shut her office door behind me.

And I couldn't tell if she was wishing me luck with the event or with the Zolotov/Sterling brother situation. Either way, I felt like I'd just stepped onto ice so thin, it would shatter with one wrong step.

* * *

"Where are you off to?" Caspian said around a mouthful of cinnamon-maple scone. He and Maxim had practically teleported to my apartment after I'd let Caz know I'd made a batch of his favorite treat.

Maxim was polishing off his third scone when I walked past the kitchen to grab my purse. He stood up from where he'd been leaning against the kitchen counter, the brutes eating the scones straight off the hot cookie sheet. He cocked a brow at me, and my cheeks heated from the way he surveyed my outfit.

"Out," I said, giving both of them a shrug.

Maxim narrowed his gaze, the usual firm line of his lips pursing just slightly. "Have a hot date?" he asked, and his normal teasing tone bordered on...what? Worry? Had Caz totally ensnared him in the whole *protect London at all costs* moto? With the jersey and the way he was looking at me now...

Nope. Not going there. There was no way in hell Maxim freaking Zolotov was interested in me in that way. I was letting Langley and Persephone's comments slip into my mind too much. And I hated the idea that if they were right... if he was taking an interest, then our friendship would be ruined. Because I adored him as a friend, but I had no interest in more.

"None of your business," I said a little playfully as I thought about how Jansen and I had gone through the same discussion weeks prior.

My heart did a little hiccup at the knowledge that I'd be seeing him in less than an hour. It wasn't a date, I knew that, but that didn't mean I hadn't put a bit more effort into my appearance tonight. With his kiss still searing my thoughts every second of the day, and even worse at night, I figured it couldn't hurt to play up my features. Sleek black pencil pants that hugged my curves and a breezy white silk blouse that may have shown off more cleavage than I had in...forever. Savannah's suggestion, and for once, I was taking it. Usually, I stuck to more casual clothing, not even a thought in my mind on gaining a man's attention.

But Jansen?

That kiss, his smirk, the way he could get under my skin and make me laugh within the same breath? I'd be lying if I said I didn't want him to *see* me.

"You have a date?" Caz met me halfway to the door, cinnamon scone crumbs trailing behind him. I sighed but ignored the mess.

"Yes," I said, my tone pure snark.

"With who?"

"Oh, a few guys," I said. "You wouldn't know them. They're all football players."

Maxim suppressed a grunt, and I think that may have been the first time I'd ever seen him come close to laughing.

Caz, on the other hand, was not amused. "London—"

"Save it, big brother," I cut him off, patting his chest. "You know I'm joking." I reached for the door, rolling my eyes at the way his shoulders loosened. "They're actually hockey players," I called as I hurried out the door.

Caspian's grunt of disapproval sounded through the closed door, and I couldn't help but laugh at how easy he was to rile up. Served him right for always threatening to slaughter any guy I ever dated who didn't live up to his expectations of who was worthy of me—which landed somewhere between being a Greek God or a sparkly vampire. An impossible hero who could protect and shelter his weak and helpless baby sister.

Quite frankly, I'd prefer a fallen angel who'd shred me apart in the most delicious way, but then again, maybe I'd been reading too much paranormal romance.

With fantasies on the brain, I headed to where Sterling had suggested we meet, my heart racing from just the knowledge that I'd see him soon. I couldn't deny the excitement or the tiny hint of fear at whatever he had planned.

Not fear of him, of course. But fear itself. Panic. The ice-cold things that took hold of my lungs and my mind whenever I was put in a confined situation.

And right beneath all that, it was...something that quite possibly could be stronger than my fear.

Desire.

Something I never thought I'd have a remote problem with after my horribly awkward and sole sexual encounter. A cold shiver wracked my body just thinking about that ten minutes.

I shook my head, forcing the memory away, and went ahead and let that desire unfurl in the pit of my stomach. I mean, no one could really blame me, right? Jansen Sterling was delectable on his own—those crushing blue eyes that saw through all my defenses, the hard lines of his muscles, the teases of blank ink over his arm, his chest, his neck. God, even without knowing what it felt like to kiss him—who *wouldn't* want him?

But I *did* know what it felt like—fire and sparks and a swirling craving that went beyond my rational reasoning. His kiss had been powerful enough to take the edge off what had been gearing up to be one hell of a panic attack. I'd had enough of them to know the different levels of severity— some I could handle on my own with some tried and true breathing techniques my therapist had taught me. Others, I'd need to pop one of the pills she'd prescribed me for when I could see nothing but black walls closing in around me. The meds took about twenty minutes to calm my mind enough to think through the problem, but it was a hell of a lot better than crumbling into a ball of blind panic, icy whispers in my mind that I'd never get out, never survive. That the panic and terror would never end.

I'd almost gone to *that* full maximum in the elevator.

But…I hadn't.

Was that Jansen? Did he have some magical soothing effect that helped me? Or was I simply getting better at managing the fear?

I didn't have a solid answer, even as I walked up to the movie theater where Jansen stood outside.

Damn, he looked good. Dark jeans hugged his massive, powerful legs, and a tight black t-shirt clung to his chest, leaving very little to the imagination of what lay beneath. Sure, I'd caught glimpses of him before and after practice, those times where he'd leave the arena gym sans shirt, but I didn't know what his skin felt like. What the muscles beneath it felt like. What his collection of tattoos created or the meaning behind them.

And I *wanted* to know.

Which was almost as terrifying as where he was about to take me.

"You look beautiful," he said as I stopped before him.

My heart did that flutter thing, but I shrugged. "Well, if I'm going to go down like this, I figured I may as well look good while I do it."

Jansen laughed, shaking his head. "Are movie theaters that hard for you?" he asked as he held the door open for me. I nodded, following him inside. He walked right past the ticket booth, giving a wave to the young kid behind it before heading down the long theater hall. "I figured with the openness of the space, it wouldn't be as bad," he said, holding open the theater door for me.

Ice prickled down my spine, and my chest clenched.

No windows.

Only two exits.

Hundreds of people there to witness my panic—

"Hey," he said, cutting into my racing thoughts. He stepped into my space until all I could see or smell or *feel* was him. Cupping my cheeks with such gentleness, he met my gaze. "It's empty," he said. "I know you said you crowds weren't an issue, but I figured this would be easier."

I raised my brows, leaning into his delicate touch. How could someone so strong be so...tender? A warm shiver chased away the ice. "Empty?"

Jansen nodded, dropping his hands from my face. I almost whimpered at the lack of contact, but he held out his hand for me to take it.

A gesture.

My choice. He wouldn't haul me in there if I actually didn't want to go. Just like at the amusement park. He was here to help me, guide me, support me.

I sucked in a deep breath, resolved in the notion that half the battle with the panic was that those who witnessed it didn't understand it. Couldn't or wouldn't understand it. The fact that Jansen not only knew about what happened to me that I couldn't control but took the care and time to support me through it? It was enough to make my knees weak for an entirely different reason than what we were about to do.

"When was the last time you saw a movie?" he asked as I took his hand.

He led us into the darkened theater, and I blew out a breath. Every seat in the place was empty. Just like he'd said. "I stream at home all the time," I answered him, my eyes wide as I took in the vacant, windowless space. "You rented out the entire theater?"

"Of course, I did," he answered like it was the most obvious solution in the world. He motioned to a couple of seats in the front row—floor seats, close to both exits. God, I might've fallen for him just a little for that gesture alone.

But I couldn't. Because this…this wasn't a date. This was two colleagues working out a mutual agreement in order to better our careers. He cooperated and improved his image for his first season back with the Reapers, and I nailed my first major assignment from Langley. Win-win.

Colleagues who sometimes kissed in intense and severe situations. And I was sure the kiss had just been another day in the life of Jansen Sterling for him, but for me? It had shaken awake something inside of me I'd never felt before. An all-consuming hunger. A tingling ache I couldn't soothe myself.

"When was the last time?" he asked again as I settled into the leather seat next to him. The giant screen flared to life, illuminating the room with upcoming attractions.

"Sixteen," I said, wringing my hands. I tried to force myself not to think about the thick, dark walls. The lack of exterior air. How hard it would be to get out if there had been a crowd of people here.

"I thought the claustrophobia started younger than that?"

"It did," I said, not wanting to rehash that particular memory with him again. "But my high school boyfriend at the time, didn't take it seriously. He knew about it, but not in a way that gave him any real insight to what it would put me through." I sighed. "He said he had a surprise for me, and when we ended up at the theater, I was shocked. My panic flared, but he goaded me into going. A ton of his friends were there, and I didn't want to make a scene, so he tugged me inside, forced me to sit in the very top row, and…" My chest tightened at the memory. The way I'd had to run out of the place, nearly falling down the full flight of stairs as I did. The way I'd sat outside, tucked against the building's brick wall, tears streaming down my face as I tried and failed to get my body to stop shaking. "I didn't really see much of the movie," I said.

Sterling's eyes were sincere as they met mine. "You know we can leave whenever you need to," he said, and I nodded.

I did know that.

Somehow, I knew Sterling would never push me like my ex did.

"You seem to be doing pretty well already," he added, that smirk shaping his lips. "The previews are over, and you look downright calm."

I huffed a laugh, forcing my hands to the armrests instead of wringing them out again. I wasn't close to calm, but I wasn't barreling down the freeway to an attack either.

Baby steps.

And with Jansen at my side? It didn't seem such a lonely, dark place to be.

Thirty minutes into the movie, I couldn't concentrate. My knee bounced lightly, and I shifted my position about a dozen times. It wasn't that the movie was bad, in fact, it was super interesting with great acting and a tight plot. And it wasn't exactly the dark walls bothering me either.

It was Jansen.

His laugh, the way his bicep brushed against my arm, or his thigh pressed lightly into mine. God, maybe I *was* back in high school, crushing on the hot jock who made me laugh. I might as well be with how my thoughts were racing. Flashing from the way the theater made me feel, and then how *he* made me feel. The two emotions clashing in a battle that threatened to make me scream.

The theater being empty helped a ton with me being able to control the dark thoughts that tried to squeeze their way into my mind. I felt that slightly trapped sensation, but I *knew* I could get out of this room because no one would be in my way when rushing for the door. That alone should have allowed me to relax enough to enjoy the movie, but every time Jansen moved or laughed or breathed I caught his scent, felt the electric crackles from his accidental touch, and basically did somersaults inside.

His kiss replayed over and over so much that I soon had no clue what was happening on the screen.

And I just…didn't care.

I wanted.

Like, full-on, can't breathe without touching him, *wanted*.

The sensation was so new and exhilarating I couldn't think straight. Couldn't remind myself of all the reasons why I shouldn't, why we couldn't…

"You okay, London?" Sterling whispered, his lips close to my ear. Warm chills burst along the skin of my neck.

I turned my head, my eyes locking with his. "I don't know," I admitted, my eyes flashing from his lips to his eyes and back again. God, I was practically writhing in my seat.

He shifted toward me, his focus fully on me now. "We can go," he said. "You say the word." He gently laid his strong, warm hands over my forearms, the gesture both comforting and igniting at the same damn time.

Just. Like. *Him.*

"London?" he asked, arching a brow when I hadn't said anything. Something crackled behind his blue gaze, some awareness as he realized how close our faces were, how my body was turned toward his, how I hadn't pulled away at his sudden nearness. "Tell me what you need," he said, his voice taking on a gravely tone that *did* things to my body.

Yep.

I wanted more of *that.*

In a blink, I succumbed to the drumming, pounding, pulsing *need* in my body—ignoring the pleas of my rational mind and simply…*being.*

My hands flew to his neck, and I yanked his mouth to mine. He came willingly, a low growl rumbling in his chest from the contact. I fisted his shirt, holding him close while I crushed my lips against his, holding absolutely nothing back.

And when he jerked back the armrest between us? Snaking an arm around my waist to haul me to him?

I saw stars.

7

STERLING

*H*oly shit, London was kissing me. I shoved the armrest between our seats up, then gripped her hips and tugged, pulling her onto my lap so I could get closer.

There wasn't a *close enough* when it came to this woman. I had the feeling that I could drive my tongue, my fingers, my cock deep inside her body and still wouldn't be satisfied until I reached her soul.

She gasped as my tongue sank deep inside the sweet recess of her mouth, and she swung her knee over my thigh, straddling me.

Fuck yes. It had been a week since we'd been at the amusement park, and I'd been dreaming about this moment ever since. She wasn't scared or in the throes of a panic attack. She wasn't looking for a diversion or a distraction.

She'd kissed me because she'd wanted to, and if the way she settled in my lap and rocked her hips over mine was any indication—she was as into this as I was.

I speared my hands through the long, silken strands of her hair to cradle her head, then kissed her breathless, stroking my tongue against hers. She tasted just as sweet as I remembered, just as addictive, and I was hooked.

"London," I groaned against her lips.

"I love kissing you," she admitted in a rushed whisper before sucking on my lower lip and wrapping her arms around my neck.

Damn, that felt *good*.

I kissed her hard and long until we were both panting. "You have no idea how badly I want to put my hands on you."

"So put your hands on me." She tugged at my hair, urging my mouth back to hers, and I followed willingly, sinking into her mouth and abandoning another degree of my restraint.

She gasped when I set my lips to her neck, and the sound went straight to my dick, taking me from the semi I always seemed to have around her, to fully, painfully hard. I kissed down her throat and across her collarbone, nudging the material of her blouse out of the way so I could worship her skin with my mouth.

Her hips ground over mine again, the pleasure of it making me moan as I palmed her waist with one hand and tugged on her hair with the other, exposing more of that gorgeous neck.

"What are you doing to me?" She moaned as I sucked on the little section of her skin where her neck met her shoulders.

"What does it feel like I'm doing to you, London?" My hand slid to the curve of her hip.

"Driving me wild." Her grip tightened in my hair. "You make me feel…"

"What?" I prompted when she trailed off.

We locked eyes as the light around us flickered with the motion on the big screen. I'd chosen some romcom to keep her laughing just in case the theater triggered an attack, but I'd been too focused on her to remotely pay attention to the plot. Besides, everything I cared about was in my arms right now.

She bit her lower lip, and I leaned in and sucked it free.

"I make you feel what?" I asked again, gripping her hips and pulling her closer.

She sucked in a breath at the contact as my dick lined up with the seam of her pants. Thank fuck she wasn't in a skirt. Her pants gave us one more barrier just in case my cock actually punched through the fabric of my jeans just like it was threatening to.

"Needy," she whispered. "Hot. Reckless." Her gaze dropped to my lips. "I've never been the reckless type, Jansen, but I swear you kiss all my common sense away."

"Reckless, huh?" I grinned. London and reckless were two words I never would have paired, but I was all for it.

She nodded, and then we were kissing again, hotter and deeper than before. There was an urgency to it, a desperation as it became an openly carnal exchange. She slipped her hands under my shirt and traced the lines of my abs, my pecs, her fingers softer than the kiss of a butterfly's wings.

"Fuck, London," I growled. The feel of her hands on my skin sent my pulse skyrocketing. "Tell me what you want." Was it a consent thing? Absolutely. But damn, if I didn't want to hear that prim little mouth say something dirty.

"I…" She swallowed. "I want you to touch me."

"Good, because I really fucking want to touch you." I pulled her into another kiss, then lifted a hand to the swell of her breast, palming the exquisite mound and squeezing gently. "Like this?"

"God, yes." She rocked against me, pushing her breast into my hand and the juncture of her thighs against my cock.

My dick jumped at the feel of how hot she was through layers of fabric between us. *Settle the hell down. You're not going to fuck her in a movie theater.*

London deserved better—if she even wanted to go there with me. She deserved candles and roses and a fucking bed. Yet here she was, rolling her hips over mine as I flicked open the first button on her blouse, then the second.

I kept my gaze locked on hers as my hand swept inside her shirt, then her bra, until there was nothing between her flesh and my fingers. She nodded, then groaned when I tweaked the bud, rolling and pinching.

"Fuck, I want to taste you," I groaned, leaning in to kiss her neck. Getting my hands on her in this theater was one thing, but there was no chance I was exposing her skin to anyone who might walk in. *Mine.*

"Jansen," she moaned, her hips rocking faster. "You're setting me on fire. I need…I need…" Her hips shifted over mine, her body telling me exactly what she needed.

"What do you need?" I plucked her nipple, and she cried out, the sound swallowed by the sound of the movie.

"More." She gripped the back of my head and brought it to her breast.

Fuck it. Her blouse could keep her covered as long as I was careful. I lifted her breast from the cup of her bra, then angled the opening of her shirt and sucked the pearled peak between my lips.

"Jansen!" She urged me on, holding my head as my tongue lashed at her hard, swollen nipple, alternating sweet strokes with hard sucks.

My dick leapt, pulsing in time with my heartbeat as I worked one breast, then the other, until she was heavy and swollen in my hands. If she had me this turned on by touch alone, what was it going to be like when I had her under me? When I could see her laid out beneath me like an offering?

She ground against my dick, seeking the friction she needed, and she gasped when I thrust back against her. "Again," she demanded.

I rocked my hips, and she moaned.

"You're killing me," I groaned testing her nipple with my teeth.

"I didn't know it could feel like this." She cupped my face, and I released her breast so I could look into those gorgeous eyes. They were glazed with lust, but there was also an element of wonder there.

"Feel like what?" I palmed her ass and squeezed.

"Like I'll die if you don't touch me. I've never wanted anyone like this." She swirled her hips, and I nearly saw stars. Fuck, the woman was going to make me come without even touching my cock.

"I *am* touching you," I said with a kiss, sliding my hands back to her hips.

"Here." She gripped one of my wrists and put my fingers right between her fucking thighs.

"London. God, baby."

"Please," she begged.

The plea broke whatever was left of my sense of chivalry. If she wanted me to touch her, then *fuck yes*. At least one of us could get some relief.

I undid the button of her pants and slid the zipper down while she nodded her encouragement, resting her forehead against mine. Then I took her mouth in a hot, wet kiss, and sent my fingers down the smooth skin of her tight stomach, pushing past the silk barrier of her panties and into the scorching heat of her.

"*Fuck*, baby. You're soaking wet." She coated my fingers, all hot and slick as I dipped to her entrance.

She whimpered, bracing her hands on my shoulders and digging in with her sharp little nails. I wanted her to grab harder, to leave marks so when we left this theater, I knew this had actually happened, and I wasn't in just another dream.

I stroked her from entrance to clit, swirling over that little bundle of nerves with two fingers.

The sound of her whimper was enough to fuel my fantasies for the next month. She was so incredibly responsive, so honest in her needs and wants that I lost myself in the act of pleasuring her. I'd always been about mutual enjoyment when it came to the bedroom, but I'd never been so focused, so driven to get someone off the way I was with London.

My entire body burned with the need to see her come apart, to be the one that took her to that edge and pushed her over it.

I rolled my fingers over her clit, stroking and teasing the flesh, then I slid to her entrance and sank two fingers inside her. My kiss swallowed her cry as she clenched around me.

She was so fucking tight that she gripped my fingers like a vise as I stroked in and out of her, fucking her mouth at the same rhythm with my tongue, slow and deep. Her thighs tensed around my legs as she rode my hand, and I pressed the heel of my palm hard against her clit so she ground against it.

"Jansen!" She broke the kiss with a gasp as her muscles locked, then trembled.

"You're so fucking beautiful like this," I whispered. "So hot and tight around my fingers, London. Come for me." I curled my fingers inward slightly and thrust faster, sending her into the throes of an orgasm.

She screamed, but I caught it with a kiss as she came apart over and over. I stroked her through, bringing her down slowly until she shuddered one last time and went limp against me.

"What the hell was that?" she mumbled into my neck, the last word breaking when I slid my fingers from the warmth of her pussy.

"Never had an orgasm before?" I teased, my fingers shaking slightly as I managed to button her pants and zip her up.

Fuck, I was a mess. My heart was racing, and my breathing sounded like I'd just run a fucking marathon.

Get some control, Sterling.

"Not with a guy," she muttered, then yanked her head up, her eyes flying wide. "I mean, not with a girl, either. Not that there's anything wrong with girls who do, of course. I just prefer men. Well, prefer *you*."

I smiled and brushed my thumb over her lip.

"Never?" How the hell was that possible? London was traffic-stopping beautiful, whip-smart, and had a body that begged to be stroked.

"Never." She shook her head slowly.

"Seriously?" It had to be asked. I couldn't imagine anyone getting London under their hands and not spending hours figuring out exactly what made her body purr.

"I've dated—I'm not a nun or anything, but I've never *wanted* like that." She looped her arms around my neck. "You, however, I wanted in the elevator. You probably could have pushed me against the wall, and I would have climbed you like a ladder." Her eyebrows rose.

A slow smile spread across my face. "Then we would have been in perfect agreement. Not sure it would have looked too good once the guys got the doors open, though."

She huffed a laugh and stroked her fingers through the ends of my hair.

My mind started tripping all over itself at the thought of feeling her come again and again. Next time I'd do it with my tongue and lips, and if it freaked her out too much to feel restrained, she could ride my fucking face all night long. My dick screamed in agreement.

"What?" she asked softly, looking at me with a slight wrinkle of confusion.

"Oh, nothing. I'm just planning all the different ways I'm going to make you come." After my mouth, I'd use my cock when she was ready. How many times could I get her there if I had all night with her?

Before she could react, the credits rolled, and the lights came up in the theater.

"Um. How did you like the movie?" she asked, her cheeks flushed and her eyes bright.

"Best show of my life."

It was.

* * *

The next night we took on Anaheim at home and squeaked out a four-to-three win. I'd spent the majority of the game in net, and sweat poured down my body in rivulets as we made our way to the locker room.

The sound of the cheering crowd faded when I passed through the door, but the guys were just as loud in their celebration.

"You were on fire!" Briggs slapped my back as we sank to the bench in front of our lockers.

"You saved my ass in the third period. I lost sight of the puck for a good two seconds," I admitted. The guy was a defense god.

"Just doing my job." He shook it off like he always did. He may have gone third pick in the first round of the draft, but he was humble as they came.

Foster, on the other hand, had a shit-eating grin as he took his seat across the room from us. Between his speed and Maxim's accuracy, they'd put two of the points on the board. Brogan, who was silently ripping off his gear like it had personally offended him, had brought in the third.

"You don't think I know that?" Maxim growled, his voice standing out in a moment of quiet. "Well, we won, so it's going to have to be good enough," he said into his cell phone, switching into Russian as his voice escalated. He finished up his conversation just as I headed for the shower, sending me off with a glare as he threw his phone into his bag so hard I would have taken bets that it didn't survive the trip.

Whatever.

I showered off and got dressed, hanging my gear to dry.

"You want to head to *Scythe*?" Briggs asked, yanking a shirt over his head. "I think some of the guys are headed that way."

"Some of us have dates," Maxim intruded, his bag slung over his shoulder. "I'll personally be at dinner with London, but I asked Caz to join us, too." His mouth quirked up in a smirk that made me want to punch it off his fucking face.

He's her brother's best friend, I reminded myself.

"Have a good time," I managed to say, sliding my wallet into my back pocket.

"Look at you getting all mature," Briggs joked under his breath.

"Oh, I will." Maxim smiled, but it sure as fuck wasn't friendly. "Have you given up chasing after her yet? I'd hate to think I won her by default."

My blood boiled, and I had to lock my jaw to keep from running my mouth. London and I weren't official. Hell, she hadn't even given me the okay to go public about us yet. What we had—whatever we called it—was ours.

"You won't win her at all." I shrugged. "She's out of both of our leagues." Wasn't that the honest truth?

Maxim scoffed and walked out of the locker room.

"He wouldn't have said that shit if Foster was still in here," Briggs muttered. "I still can't understand how you're genetically linked."

"You see," Greene said, throwing his arm around Brigg's shoulder. "When a man loves a woman—"

"Shut the fuck up," I snapped. "He never loved her." Love had never been the word Mom used. I grabbed my keys and walked out of the locker room with Briggs by my side, taking a deep breath in the hallway and making my way past the outstretched microphones from reporters and grasping hands of puck bunnies who just wanted a piece.

London was at the end of the hall, standing with Persephone and Langley.

Our eyes locked, and she tugged her bottom lip between her teeth, trying to hide a smile. "Good game, Sterling. You too, Briggs," she said as we passed the group.

"Thanks," he answered, flashing a smile that didn't quite reach his eyes.

"Have fun at dinner." I gave her a wave and bit back the nauseating jealousy that crept up my throat. We hadn't been alone in almost a week. She was always working or with Foster, and I was always working or traveling…with Foster.

Either way, it was physically painful to walk away from her without so much as touching her hand, but I managed.

"Don't do it," Briggs said as we made our way into the players' parking lot.

"Don't do what?" I hit the button on my remote and unlocked my car.

Briggs shook his head. "You honestly think anyone in there couldn't see the level of eye-fucking going on in that hallway? I almost asked if you needed a condom."

"Uh." I paused. *Shit*. Honestly, I thought we'd been pretty good about hiding it.

"Look. The unwritten code of not fucking someone's sister is there for a reason." His tone changed, going tight. "Trust me. If it's between the girl and the team, you choose the team. Choosing the girl only gets you fucked over."

Well, then. "I'm not fucking anyone," I said honestly. "And I sure as hell didn't hear you giving Maxim the same speech."

He laced his fingers behind his head. "Because I don't give a shit if Maxim gets the fuck beaten out of him by Foster, or traded off to the minors."

"Is that what happened to you?"

His face went blank. "I'm just saying that you don't shit where you eat, and the Reapers feed you, Sterling."

"I get it." I did. But I also didn't give a fuck. I'd seen Cannon marry Persephone, and Axel and Langley were the picture of domestic bliss.

The door opened, and Foster walked out with his arm around London, laughing at something she'd said while Maxim followed them.

The nausea in my gut churned into something that burned as I watched the three of them drive away. She hadn't even looked my direction once.

Briggs looked at me knowingly and then climbed into his car.

I'd never been a guy who was hung up on labels, but damn, what the hell was going on with London and me?

8

LONDON

*T*he crisp fall air had way more of a bite to it in Chicago than it did in Charleston. The wind was sharp against my cheeks, stinging them to a rosy red as I stood outside the hotel.

But despite the chill, heat flooded my skin beneath my too-light jacket.

Because Maxim Stolov and Jansen Sterling were posing for post-win promos—the historic hotel's clean and classic architecture providing an awesome backdrop.

The photographer had the brothers posing in their post-game gear—black Reaper athletic pants and white Under Armour long sleeve shirts. They were both freshly showered, the evidence still clear from Jansen's slightly damp hair. I had no idea how he wasn't freezing, but he didn't seemed bothered by the kiss of cold in the air.

He didn't seem bothered by *anything*, actually. From the second I'd grabbed the two for their promos, he'd adapted this cold kind of calm that raised the hairs on the back of my neck. His crushing blue eyes were normally filled with emotion, whether it be a sensual look meant to drive me crazy, or a teasing flirt to make me laugh, or a rage-fueled stare with just a hint of pain whenever Maxim came around.

But not here.

Not for the camera.

He'd kept good on his word—not even flinching when the photographer had them stand back to back, arms crossed over their massive chests.

In this snapshot in time, they actually *looked* like brothers. Not so much their physical appearance, which was slightly varied, but in the *way* they both stared down the camera. Fierce, hungry, and cocky after an away game win. They looked like they might actually grab a drink at the bar after this—their features were that smooth.

Professionals, the two of them.

But, God, could they be more gorgeous? The wealth of muscles and sharp eyes was indeed the source of heat flushing my skin—the brothers anyone would have a hard time ignoring. Langley had been right when she said the promos would boost the Reaper image. Maxim and Sterling were impossible not to appreciate, to admire...to *want*.

My eyes naturally gravitated toward Jansen, and I worried my bottom lip between my teeth. I swear I could still *taste* him despite it being a week since he'd thoroughly kissed and wrecked me in the movie theater. And this time...it wasn't because I'd *needed* the distraction, but *him*. I'd needed him on a level I still didn't understand. Craved his kiss like a starved woman.

And, if I was being honest with myself, it wasn't just his searing kisses or his electric touch that had made me come harder than I ever had in my life.

It was the way he listened, the way he took the time to genuinely understand me and the fear that gripped me without any hint of judgment. The way he made me laugh right after he rattled off a comment that made me want to slap him. I *enjoyed* it—the push-pull, the give and take between us. It was fun...and it had been such a long time since a man and I had fun like that.

"Few more," the photographer called out, and I blinked out of my unabashed barely-contained drool fest. "Could you two face me now, almost shoulder to shoulder?"

The brothers moved eerily similar, their muscled bodies obviously strong but also fluid as they turned toward the camera. Jansen's eyes flickered with a mere hint of the pain I often caught him burying beneath the barely contained hate for Maxim, but it was gone in a blink.

My chest tightened, and I once again wished he would tell me the truth about why they hated each other. I could likely grill Maxim on the circumstances—he had grown more and more open toward me in the weeks since being signed with the Reapers. But I wanted to hear it from Jansen. Wanted to hear his side of things, which no doubt would be different than Maxim's version. Because isn't that how family hatred always festered? Not being able to agree or compromise or understand the other? What had happened between them to make the space between them a canyon despite being shoulder to shoulder now?

And, damn me, but I wanted to *help.* I wanted to ease the strain that radiated from him when he thought no one was looking.

"Either one of you want to do a smile shot?" the photographer asked, and I choked back a laugh.

Jansen's eyes shifted, locking on mine, and he gave just the barest hint of a smirk. The one that had driven me crazy since the elevator—all confidence and sex and undiluted *fun.* My cheeks flushed, and I tried like hell to ignore the ache now radiating between my thighs.

From. Just. A. *Smirk.*

I shook my head when he arched a brow, just slightly, as if he could *sense* where my thoughts had taken me. Not wanting him to see right through me, I broke our gaze, glancing at Maxim.

His eyes were on me too, but no playful smirk shaped his lips. No, Maxim's mouth promised destruction—pure, soul-wrecking destruction for anyone who dared to get too close to him. Yet his eyes, so much lighter blue than Jansen's, churned with something I couldn't read as he looked at me. I tilted my head in question, wondering what that silent look meant.

And then he *winked.*

Maxim actually winked.

It was so...unexpected that my lips parted open, an uncontainable laugh flying past them.

Maxim's eyes smiled, his lips barely giving anything away.

And Jansen?

He glanced between the two of us, a look of utter bitterness churning in his eyes before he locked it down. The muscle in his jaw ticked, and I recoiled internally from the shift from his playful smirk to this…iciness.

I furrowed my brow, trying to catch his gaze, but he refused to look at me.

"That's all we need, guys, thanks," the photographer said as he packed up his gear. I made sure to thank him and his crew, doing my best not to track Jansen's every move.

Which was in the opposite direction.

And I would've chased after him, but I had a line of fans waiting on the other side of a red-velvet rope to do a meet and greet with him, Maxim, Cannon, and Axel.

Cannon and Axel were chatting near the group of fans, waiting patiently for me to come to them with instructions and supplies. Maxim hurried over to me, nodding to the group.

"We're supposed to be over there, right?" he asked, and I nodded. "You okay?"

I drew my gaze away from Jansen, who leaned against the white stone of the hotel, his eyes distant.

"Yes," I said, a surge of anger sizzling in my blood. Why the cold shoulder? Because I had *glanced* at his brother who happened to be doing his best to make me laugh? In a *friend* way? Why did that earn me a disgusted gaze? Jansen hadn't asked for me in any real capacity—sure, he was helping me through my fears, but I was helping him with his career. If he wanted to put some *claim* on me, which I shouldn't even be thinking about, then he should've said so after he'd made me come with just his fingers. Not wait until I smiled at another man and go all primal caveman on me.

"Sterling?" I called to him, not giving him the satisfaction of waiting for him. I headed over to the group of fans with Maxim following at my side.

"Omigod," a redhead said, practically bouncing on her toes as she looked past me. "That's Jansen Sterling. He's as hot as his pictures!" She glanced down at her friend, who was staring awestruck at Maxim. "Sterling is single, right, Alice?"

The awestruck girl nodded. "According to the *Reapers Rocking Roster* group, he's not attached."

A cold spike of ice shot through the center of my chest.

Don't. I chided myself. Hadn't I just been internally ranting about Jansen and I owing nothing to each other beyond the terms we set?

The redhead fluffed her hair, popping out her chest as her eyes widened behind me.

I didn't need to turn around to know who now stood behind me—I could *feel* him there. Feel the heat from his body, the delicious prickle of electricity against my skin that happened any time he was near me.

"London?" Maxim asked from my left, Cannon and Axel now striding toward us. "The sharpies?"

I blinked out my cold-infused glare on the girls, and reminded myself who I was in this moment—London Foster, Reapers Game Day Event Coordinator.

Not, London Foster—majorly crushing on Jansen Sterling while simultaneously wanting to throttle him. And these fans, regardless of their comments, were important. They loved the Reapers, had waited out in the cold for just a glimpse of them, and I would do my damn job.

"Of course," I said, popping on my invisible career hat. I grabbed the handful of sharpies and headshot photos from my bag, passing them out to Maxim, Cannon, and Axel. Then I sucked in a sharp breath, spinning to face Jansen. Or, his chest, rather, since that was how close he stood behind me. I stepped back, extending the items toward him.

His eyes bored into mine, and I had the urge to melt under that stare. To let my knees give out like they wanted and simply fall into those arms that I knew were so damn strong.

But I steeled my spine.

Even as his fingers brushed mine when he took the pictures and pens from me, I didn't give into that trembling ache.

"Thanks," he said, his voice pure gravel as he took them and stepped around me like I was nothing more than a piece of furniture. Certainly not a friend, or a woman he'd kissed senseless on not one, but *two* separate occasions. Not to mention had his hands on me, *in* me.

Probably second nature to him.

My shoulders dropped at my own stupidity. Of course, the kisses we shared weren't life-altering to him. Why would they be? He'd been an NHL star for a hot minute now and had women falling at his feet without him saying a word. Just because they'd meant something to me, didn't mean the same for him. And I couldn't *truly* be mad about that. Not when he was free to do whatever he pleased, and so was I.

Then why do I feel so...awful?

About the girls fawning over him like he was a prize to be won.

About the way his gaze had burned when he'd looked so... disappointed in me when Maxim made me laugh.

About wanting him when I knew I shouldn't.

Everything bunched and tensed inside me. A pot of water about to boil over.

I backed away from the players and the fans, allowing them to do their thing while I tried like hell to get a grip on my breathing.

Maxim was the first to finish since he'd been the first to start, and he walked over to where I waited patiently near the entrance of the building. "What are you doing tonight?" he asked.

"Caspian has you checking up on me, doesn't he?" I asked, eying Maxim. Caspian had gone straight to his room after the game to power rest for the celebration later. He didn't have any obligations like Maxim and Sterling had, so he was free.

"Why would you think that?" Maxim tilted his head.

I shook mine. "Because Caz's obsession with keeping tabs on me has doubled since we work for the same team," I said. And I knew his heart was in the right place. It had always been in the right place. Ever since that day he lost me in the storm cellar.

A cold chill raced along my spine.

"Well," Maxim said, drawing my attention. "Not everything I do is at your brother's behest." I laughed again, the reaction free and easy when he used words like *behest*. "She laughs again," he said, and he *almost* looked like he might smile. Almost.

"So?" I reeled in my laughter. "You're being unusually funny and cheerful today. I'm not used to it."

Something flickered in his gaze, a darkness swirling there for a second before it was gone. "I can be…cheerful," he argued, but he nearly tripped over the word. "Sometimes."

I smiled at him, grateful for the distraction since Jansen was *still* talking to the redhead. Axel and Cannon had already wrapped up and headed inside the hotel. And I couldn't escape to the comforts of my room until I'd officially closed the fan event.

"You don't have to be cheerful," I said, forcing myself to focus on him. It shouldn't be that hard—he was gorgeous, my brother's best friend, and despite being a broody man of few words, he'd been sparing me a few.

But it *was* hard. Because each second I stood there and those women kept boldly reaching over the rope to touch Jansen, I wanted to throttle them. And I had *no* right to do or think that.

"It's okay to be exactly who you are," I continued, glancing up at him. That was one thing the brothers shared—they were freaking tall. "I know we asked you and Sterling for some slack during promos, but you shouldn't try and force yourself to be anything other than how you feel." Savannah had taught me that. It had taken me a while, but slowly I'd learned it was okay to be me—awkward, career-driven, *me.*

Maxim shifted, sliding his hands into his pockets. Something distant colored his eyes, a far-off gaze I suddenly felt I shouldn't be privy to. "Not everyone thinks so," he said, his voice low, rough. "Some people believe it's perfection or nothing. Please the masses or your worth holds no value."

My lips tugged down at the corners as I studied him. Who could possibly think Maxim was anything but a perfect specimen? He was an NHL legend, descended from practically hockey royalty. He could land any sponsorship he wanted, any woman he wanted, and had a tight-knit circle of friends eho trusted him.

I cast a glance toward Jansen, wondering if Maxim meant the jab toward him. But that didn't make any sense because Jansen's opinion had never appealed to Maxim before.

The mystery of the brothers deepened, but I didn't have second to register it as hope flared in my chest when Jansen turned away from the redhead, heading our direction.

"You never answered my question," Maxim said, drawing my attention back to him.

"What was it again?" I asked, flashing him an apologetic look.

"What are you doing tonight?"

Jansen slowed as he came within hearing distance of us.

"We're going to this local bar," Maxim continued. "Want me to swing by your room and pick you up on our way out?"

"I…" I floundered in my own head as I watched Jansen stop and turn, changing his path from toward us—toward *me*—and heading inside the hotel instead.

I blinked a few times. A drink sounded exactly like what I needed, but drinking with my brother and his friends wasn't exactly a night off. "I have to close out this event," I said, motioning to the fans who wore smiles and glazed looks. It was nice, seeing them so happy.

Except maybe for the redhead, because she looked downright devious as she chatted with her friend.

"And then I think I'll just crash," I continued. "Thanks for the offer, though. I'm sure you and Caz will have a great time." Maxim nodded, taking a step back. "Not too much though," I said, eying him. "Hangovers on the plane are a bitch."

His eyes did that squint thing that they did when he looked like he might laugh but wasn't physically capable. "You have my number if you change your mind," he said before turning into the hotel.

I hurried over to the crowd, thanking them for coming and wishing them all well. Most of them dispersed, holding their autographed photos to their chests like prized pieces of gold. Two fans in particular, though, headed *inside* the hotel instead of away from it.

I followed in behind them, having completed my duties for the night. And after the tension storm Jansen had delivered, I was more than ready for a scalding shower and a good night's sleep. Maybe I'd rent a movie and zone out—

"Omigod, did he actually invite you up to his room?" the awestruck friend from earlier asked her redhead friend as they hurried into the elevator I'd just boarded.

Oh, kill me now.

I assumed the enthusiastic pair had been headed toward the hotel bar—the easiest place to find the single Reapers looking for a good, and consensual, time. But no, here they were, crowding the already small space. Elevators were a part of life, despite my fear, and I'd gotten really great at only boarding the ones that had zero to one person inside. All I had to do was count to twenty and the doors would open.

But these two? They practically suffocated the space—their voices loud and this side of slurred, like they'd started the party before the fan event.

"He didn't exactly come out and invite me," the redhead said, twirling a spiral curl of hair in her hand. "But I could tell he wanted me to. The look in his eyes? It was pure lust. How can I *not* show up to his room."

Ice shards bit into my stomach. Thirteen more seconds, and the doors would open.

"But he didn't give you his room number?" The awestruck friend seemed to sober a bit.

"No."

"Then how did you get it?"

Yes, how indeed? There were genuine fans, and then there was this…she was crossing a major line.

"I overheard him telling the concierge to send up some drinks," she said. "It was like he *wanted* me to hear it."

Jesus, this girl was delusional.

Right?

I hated the doubt creeping into my blood, the whispers in the back of my head saying maybe Jansen was playing a game with the fan.

But no, that wasn't right. Not at all.

And not because he *couldn't* indulge in willing conquests, but because if he wanted the girl, he'd absolutely be straight forward and tell her. He was a flirt by nature, a tease at the best of times, and a downright scoundrel at the worst.

And you enjoy every single version of him.

True, but I didn't have to tell him that.

"What are you going to do if he doesn't like you showing up?" the friend asked, and the doors mercifully swung open.

I bolted through them, gulping down the air in the hallway, my eyes finding the large window at the end of it out of sheer instinct. My nerves untangled, a sense of solidness returning to my limbs as I headed toward my door.

"One, how could he not?" the redhead continued as they stepped out of the elevator. "Second, if he isn't hospitable at first, I'm sure I can convince him to let me in."

"I think we drank too much," the friend said. "Because seriously, what if he doesn't? What if he shuts the door in your face?" At least her friend was sounding somewhat reasonable.

"Then I'll blast that shit all over social media," the redhead said with a shrug.

Oh, fuck that—

I spun on my heels, stopping the direction I'd been heading toward my room, and damn near stomping to where the girls were going straight toward Jansen's.

"Excuse me," I said just as the redhead knocked on his door.

She pinched her brow as she looked at me. "Oh," she said, recognition flaring in her glazed eyes. "We don't need any more headshots or anything. We're good. You can go."

I blew out a sharp breath, telling my adrenaline to chill the fuck out. "No, you're not good. Not even close."

Her lips popped into an O as she glared at me. Her friend tugged on her arm, trying to get her to go. A shuffling sounded behind the door.

"I'm going to give you this one shot," I said, just as I heard the doorknob click. "Leave. Walk your ass out of this hotel with a little dignity."

She popped a hand on her hip. "And if I don't?"

The door creaked open, and Jansen stood there, eyes darting between the three of us.

"I'll call security and let *them* haul you out of here."

"For what?" she snapped.

I ignored the way Jansen folded his arms over his chest, an amused look on his face that screamed he was *dying* to know what I'd do next.

Instead, I stepped forward, a few mere inches from the girl's face. "For threatening to slander one of my players if they deem you unworthy, which trust me, in his case?" I jerked my head toward him without looking. "You absolutely aren't worthy."

She gaped at me, all the while her friend was still tugging on her to go.

"Your call," I said, waiting.

She glanced at Jansen, and one look from him deflated every ounce of arrogance she'd had prior. "Whatever," she scoffed, then shook off her friend's hand and stomped past me.

"If I hear a word about this on the sites, it won't just be *me* who hunts you down!" I called after her, knowing Langley and Persephone would use all their resources to bring down any lies she may try and post about Jansen. "I have eyes everywhere!"

The girls upped their pace toward the elevator bank around the corner, but the adrenaline in my blood had my hands shaking.

"Well, that may have been the sexiest and most adorable thing I've ever seen in my life," Jansen said, his voice all calm tease.

I brought my eyes to his, and something inside me tensed and went loose at the same time. The coldness was still there, but above it laid a layer of intrigue and...something else I couldn't place.

"Adorable?" I almost hissed. "That woman was planning to slander your name if you didn't fuck her." Trash. Absolute *trash*.

He cocked a brow at me and pushed his back against the door to fully open it. "You look like you could use a drink."

I gaped up at him, shocked that he hadn't immediately been offended by the threat from the woman, or at least surprised.

The wind rushed out of me. I wasn't new to the celebrity athlete lifestyle, but was it such a commonplace occurrence that he wasn't even fazed by it anymore? God, how hard would that be to deal with? The constant knowledge of if you do the right thing, you still might be damned by the media, by jilted fans.

I pushed past him, fire still in my blood over the entire situation. He huffed a laugh, closing the door behind him.

"Thought you were going out with Maxim tonight," he said, leaning against the door, his eyes flickering with amusement and intrigue and...*want*.

I scrunched my brow, holding my arms out horizontally to indicate the room in which I now stood. "How about that drink?"

9

STERLING

$\mathcal{L}$ondon walked into my room with her head held high and threw her purse on my dresser. Tension wafted off the woman in waves. If I hadn't known better, I would have called it jealousy.

I shut the door and leaned back against it, enjoying the sight of her bent over to root through the mini fridge. That ass deserved to have songs written about it, and it was currently covered by a pencil skirt that screamed sexy librarian. Add her buttoned-up blouse and twisted-up hair, and she was a walking, talking fantasy.

"Apple juice. Orange juice," she muttered, pushing bottles around. "Water." Her head popped up, and she glared in my direction. "Where is this drink you offered?"

"You think I drink alcohol during the actual season? That's cute." The corner of my mouth lifted into a smirk.

Her mouth opened and shut a few times, but eventually, she shook her head and took an apple juice out of the fridge. "I don't know how you're just…calm about all that?"

I folded my arms over my chest. "Calm about what? The fact that I had to spend a half-hour posing for pictures next to an asshole I happen to share some genes with, or the women at my door who were hoping to fuck me?"

She considered her answer for a few seconds as she opened the bottle of juice. "Yes. All of it."

"I tolerate Maxim because you asked me to. It's as plain and simple as that." My stomach churned every fucking minute of it, but I did it.

"Is it really that hard?" She slumped back, perching on the edge of the desk. "I'm going to break my own rule here for a second, but he's been Caspian's best friend for two years. He's not that bad of a guy."

"Not that bad of a guy," I repeated slowly, reminding myself that our family dynamic wasn't exactly something that most people understood, mostly because we didn't *have* a family.

"He's not! Okay, maybe he's arrogant and a little aloof until you know him"—she cocked her head to the side— "and to be honest, I don't think I've ever seen him with the same woman twice, but you might actually like him if you got to know him."

I scoffed. "Not happening."

"Jansen…" She sighed like I was disappointing her or some shit.

"London, you don't know the first fucking thing about my family, which, by the way, consists of my mom, grandparents, and *me*." My forehead puckered. "And fine, Greg, my stepfather, whom my mom married my junior year in college. But that's it. Maxim isn't my family, I don't care how much you like him."

"He's your brother!"

"No, he's not." I moved forward, raking my hands over my hair. "And if you had been there when I had to call my mom and tell her that not only was he on my team, but I was being put with him for promotional purposes, you might have another view of this subject." I'd never forget the way her breath had stuttered, and she'd gone silent. "That being said, choosing to get your hackles up about the women outside my door is a much safer fight to pick if you're feeling feisty over there, London."

"Feisty?" She threw back the apple juice like it was a beer and clunked it down on the desk beside her. "I'm not trying to pick a fight."

"Yes, you are." I leaned against the dresser and gripped the edges, keeping a safe distance away from her. It had been almost two weeks since our little theater date, and this was the first time she'd approached me. The first time she'd talked to me when it wasn't in a professional capacity, and while I liked to think I was a pretty confident guy, her little hot and cold routine was a mindfuck. "You've been around professional hockey enough to know that there are willing women in every arena, every hotel, and every hallway, so why is the fact that you managed to run off the two at my door getting you all prickly?"

"*Run off*? Wait, were you interested in them?" She sputtered, her eyes sharpening like little daggers as her spine went stiff.

"If I had been, would that have been a problem for you?" I wasn't. I hadn't so much as breathed in the direction of another woman from the moment I'd seen her in the elevator. She'd owned me from that moment on.

"I...I...." Color flushed from her neck up to her cheeks, and her gaze darted between my eyes and my lips. She wanted me.

Good, the feeling was mutual.

"Because you say the word, and I'll get online and change all my social media statuses to *in a relationship*." My fingers dug into the wood. It didn't matter how badly I wanted to launch myself across the few feet that separated us and kiss the ever-loving shit out of her, I wasn't budging. Not until she admitted what had her sexy little panties in a twist. "Until then, why should it matter who I sleep with?" How far did I need to push her until she snapped and admitted what she wanted?

"Because random hookups are just...dirty and impersonal!" she fired back, shifting her weight.

"Hey, dirty can be good, and last time I checked, you're the woman who climbed into my lap and came so hard the theater next door probably thought it was part of the sound effects." I arched an eyebrow, ignoring the way my dick hardened at the memory.

"We're not random!" She huffed an angry sigh. "And besides, there were *two* of them. What were they going to do, take turns?"

I let a slow grin slide across my face. She was so jealous I half expected her face to turn green at any second, and I was loving every minute of it. "Who said I couldn't handle both at once?"

"You. Can. Not. Be. Serious." The look of pure shock on London's face was well worth the annoyance of having the two puck bunnies hunt me down.

"Well, I mean, I'm not sure what college was like for you…" I shrugged.

"It sure as hell wasn't orgies in the frat house!" She pushed off the desk.

"I wasn't in a frat, but if you need to argue locations—"

"You can't be serious!" Her cheeks went from pink to red as she marched closer, stopping when the toes of her high heels were an inch from my bare feet.

Fucking adorable.

"Oh, come on, London. Are you telling me you didn't have a one-night stand or two while you were in college? Are you seriously as perfect as you seem?" I tilted my face down toward hers as she stared up at me with fire in her eyes. Fuck, her lips were kissable, even when pursed.

"Perfection has nothing to do with it. Sex is way overrated." She arched her eyebrow.

"Then you've been sleeping with the wrong people."

"*People*? I've had sex all of *one* time, thank you very much!" She put her fists on her hips and glared at me with everything she had.

"Once." My eyebrows skyrocketed as pieces fell into place.

"Once." She nodded. "And I'd say he couldn't have gotten off me fast enough, but well…" Her nose crinkled. "It really was pretty fast now that I'm thinking about it. Awkward as hell, too. Trust me, it didn't exactly leave me begging for more. Like I said, it's overrated. If you were a woman, you'd get it."

Awkward? Fast? *Overrated?* I was torn between laughing that some idiot had the privilege of getting London under him and blew it completely—pun intended, and finding that same guy and punching him in the face for leaving her with such a sour taste for sex. My cock argued for a third option of showing her exactly how good sex could be, pushing against the fabric of my athletic pants, which weren't hiding much.

"Is that what you'd call what happened between us in the theater?" I gripped her hips and pulled her against me. "Overrated?"

"That was different." She gasped, her hands coming up to my chest to brace herself.

"How?" My hands shifted to her ass.

"Because it wasn't...sex." Her breasts crushed against my chest as she leaned in, running her tongue over her bottom lip.

"Wasn't it?" I moved my hand down her thigh until I found the sexy little slit up the back of her skirt. Then it was her bare skin beneath my fingers.

Her breath stuttered, and she moved into my touch. "That was...something else."

"Huh." I locked eyes with her, watching for any sign of refusal, then brought my hand between her thighs and found her underwear already damp. "You're wet, London." Keeping my voice level and my control firmly locked in place should have earned me a gold medal or some shit. Just the feel of her heat through the silk of her thong was enough to tighten my balls.

"Jansen," she whispered in a plea, clutching fistfuls of my shirt.

"You want this?" I slid my fingers under her thong, just lightly skimming her swollen flesh.

She nodded slowly, her glacier-blue eyes glazing over in need.

I plunged two fingers inside her and groaned at how ready she was for me. "Feel this?" I pumped my fingers in and out slowly.

"Oh *God,*" she moaned, her forehead falling against my chest.

"I'd consider this sex since I'm fucking you with my fingers." I brushed the shell of her ear with my lips, then raked my teeth over her skin.

She whimpered as I stroked her deep, mimicking exactly what I wanted to do with my cock.

"You're not random." Fuck, my voice sounded like it had been dragged across a skate sharpener. "You're not a hookup. You have no reason to be jealous of those hallway puck bunnies, London."

"I'm not jealous," she muttered, then moaned.

I stilled my fingers.

"Jansen!" she complained.

"I'm jealous of everyone who gets to breathe the same air you do. It's not a weakness to admit that you want someone." I withdrew my hand inch by inch until my fingers hovered on the edge of her pussy.

"Fine," she whispered, then sucked in a deep breath and tilted her face to mine. "I want you. I always want you. I look at you—or even just think about you, and I want you." Her face was a gorgeous mix of need and frustration.

"Then we're on equal footing, London, because that's exactly how bad I want you." I gripped her ass and lifted her against me, then kissed her with the full force of the hunger that had kept me on edge for *months*.

She opened for my tongue, and I swept inside, kissing her deep. Her nails dug into the back of my neck as she tilted her head and moaned, claiming my mouth the same way I'd done to hers. I heard the soft *clunk* of her shoes falling to the floor, but her skirt was too tight to wind her legs around my waist, but damn if she wasn't trying.

I walked us forward and laid her out on the bed, keeping my weight off her as I sucked my way down her throat.

"Take it off," she urged, arching as my fingers flicked the buttons of her blouse free. The sides fell away, revealing the white lace cupped swells of her breasts.

"Beautiful," I muttered, already running my mouth along those lace cups. "You're so fucking gorgeous, London."

She twisted in my arms and got the rest of her blouse off, then threw it to the floor. "Show me."

I paused, my gaze flying to meet hers. "Show you that you're gorgeous?"

A smile flashed across her face, but she shook her head. "No. Show me that sex isn't overrated. I want you. All of you."

The breath left my lungs in a rush, but I locked down every muscle except my dick. He was throbbing, and there was nothing I could do about it. "We don't have to have sex for me to show you just how good it can be for you."

"Are you telling me no?" A playful spark lit in those beautiful blue eyes. It wasn't like she couldn't feel exactly how much I wanted her against her thigh.

"I'm telling you that I don't want you to feel rushed or like you have some point to prove." What we had was too important to fuck up.

"Huh." She rolled to her side, then arched her hips, shimmying out of her skirt.

Legs. Holy, fucking legs. They were lean and toned and went on for days. I was still staring at them, awestruck, when she rose up on her knees and unfastened her bra, dropping it to the floor with the rest of her clothes. "Do I look rushed to you?" she asked, tilting her head.

"You look...incredible," I managed to answer. Her breasts were high and firm, with rose-colored nipples that were already pearled into hard tips.

My mouth watered as I sat up.

She lifted her hands to her hair, pulling out a few long pins and dropping those, too. Her hair fell, long, dark, and luscious, to shield her breasts as she shook the tresses free.

"Do I sound like I have a point to prove?" She leaned forward, grabbed the fabric of my shirt, and lifted it over my head. Her indrawn breath made me feel like a fucking god as her gaze skimmed the lines of my torso. "Wow, Jansen..." Her fingertips traced the lines of my pecs.

"You sound like a woman who knows exactly what she wants." I caught her hands against my chest, trapping them there. If she went any farther south, this would be over way before I wanted.

"Good. Now use that flawless body of yours and show me what I've been missing out on." She brought her mouth to mine and traced the seam of my lips with her tongue.

I pounced, taking her beneath me as I kissed her breathless. My hands shaped the soft mounds of her breasts, my thumbs teasing her nipples as our kiss blazed out of control, taking on an urgency that made my heart pound.

"I'm going to make you come so hard so you won't be able to say my name without getting wet," I promised, moving from her mouth to her breasts.

"Promises," she teased, then gasped as I sucked one peak into my mouth and worshipped it with my tongue and lips.

"I can't wait to taste every inch of you." I moved to the other breast so I could give it the same attention. Taking my time, I lingered until both of her nipples were swollen and sensitive before moving down the plane of her stomach.

Her fingers tangled in my hair as I learned her curves with my hands and mouth, leaving none of her skin untouched. When I reached her white, lace thong, I hooked my fingers through the flimsy straps at her hips and looked up into her eyes.

She nodded and arched.

I dragged the scrap of fabric down those impossibly long legs, then began working my way back up, kneading and stroking the muscles of her calves, her knees, her thighs. I grazed over the sweet cleft of her pussy, but didn't give her what she wanted until she was an undulating, panting mass of need.

"Jansen," she pled, tugging on my hair.

"What do you want, baby?" I kissed her inner thigh and leaned hard into the bed, hoping my dick would get the not-so-subtle message that it wasn't play time. Not yet.

"Get up here and touch me!" She tugged again.

"I like it right where I am." I kept my eyes locked on hers as I spread her thighs wider, settling them over my shoulders. Then I leaned forward and ran my tongue over her pussy.

She cried out, her hips bucking. "Oh my God."

"Eyes on me." The command was soft, but she followed it. My tongue skimmed the opening of her pussy, and then I licked up to her clit, giving it a flick.

She gasped, rolling her hips.

"Feel that? It's only going to get better," I promised with another tongued circle around that tight little bud. "You taste so damned sweet, London." Honey and citrus slid down my throat as I lapped at her.

"Jansen," she moaned, her eyes sliding shut.

"Watch me, baby. Watch how much I love eating you." I blew softly over her wet flesh, and she whimpered before doing exactly as I'd asked, her eyes finding mine. I gave her a long, hard lick in reward, then got down to working my girl into a frenzy.

I devoured her with the hunger of a starving man, licking and sucking at her clit before stabbing deep and fucking her with my tongue, her cries like music in my ears as she keened higher, her legs tightening against my back.

She was so tight I felt her constrict along my tongue, and I groaned as she rocked her hips, riding my face as I pushed her relentlessly toward the brink of orgasm. Her breaths came faster, her breath catching as her thighs trembled.

I rubbed my thumb over her clit and sent her reeling, screaming my name before she released my hair to muffle her cries with a fist. While the waves still rolling through her, her hips swiveling, I lifted my mouth to her clit and sank two fingers deep inside her.

She moaned, and I worked her toward a second orgasm, pumping deep and adding a third finger to make sure she was ready for me. London's body was perfect, but she was small, tight, and the last thing I was going to do was hurt her.

"What are you doing to me?" Her head thrashed above me as her muscles coiled again.

"Did you want me to stop?" I offered, unable to crack a smile. My entire body was wound so fucking tight that snapping was a real possibility.

"Never," she groaned, grabbing fistfuls of the covers.

I sucked her clit between my lips and lashed at it with my tongue. She came again, her back bowing off the bed. My fingers stroked her down easy, then withdrew from her slick heat.

It took all of thirty seconds to grab a condom from my bag and shed my clothes, and her arms were open, reaching for me as I hovered above her.

"Are you sure?" I asked.

"Absolutely." She grabbed the condom from my hands and ripped it open, then looked down between us with wide eyes. "I've never—"

"Let me." I took the thin plastic and rolled it on. "If you put your hands on me right now, it would be game over for this round."

She smiled as I settled between her thighs, looping her arms around my neck. "Do I at least get a turn to touch you?"

"You can have as many turns as you want," I offered as my cock nudged her entrance, but then a groan slipped from my lips at the sight and feel of her. She was flushed and pink and had the glow of a satisfied woman coupled with the hope in her eyes that there just might be more to come. My control was hanging by the barest of threads, but something she'd said tickled the back of my brain. "Are you okay like this? Am I too heavy on top of you?"

She shook her head and hooked an ankle over my waist. "You're perfect. Now take me, Jansen." Her hips rocked slightly.

I rolled mine slow and steady, pushing through the velvet muscles of the tightest pussy I'd ever felt in my life until she took me completely.

She gasped, but there was no pain in her eyes as I gave her a moment to adjust, sweat beading in a fine layer on my skin from the effort of holding back and fighting every instinct in my body to move.

"You feel incredible," she whispered then arched up to kiss me.

I sank into the kiss as I rocked my hips gently, setting an easy, soft pace. She was so damned small, and I wasn't exactly a little guy. She moaned into the kiss and met me thrust for thrust.

Slow. Easy. Gentle. I was dying, *dying*, at the pleasure of being inside her. My entire body was alive and humming with electricity.

"You won't break me, Jansen." She skimmed her hands down my sides until she grasped my ass.

"I'm. Trying. To. Be—"

"Just be you. Stop holding back." She forced her hips up and pulled me into her on the next thrust, sending me hard and deep. I groaned. So did she.

That sound unraveled the last of my control.

I took her with hard, deep, long strokes that brought me close to the stars with every thrust. She squeezed tight around me, meeting me for every move, our bodies sliding and colliding over and over.

It was too good. Too hot. Too consuming. I couldn't stop. Her whimpers turned to soft, keening little cries as she scratched at my back, urging me on. When her body drew tight again, her eyes flaring slightly as if surprised, I pushed the back of her thigh, opening her wider, and stroked even deeper.

"Jansen..." She clutched my shoulders as her legs shook, and I worked my fingers between us as I took her faster, climbing that same peak with her as lightning shot down my spine. I strummed her clit and felt her convulse around my cock just as my own orgasm took hold, shooting me straight to the stars.

I think I blacked out for a minute because when I came to, I'd shifted so she was at my side, both of our chests heaving as we struggled to catch our breath.

"That was…" She stroked her thumb across my lower lip. "That was not overrated."

I laughed and pulled her close. "That was the best I've ever had in my life. And maybe the loudest," I teased.

She grinned, but then it slipped slightly. "You don't think anyone heard me, do you?"

"I think we're okay." Hotel walls were only so thick, but I doubted anyone would recognize London's cries, especially since I was the only guy to get her screaming like that.

"Good." Worry dulled the heavy-lidded satisfaction in her eyes. "We just have to keep this quiet. I don't even want to think about what Caz or—"

I kissed her softly, stopping her words. "London, I have no problem keeping this between us. But baby, I need it to be just that—between us." My fingers brushed back her hair, and I cradled her head. "I don't know what this is, but I do know I'm sick at the thought of anyone else touching you."

She pushed at my chest, and I let her roll me to my back as she smiled down at me. "Then the same goes for you."

"Already does." I pulled her into another kiss and we started all over again.

By the time I woke the next morning, it was seven a.m., and my bed was empty, which made sense seeing that London was hell-bent on keeping our private activities, well, private. Didn't mean that waking up without her didn't suck. It did.

I showered, dressed, and headed down to the lobby to grab breakfast. We had the second game of the series today, and I wasn't the last Reaper to the private dining room, but I wasn't exactly the first, either.

"Saved you a seat," Briggs said, smacking me on the back as he walked by with his food, pointing toward the table in the corner where Cannon and Sawyer already sat.

A laugh I'd know anywhere sounded from the opposite side of the room, and my gaze found her with all the effort of a compass and the North Pole.

London sat with her brother on one side and Maxim on the other, laughing at something Caz had said. Her cheeks were pink, and her eyes bright as they locked with mine.

Too many emotions to name barreled through me.

I wanted to kiss her, to ask how she was feeling. Hell, I wanted to carry her back up to my room and go for round five…or was it six? But more than all that, I wanted to be the one she was laughing with at breakfast.

How could I feel so incredibly connected to someone from this far across the room and yet worlds apart?

She gave me a smile, but then Maxim leaned in close to talk to her, wrapping his arm around the back of her chair.

Her gaze fell from mine, severing our connection.

I waited a breath, then two, hoping she'd look over, hoping she felt the same inexplicable pull that I did, but…nothing.

Something in my chest chilled and drew tight.

Why? I'd agreed to keep our relationship quiet. What did it matter if everyone knew as long as she and I did? There was less pressure this way, and whatever made her comfortable was okay by me, that's how badly I wanted to keep her.

But that's when it hit me.

We weren't just quiet or discreet.

We were something a little dirtier—a secret.

10

LONDON

"I don't know what to do," I groaned as I sank onto Savannah's couch. I shoved one of her throw pillows against my face, muffling a scream.

"Whoa," a familiar male voice said, shocking me. I dropped the pillow to see Hendrix, frozen two steps into the living room. "What kind of a situation did I just walk in on here, babe?" he asked Savannah, who had her legs curled up under her on the chair across from me. "Is it an ice cream and brownies thing or a whiskey and ice thing?"

I choked on a laugh, smoothing out the wrinkled pillow.

Savannah waved him off. "It's just a normal thing, Holly-wood. But I'd absolutely take a brownie." She winked at him. He snapped his fingers, pointing to both of us before practically sprinting to the kitchen.

My heart warmed a fraction, calming some of the infuriating tension that had collected in my muscles. "Using those wide receiver skills to rustle up treats?" I nodded, smiling at my friend. "Not a bad man at all."

She bit her lower lip, her features nearly drowning in true-love dust. "He is. But Hendrix's extensive skill list isn't what we're discussing."

I blew out a breath. "It's been *seven* days," I said, but it sounded like a whine.

Seven days since I'd had the most incredible, world-shaking, mind-blowing sex of my life. Like...I wasn't sure it got better than that. Ever. My skin flushed just thinking about him, about the things he'd done to my body, the places he'd taken me with just his tongue.

"Tell me about that little trick he did with his mouth again," she said, and I laughed again. God, it was so great to have a friend like her.

"You're shameless," I said, shaking my head.

She shrugged.

"He hasn't called." Or texted or even acted like I existed. It twisted something inside me. "He's been *off* since the breakfast in Chicago." The same morning-after breakfast. I'd decided to sit with Caz—one, because he'd made it to the room before Jansen—but also because I didn't want Caz going after him.

It hadn't been a *choice* thing, it'd been a professional thing. I wasn't sure what we were to each other, and until I was, I wouldn't flash what we'd done to the entire team, least of all my brother. That was drama Jansen didn't need for sure.

"What a dick," Savannah hissed.

"Who's a dick?" Hendrix asked as he came back into the room. He set down a plate of brownies on the coffee table between us, then handed me a sparkling water.

"Sterling," Savannah said at the same time I said, "Thank you."

Hendrix whistled, his eyebrows raised as he took a seat. "That doesn't sound like Sterling," he said, leaning back in the chair next to Savannah.

I snatched a brownie off the table, taking two bites. It was almost enough chocolate to cool the anger and confusion simmering in my blood.

"So walk me through it again," Savannah said, her brow pinched.

I finished chewing, took a sip of the drink, then set everything back on the table. "We..." I glanced at Hendrix, who waggled his eyebrows at me with a teasing look. "We had a *night* together," I said, and he snorted. "And the next morning..." I sighed. "Well, I don't know exactly what I did wrong." The knowledge curled up inside me like dried flower petals. I had practically zero experience with sex. Maybe I hadn't been good enough for him. But he'd seemed so enthusiastic in the heat of the moment...maybe that had been for my benefit too. I pinched the bridge of my nose. "I tried to talk to him on the plane, but he gave me the cold shoulder. I've been trying to catch him in the arena, but he's always just heading out. And he's ignored my texts."

Hendrix hissed through his teeth, and Savannah smacked his chest.

"You didn't do anything wrong," she said, and Hendrix practically hid behind his bottle of water.

"Maybe I did. You know I don't have that much...experience."

141

"It doesn't matter," she argued. "From what you told me he was more than into it."

"I should probably go," Hendrix said, but Savannah shook her head.

"You can talk about sex without hiding, Hollywood. You basically have a master's degree in the subject." She flashed him a look that made me want to cover my face with the pillow again.

This all should be incredibly mortifying, but Savannah was my family. And Hendrix was the love of her life, so that made him family too. Plus, he *did* have an insight to the male mind. Maybe he could tell me why Jansen was flaking on me out of nowhere.

"Yes," I said. "Please stay." His brows raised at my request. I looked down at my nails. "Do you think it's because I wasn't...knowledgeable?"

"God, no," Hendrix blurted out, shaking his head. "Trust me. It doesn't matter if you've never had sex before or you've had it with a thousand people. With the right person, experience isn't necessary. It comes down to *instinct*."

I nodded, a little bit of relief pooling inside me. I *had* given over solely to the instincts and demands of my body. And we'd crashed together like the most brilliant, electrifying storm.

"What's up his ass then, I wonder?" Savannah asked, eyes darting between the two of us. Something clicked, and she tilted her head. "Did you do anything with Maxim?"

"What?" I snapped. "No! Of course not—"

"I didn't mean sexually," Savannah laughed.

"Oh, for fuck's sake, London," Hendrix grumbled. "Tell me you're not dating *both* brothers." I gaped at him, and he quickly raised his hands in defense. "Not that you don't have every *right* to do that. More like, they seem like they'd kill each other on a good day, let alone if they had to *share*."

A shiver ran the length of my spine at the thought. Trying to juggle both brothers would be about as easy as nuclear fusion. "No. There is *nothing* going on with Maxim and me. Why does everyone assume there is?"

"He's at your apartment a lot," Savannah said, then hurried on when I flashed her a glare. "And *I* know it's because Caz is always there too. But does Sterling know that?"

I parted my lips, then shut them.

Was that it?

Could he possibly think I was trying to play them both? God, what kind of person did he think I was? If I were to openly date two men—two *brothers*, no less—I would be absolutely up front about it. Hell, I didn't even know if what Jansen and I were doing could be considered *dating* or if he even wanted it to be labeled.

My mind raced backward, thinking of all the times Maxim and I had been seen together in the last week. There was breakfast in Chicago—*with* Caz too—and the plane ride, I'd sat next to both of them. The following practice Maxim had teased me about not wearing the jersey he'd gifted me, and Jansen had definitely been in earshot.

I pinched the bridge of my nose. Surely, Jansen was smart enough to know better, right?

"I don't even know what we are to each other. And it's not like I can confess a working relationship to Asher-freaking-Silas without knowing if this is even a thing or not." I sighed.

Did I want it to be a thing?

God, I did. I could feel that in how unsettled I'd felt since he'd been so distant.

"How do I fix things?" I asked.

"Sex always works for me," Hendrix said, and Savannah laughed. "What?" he asked. "They clearly need to set up some rules. Stick to them, and everything will work out."

Savannah snorted. "Yeah, rules are meant to be broken." She leaned over the armrest, grazing a finger over his forearm. "Or have you forgotten?"

He grinned at her, and I suddenly wished for the ability to teleport the hell out of there.

"I remember everything," he said.

"Okay, this has been fun," I said, pushing to stand. "I have to go Caz's barbecue. I'm already late as it is."

"You were stalling on purpose," Savannah said, standing up to hug me.

"Of course, I was," I said, squeezing her back.

She released me but held my gaze. "You like him."

Not a question, but I nodded anyway.

"Then you have to talk to him."

"I've been trying—"

"Make him listen," she said. "Be more direct. Lay out exactly what you want, whatever that may be, and it'll be his decision whether or not that's okay with him. And at least you'll know."

Right. Not knowing what he wanted or why he was upset with me was half as painful as not being able to joke or laugh with him like we'd been doing before that night. I'd grown used to his teasing texts and phone conversations that lasted far past bedtime.

"Okay," I said, sucking in all the confidence I could muster. "How do you propose I get him to talk to me?"

"Sex. Always. Works!" Hendrix chimed in, and Savannah and I laughed.

"Great," I said, shaking my head. "Wish me luck." I turned for her door, closing it softly behind me.

I sure as hell was going to need it.

Caspian's home in Reaper Village was finally starting to look the part. Pictures of our family in various stages over the years decorated the halls, and he'd had someone come in and decorate for him because I knew he was clueless when it came to selecting furniture. But the home was full of carefully selected pieces, all looking *so* Caz that I wondered who he hired. The person obviously was an expert.

I made my way through the house, waving to Langley and Persephone who lounged in the front room with their hulking husbands. The sliding glass door to the backyard was open, happy voices filtering inside from half the Reapers who dominated the space.

It didn't take more than thirty seconds to spot him.

Looking ten degrees of amazing in a pair of jeans and a white thermal, he chatted with Briggs and Demon across the yard. I was surprised I managed to stop to chat with Caz—who stood before the grill—when everything in my body *begged* me to run across the yard and demand Jansen to talk to me.

Luckily, I maintained some shred of dignity. "Smells good, brother," I said, patting his back as he flipped a half dozen steaks on the grates.

He wrapped me in a quick side hug. "I'm a master chef," he said, then waved his tongs toward the tables on the other side of the patio. Each one was piled high with side dishes, drinks, and desserts. "Help yourself," he said.

"Thanks," I said, but my mind was so not on food.

Or my brother, for that matter.

They were on the man who was now staring at me from across the yard.

Those crushing blue eyes had the ability to shred me or save me.

Now or never.

I straightened my spine and headed his direction.

It's fine.

Whatever he says will be fine.

I tried to grill the notion into my head, but I couldn't stop my heart from trembling as I stopped before him.

"Hi," I said, and the look he gave me…

God, the man had some nerve to look at me like that. Like he didn't have a clue why I was seeking him out.

"How's it going?" I tried again.

Brigg's brows raised when Sterling didn't say anything, and I flashed him an apologetic look. Because you know what?

Fuck. *This.*

I boldly reached out and grabbed Jansen's arm, tugging him in the opposite direction. I knew full well if he didn't *want* to follow me, he wouldn't. But he *did.*

"I'm going to steal him for a minute," I called over my shoulder to Briggs, who waved me off with the beer in his hand.

I traveled around the side of the house, opening the gate and passing through it. Jansen shut it behind us, and I nearly groaned when I spotted at least four more Reapers and their dates hanging out on the front porch. Worrying my bottom lip between my teeth, I spun to face him. "Where can we go to talk that won't be overhead by the entire team?"

Something cracked in his steely gaze—maybe it was the wild desperation in my voice. He cocked a brow and pointed at a house just down the street. "I live two houses down."

My jaw dropped. How had I not known that? "You live—" I cut myself off, shaking my head. I grabbed his arm again, hauling him to the home he'd pointed at. If any of the Reapers saw or cared, they didn't let on.

Jansen quickly opened his front door, laughing under his breath as I hauled him inside his own place.

"You *have* to stop dragging me places," he said, but there was the familiar tease I knew and loved in his tone.

"Well, you always come so..." My eyes widened as the words left my mouth, and I cringed slightly as I stopped inside his entryway.

"I think you mean I always deliver," he fired back, tossing his keys onto a small wooden table tucked up against the main hallway wall.

Heat flushed my cheeks. I couldn't argue with him. Couldn't fire back some well-thought retort. I had no doubt Jansen *always* delivered. I was still reeling from the aftermath of what he'd done to me.

I glanced around his home, noting how the model was similar to Caz's in build, but not in style. Where Caz had carefully selected pieces by someone who obviously knew what they were doing, Jansen's home was filled with things that looked like him. Clean, comfy couches, rich wooden shelves, crisp paint. A complex collection of sharps and softs that was as exciting as it was inviting.

And it *smelled* like him. All mandarin and sage and *God,* why had I asked to come here?

"Your home is beautiful," I said, folding my arms over my chest as we lingered in his entryway. A set of stairs rested just to my left, and I shivered at the idea of his bedroom being just up them.

"Thanks," he said, his tone back to what it'd been the whole week. Cold. Calm. Bored even.

No beating around the bush, then. Got it.

Well, here goes nothing.

"You've been frosty toward me," I blurted the words but refused to lose his gaze.

He raised his brows. "*Me*? Cold?"

"Yes," I said, exasperated. "Why?" A knot formed in my throat. Fuck, what if he said it was because he'd had me and now wanted nothing to do with me? That I wasn't worth the hassle that would eventually come when my brother found out, my bosses.

He's not like that, some hopeful bitch whispered in the back of my mind.

"I'm not the one who ignores you in public," he fired back.

I gaped at him. "You have been!" I shook my head. "And I haven't been ignoring you—"

"You practically acted like you didn't know me the morning after," he cut me off. "Like I was *no one*. Like I hadn't been inside you every way possible hours before. Like—"

"Are you *kidding* me?" I stopped him, stepping into his space. Heat buzzed off of him in waves, and dammit, it made me *ache*. "I'm trying to be a professional! What did you want me to do? Straddle you in the banquet room? Cuddle up in the seat next to you and stare at you with moony eyes?" I smacked my hands on my thighs. "I don't even know what you really want beyond you asking that no one else touch me! And you what? Wanted me to *out* you to your coach, our bosses? My brother and everyone who could potentially fire me or mess with your contract without us at least having a discussion about it?"

His mouth snapped shut, his eyes flaring as he stared down at me. There was only an inch of space between us, and every inch of my body cried out for his.

"Do you get how hard that is?" I asked, calming my rant.

"What?" His tone was pure gravel.

"Acting professional with you when my feelings are *anything* but."

He moved closer, and I retreated, the look in his eyes wholly glazed and primal. My spine kissed the wall next to the stairs, but I didn't break our gaze. Every nerve ending came alive as he caged me in with a hand on either side of my head.

"What do *you* want, London?" he asked, his words a whisper between us.

"I told you that night." I licked my lips, my eyes fluttering from his to his mouth and back again. "I want *you*," I said, release unraveling from my chest at the admission. "I know we shouldn't. I know the risks with our jobs, my brother, everything. I know I'm the hard choice—the hassle, the lack of experience. I know you could have any woman you want—"

He crushed his mouth against mine with a kiss so dominant and primal I *whimpered*. My hands flew to his shirt, fisting it as I held on to him. He parted my lips with his tongue, taking my mouth in sweeping strokes and teasing flicks.

God, kissing him felt like breathing after being underwater for too long. Felt like it was necessary for my survival to feel his mouth against mine.

He jerked his head back, sucking a sharp breath as his eyes met mine. "Say it again," he demanded, flicking his tongue over my bottom lip.

My thighs clenched, an ache wrenching deep in my core. "I *want* you, Jansen," I said, not needing him to clarify. "No one else." His eyes guttered, and he slanted his mouth over mine, claiming it enough to steal the breath from my lungs.

He took my mouth with starvation and relief and it...*broke* me.

Because he'd *needed* to hear me say it. Needed to hear me say I *wanted* him for him. The reasoning behind that need hadn't been shared with me yet, but it was enough to make my heart ache for him as much as my body.

Who *wouldn't* want this man? This strong, smart, funny man with so much depth and passion to him? Who wouldn't rip apart their very lives to be with him? As I was clearly doing now—because there were risks, stakes to what we were doing, and most definitely consequences, but I just didn't care.

"I," I said, breaking our kiss for just a moment. "Want." I tugged at the hem of his shirt, and he pulled it over his head with one arm. "You," I finished on a gasp as I ran my fingers over his chest.

He deserved to hear it again and again.

As many times as he needed for it to sink in.

"I want your teasing words," I said, breathless. "I want your challenges, your jokes. I want your eyes on me in the arena. And I have an impossible time watching anyone else on the ice. Jansen, I want every single piece of you."

"*London,*" he breathed my name, and I smiled up at him, my heart racing as every nerve in my body became a live wire.

I dug my fingers into his biceps, shifting and tugging until he spun, our positions replaced. He smirked down at me as he *let* me push him against the wall. But that smirk vanished as I dropped to my knees before him.

My fingers flew to his jeans, making quick work of the zipper and button. I yanked them and his boxer briefs down, practically moaning as his hard length sprang free.

Butterflies flapped in my stomach as I gripped his considerable length in my hand, my lips inching nearing. I'd never done this before, but my body, my soul, was screaming to devour this man. To show him what he meant to me.

So I dove in headfirst, wrapping my lips around the head of his cock and sliding it right on it.

"Fuck!" he hissed, his fingers tangling in my hair as I moved my mouth on him.

He flexed inside my mouth, his cock twitching as I flicked my tongue over the sensitive head. I moaned around him, rocking my head back and forth as I explored him. God, he tasted good—like heat and salt and Jansen. I pumped him with a hand while I sucked, working myself up just as much with every groan or growl that escaped his mouth.

Here, in this, I felt experienced. Capable of wrenching those sounds from him. His grip tightening in my hair.

I did that.

Me.

And it felt fucking amazing.

Doubt and worry dissolved in the wake of flames that consumed my body, my soul.

There was only this—Jansen, me, and the fire between us.

"Fuck, baby," he growled, his length hardening another degree in my mouth. That grip on my hair intensified, and he tugged back. His cock sprang from my mouth with a little popping sound, and in the span of a blink, Jansen hauled me to my feet. "My turn."

He stripped me bare in a matter of breaths, and before I could reach for him, he hauled me over his shoulder, giving my ass a light smack as he hurried up the stairs.

A delighted laugh ripped from my lips, and before I knew it, my back landed softly against a giant mattress.

Jansen smirked as he hovered above me, kissing his way down my neck, lingering on my bare breasts. "Fuck, I love these," he said, palming each breast, flicking one nipple before he soothed the sting with his tongue. The sensation had me writhing beneath him, desperate and greedy for what I could feel hard between us.

"Jasen," I moaned, rolling my hips upward.

He flashed me another cocky grin, planting kisses down my belly, over my hips, and—

"Omigod!" I screamed, my fingers flying to his hair as he licked me from slit to clit.

"Delicious," he growled against my sensitive, slick flesh. He plunged his tongue inside me, and I arched off the bed. He gripped my hips and held me down, working me up with teasing strokes and feather-light flicks over that swollen bud.

I fisted the sheets above my head, my mind and body whirling with the sensation of his mouth on me. Everything inside me coiled and burned with each lap of his tongue, each grip of his strong hands on my hips, each satisfied growl against my flesh.

My breaths came too quick, my head spinning, my heart racing. I thrashed beneath him, the sounds coming from my lips slightly animalistic as I felt myself being pushed closer and closer to that sweet, sharp edge.

I lifted my head, and my breath caught as I saw him gazing up at me from between my thighs. The smirk on his lips was near devilish, and those eyes? God, they were wholly glazed and churning. He lowered his mouth again, fast and sharp, sucking on my clit with just the right pressure—

My back bowed as I shattered into a thousand pieces of sparkling light.

Jansen gripped my hips as I unabashedly rode his face, seeking out that pleasure like my life depended on it. He worked me through the throes of the orgasm, my body trembling beneath him.

He raised up, stalking up my body like a prowling predator. He settled between my thighs, his hard length just grazing my entrance, the flesh soaked and swollen and aching.

"London," he said my name, running his fingers through my hair as his mouth hovered above mine. "You have to tell me to slow down if you need me to. Need to tell me if there is anything you don't like."

I blinked the stars out of my eyes, and grinned. This man. He'd never trap me, never make me feel cloistered, never push me beyond whatever limits I may have. And my heart *sighed* and swooned at his care. At the way he went out of his way to truly understand me, my needs.

And right now?

All I needed was him.

I pushed up on my elbow, wrapping my hand around the back of his head to grip a fistful of his hair. Yes, I had little to no experience with sex but with Jansen? It was pure instinct, pure primal demand. "I want you, Jansen," I said again. "I want you to do whatever you want with me. *To* me."

He shuddered against me, the motion sending hot shivers up my spine. "What if I want to take you hard and fast?"

I became liquid—all limp limbs and breathless moans.

"Then take me hard and fast."

He lowered his mouth to mine, claiming my lips with a searing kiss as he rolled his hips against me. Teasing me. I arched into it, seeking more. "What if I want to take my time?" he said against my mouth, his hands traveling down my ribs. "Worship your body until you can't stand a second more of the torture."

"Then do that," I said, yanking him to me and kissing him just as hard and hungry as he had me.

I reached my free hand down between us, shifting so I could grip his hard length. He hissed against my lips as I squeezed him.

"What if—"

"Any way. All ways. As long as it's *you*."

Jansen stilled above me, his eyes flaring like blue flames. He shifted on the bed, reaching toward a nightstand near the head—

"I want all of you, Jansen," I said, stopping him. "You already know I'm clean," I hurried to add. "And I got on the pill after that night in the hotel."

He shuddered above me. "I am too," he said. "But, London—"

"I trust you," I said. "If you don't want to then I understand. But you asked me to tell you what I wanted." I bit my bottom lip, wondering if I was asking too much. "I want to feel you inside me with no barriers."

Something snapped, some restraint he'd held himself back with.

One second, I gripped him, and the next?

He'd drawn back, rising to his knees between my legs. He hooked his hands behind my knees, yanking me to him.

And he plunged inside me in one, fast, hot, thrust.

I moaned, arching off the bed to meet him as he pulled out and thrust in again.

And again.

And again

All the while, those burning blue eyes watched me, seared me down to the very quick of my soul. I raised my hands above my head, gripping those sheets as I held that gaze. He smirked at the submissive move, and God, he looked glorious. All the hard ridges of his abs on display as he slammed into me. The whorls of ink decorating his chest, his ribs. The muscles in his arms rippling as he yanked on my legs with each thrust.

"Harder," I moaned, damn near *demanded* as I fisted those sheets.

"Fuck, London," he growled, upping his pace. "You're so tight, wet. You feel fucking amazing." He accentuated each word with a harder thrust, his cock filling every inch of me.

I arched off the bed, using his hold on me for leverage as I explored the angle. Hot *damn,* he slid in deeper, the head of his cock touching some inner spot that pulsed and sparked with each graze.

"Faster," I said, and that smirk deepened as he pounded into me.

Each stroke, each thrust, those sparks ignited to writhing flames. Consuming me, twisting me into a tight braid desperate for release.

"*Jansen,*" I breathed his name, my body a tingling, buzzing thing completely at his mercy. "God, *yes.* That. Keep. Doing. *That.*"

He pounded into me harder, his hold on my legs keeping me in place so I could feel every exquisite stroke.

"Fuck, London," he growled, driving into me like he wanted to brand himself on my skin, my body, my soul.

Everything inside me clenched with an all-consuming fire, the flames licking up my spine. I tightened and trembled, a glittering storm winding up and up until I was sure I'd shatter completely.

"Jansen," I moaned, writhing beneath him. "I'm. Going. To. Come."

"Fuck, yes," he growled, shifting his position so that he hovered closer to me. The move had his pelvis grinding against my clit with each strong, fast, pump—

I screamed his name, my entire body bursting with exquisite sparks as I completely and wholly unraveled. Jansen hardened inside me, the length of him filling me so deep, his long strokes drawing out my orgasm as he found his own release.

I shook against him, even as he lowered himself, planting a slow, languid kiss on my lips. Trembling, I released the sheets and wrapped my arms around him. He fell to my chest, our bodies sweat-slicked and blissfully, deliciously spent.

And as I ran my fingers through the dark strands of his hair, doing my best to calm my racing heart, I knew two things for certain.

One, there would never be anything as torturously wonderful as him.

And two, I was wholly and royally fucked.

Because while all I'd wanted to do was stand on my own and belong to myself, I couldn't deny that Jansen had succeeded in completely and utterly claiming me.

And realized that I didn't mind being *his.*

Not. One. Bit.

11

STERLING

"Someone's been skipping the carbs," Briggs said as I finished my squat reps and put the bar back on its stand. "I don't think I've ever seen you this shredded. You might be giving Demon over there a run for his money." He nodded toward the corner, where Brogan Grant was benching an ungodly amount of weight.

"Pretty sure that guy could bench a car if he had to," I remarked, reaching for my water bottle. Any fat I'd lost was probably due to the marathon rounds of sex London and I were having at every possible opportunity.

"True." Briggs adjusted the weights on the bar next to mine and started his own reps.

I didn't say a word about the fact that he had about twenty more pounds on his bar than I did. Briggs was just like that. Always went above but never drew attention to it.

We finished our workout, showered, and headed for the conference room, where the rest of the team was already gathering. I sank into the empty chair at Sawyer's left, and Briggs took the one next to me.

Meeting every month to discuss what team promotional events were going on was a new thing this year, but I liked that it gave the rookies a chance for some face time with fans if they got their hands in the air fast enough. Plus, it gave me an extra hour of staring at London, which was hardly something I'd argue with.

Maxim and Caz took the seats directly across from us, and I did my best to ignore them both—Maxim, because fuck him, and Caz because I was sure he'd take one look in my eyes and know I was carrying on a secret relationship with his sister behind his back.

Not cool.

Necessary, but still.

Not. Cool.

I took the stack of papers Sawyer handed me, kept one, and passed it down, elementary school style. It was an itinerary of the upcoming events and listed how many players they'd need at each one.

My name was already inked on every meet and greet, right next to Maxim's, and *oh joy*, there was a TV promo spot coming up for the Ronald McDonald House fundraiser event. *Yay.*

London came by behind us, handing out bottles of water as Langley took the floor at the end of the table, explaining why two new events had been added. Had to admit, it was hard to concentrate on anything she was saying when I knew London was approaching.

"Sawyer," she said, handing him a bottle.

"Thanks, little Foster."

She cringed, but her smile was steadfast.

"Jansen," she whispered, holding out my bottle.

I turned slightly in my chair and made the epic mistake of looking up into those gorgeous blue eyes of hers. They were pretty much my kryptonite and sucked every thought out of my head. "Thanks, London."

My hand brushed against hers, my index finger sneaking a little stroke of the inside of her wrist as I took the bottle.

Her breath caught, and we shared a smile before she moved to Briggs.

"Briggs," she muttered.

"Thank you, London."

I turned my attention to the agenda in front of me and felt the heat of Maxim's glare from across the table, which I did my best to ignore. It wasn't my fault that his side of the table had Sean, the other game day coordinator, handing out their hydration. Too bad. So sad.

"Okay, we have an event at the zoo in two weeks, and they've asked for an additional two players for that. It's basically a meet and greet. Photos. Autographs. Nothing too invasive," Langley said, looking down the table.

Rookie hands shot into the air, and I let them have it. I was getting more than my fair share of camera time lately.

Seeing that London had finished our side of the table and was walking back to Langley, I took out my cell phone but kept it beneath the table as I texted her.

ME: You have no idea how badly I want to lick you right now.

London slipped out her phone and read the message, her cheeks flushing pink as she quickly typed out a response.

LONDON: You did a thorough job this morning already.

A smile tilted the corners of my lips.

"What about you, Brogan?" Langley asked, lifting her eyebrows at him.

"No." He didn't explain or offer an apology. That was it.

Langley sighed.

"He'd probably frighten the kids off," Briggs joked.

The team laughed.

"He's not lying," Brogan replied, completely deadpan.

The laughter only grew louder.

"Oh, come on." Langley put her hands on her hips. "We've had multiple requests for you, and you turn them down every time."

"Then pick something without kids." He shrugged. "They're small and breakable and say weird shit that I never know how to respond to, and then it's just awkward for everyone involved. I'll do whatever you have coming up next that's adult-only."

"Great, so if a charity opportunity pops up at the senior center, you're our guy," Langley muttered, rolling her eyes.

ME: That black dress looks delicious on you.

London shook her head at the message, but a smile tugged at her lips.

LONDON: Pay attention and stop flirting.

ME: The dress will look even better on my floor tonight.

Her gaze popped up to meet mine, her blush rising all the way to her hairline. Then she put her phone into the pocket of her blazer and picked up an agenda, clearly doing her best to dismiss me.

I grinned. As much as I wanted to stand on top of this table and shout that London was mine, even I could admit that there were certain perks of keeping our relationship quiet. Flustering her in public was the biggest perk of them all.

"London?" Langley gave her the floor, and my girl stepped into the center position.

"Right, so you'll all note that there's a special event coming up over New Year's Eve."

The team groaned collectively.

"I know, I know," she waved us off. "But it's a part of the promotion we're doing for the Ronald McDonald house. I know that we have a bye that weekend, but I'm going to need at least half of the team there since that's how we're advertising for the tickets. And you don't have to tell me right now." She looked poignantly at Caspian. "And you're going."

He scoffed. "Am I, really?"

"I just got called *little Foster*, so yeah, you're number one on the list, buddy. Tux it up." She lifted her brows at him and smiled.

"Fine," he relented.

"Count me in, too," Maxim added, giving her a slow smirk. "If it's important to you, I'm there."

My stomach twisted painfully, and it only intensified when he glanced at me to see if I'd rise to the bait. I didn't. London knew I'd be there for her, and that was good enough for me.

The meeting came to an end, and we all filed out. As I passed London, who was pressed against the wall, close to the door, she stroked her hand across my stomach when no one was looking. My abs clenched at the touch, and my body temp rose a degree. "Five-thirty," she whispered.

I nodded and managed to keep my eyes off hers as I walked into the hallway, where Briggs was waiting with an arched eyebrow.

"Man, you have got to be more subtle than that," he lectured quietly as we walked toward the parking lot.

"I have no idea what you're talking about." I shrugged.

"She called you by your first name." He shook his head.

I blinked. "What?" We walked into the sunlight, and the team scattered, headed toward their various cars.

"She called every other player by their last name, except you." He pulled out his remote and clicked the unlock button on his G-wagon.

"So?" I unlocked my Audi.

He glanced across the lot at Caspian before continuing. "So, in my *years* on this team, everyone has only ever called you Sterling. And at that table, she called every other player by his last name...except you. If you two are going to keep whatever you're doing a secret, then you have got to cover your tracks a little better than that." He stared me down.

Shit.

I couldn't confirm or deny, not without breaking my promise to London that we'd keep this quiet, so I simply nodded and got into my car as quickly as possible. We'd have to be more careful at the arena, but at least I'd get her to myself tonight.

Two hours later, I held London's hand as we entered a corn-field maze.

She tensed as we turned a corner and were surrounded by corn stalks in every line of sight.

"If it gets to be too much, maybe look up?" I suggested, pointing to the clear blue sky above our heads. We still had a good two hours of daylight, so we'd be out of here long before it turned inky black.

"Good idea." She took a deep breath as we came to a T juncture. "Which way?"

"You choose." I lifted her hand to my lips and kissed the back of it. I'd learned that London did much better in confined spaces if it was her choice to begin with. In fact, the only area in her life where she liked to give up control was in bed with me.

There, she didn't care if I was above her, behind her, or had her pressed against a wall. She was all in, and damn did I love that about her. I loved a lot of things about her, which was making it increasingly difficult to act like we were only acquaintances at the rink.

"Let's go left," she suggested, tucking a strand of long, dark hair behind her ear.

"Left it is." We made the turn and continued into the maze. "You know I'll be at the New Year's Eve thing, right?"

"I already marked you down," she said with a nod as a mischievous smile spread across her face. "I put down Brogan, too."

"Demon?"

"He said adult-only, and it's black tie and eighteen and up, so he went on the list."

I laughed. "Oh, my brave, beautiful woman."

"He doesn't scare me." Her nose crinkled, and she led us right at the next fork. "Well, maybe he's a little intimidating, but when you grow up with Caz, you become immune to the broody, angry thing. Add Maxim to the mix—" She snapped her mouth shut.

"It's okay." I squeezed her hand for reassurance. "I just tell myself that he's two different people, and your brother's best friend, Maxim, is not the same person I share genes with."

"You always say that. *Share genes.*" She took us straight when there were three options, and we passed a family who was coming out of the left, the husband muttering in agreement that he should have listened to his wife.

"That's because it's all we share." My jaw ticked. "It's not exactly easy to look at the guy and know that he was the reason I might have a father, but don't have a dad."

She tugged me to the right, where the path turned quickly again, closing us into a dead-end. "Why didn't you say it that way before?" Her brow knit in concern and her fingers stroked over my knuckles.

"There's nothing to say," I bristled slightly but softened at the compassionate look in her eyes. "Look. You know that I didn't know about them for *years*. I know that Sergei paid my mother a lot of hush money because I wasn't exactly something he wanted advertised. He already had a family. He chose that family. And all the stuff that makes a family—love, memories, loyalty—none of that exists between Maxim and me, or his siblings. So yeah, we share genes. That's it."

Her shoulders rose and fell as she sighed, long and hard. "I'm so sorry."

"For what?" I cradled her face. "You didn't do anything."

"For putting you guys in that promo together. I would never do it knowing what I know now." Her gaze dropped.

"Hey."

Her eyes rose to meet mine, and I brushed a kiss over her lips.

"If you need something from me, I'll give it to you. That's how this works now," I said softly.

"And what do you get out of the deal?" Her hands rose to my chest.

"You."

"Is that right?" She smiled slowly.

I nodded. "This is real to me, London. I'm in. I'm so in that—"

She leaned up and kissed me, cupping the sides of my neck and effectively cutting me off in the sweetest way possible.

"Me, too," she admitted against my lips. "I want whatever this is."

"It's a relationship," I clarified, needing her to know exactly what I meant. If I was being honest, I needed to hear her say it, too.

"It's a relationship," she agreed, then kissed me softly, sucking on my lower lip.

Relief coursed through my veins, and I pulled her against me, my hands sinking into her hair as I kissed her long and deep. She tasted like the apple cider we'd had just outside the maze, and that unique, sweet flavor that was all London.

She moaned and laced her fingers behind my neck, tilting her head to give us that perfect angle as I kissed her over and over. Fuck, this never got old. Every kiss was better. We hadn't tired of each other or fallen into a routine, either. Every time I touched her somehow felt new and yet comfortably familiar at the same time. She felt like...home.

Her tongue rubbed against mine, and I lost myself in the kiss just like I did every time.

A kid laughed somewhere in the maze, and London ripped her mouth away. We were both breathing heavy and my dick was pretty much a steel pipe in my jeans.

"Let's go," she said, gripping my hand. "The faster we get out of here, the faster I can get you naked."

"Excellent plan."

We made it out of the maze without her anxiety spiking once, and I kissed her breathless against the door of my car, unable to wait another minute.

It was getting harder and harder to keep my hands to myself when we were in public, not just here at the maze, but at the arena, and on the plane on the way to away games. Briggs was right. We were slipping.

At some point, we were going to be outed.

I just hoped London was ready for it, because now that I had her, I wasn't letting her go—damn the consequences.

12

LONDON

"What is that delicious smell?" Jansen asked, letting himself in my front door with the key I'd given him a month ago under the condition that he always text first to make sure Caz wasn't here. He dropped his gear bag in the entryway, his long stride eating up the space between us in seconds. "Besides you, of course," he said, scooping me up against him. My feet dangled off the floor, and I shivered against this chest.

"Cookies," I said into his neck as I held him right back.

We'd only been apart one night, but it felt like a lifetime. We'd adapted this incredibly comfortable, exciting, intoxicating routine over the past month, and every time he "came home" to me, I lost myself a little bit more for this man.

"Snickerdoodles?" he asked, gently returning me to my feet.

I grinned up at him. "Now, why on earth would I make *your* favorite cookie," I teased, heading back to the kitchen to check the oven. They were two minutes away from being done.

He followed me, snaking his arms around me from behind. He brought my spine flush against his chest, and I arched into him, my body instinctively craving his. "Because," he said, his lips at the shell of my ear. "You know I'm a sucker for your cookies. You know I'll do anything to get a taste."

My lips parted on a gasp, heat unfurling low in my belly. It had been a month of *this*. This never-ending, never-quenched thirst for the man who simultaneously infuriated me, challenged me, and turned me into a helpless, wild string of pure *need*. And I had no idea if the inferno between us would ever settle into a softer ember, but *goddamn*, I relished what we had now.

I spun in his embrace, reaching up on my tiptoes, my mouth inching toward his. He met me halfway, but I paused, lingering in that space just above his lips. "It sounds like I have you wrapped entirely around my finger," I teased, gently taking his bottom lip between my teeth.

He growled, smoothing his hands over my hips and around to cup my ass. I squealed when he squeezed and hefted me up, forcing me to lock my ankles behind his back. He turned, situating me on my kitchen counter. "Is that right?" His voice was low, and that smirk was on his lips as he rubbed his hands up my thighs. The heat from his hands sizzled through my leggings.

"That's right," I said, nodding, my heart pounding against my chest. I tangled my fingers in his hair, drawing him to my mouth. "I bet I could ask you for anything right now, and you'd give it to me."

"Someone thinks highly of herself," he teased, grazing his nose along the line of my jaw.

I arched into the innocent touch, tracing my free hand over the thin fabric of his shirt, delighting in the muscles bunching beneath. "Well, that is your fault," I said.

He grazed his teeth over the seam of my neck, and warm chills burst along my skin. "Really?" he whispered. "Why is that?" He gripped my hips, tugging my ass to the edge of that counter, right against *him*.

"Because," I breathed the word, shuddering from the feel of him against me. "You make me feel like a goddess." And that was the damned truth. I'd come alive under him, atop him, beside him. Whether we were fucking or binge-watching, next to him, I practically sparkled. He challenged me, listened to me, understood me. He made me laugh and moan and all the things in between. I'd never had anything like this.

"You are," he growled against my skin, planting kisses over my collarbone. I pushed my chest out, giving him better access, and trembled as his head lowered toward my breasts. "Beautiful, smart, funny," he said, and sealed each word with a kiss. "A pain in the ass most days," he teased. "But you're mine."

I rocked against him, shamelessly seeking that spark already igniting between us—

A sharp beeping sounded, and I jolted against him. The timer for the cookies blared throughout the kitchen, and Jansen barked out a laugh. He pointed a finger at me. "Don't move," he ordered, stepping out from between my thighs and heading across the kitchen. He grabbed an oven mitt from the drawer and pulled the cookies out of the oven. He smirked as he set the baking sheet on the stove. "Snickerdoodles," he said, nodding like he knew he'd been right. He tossed the mitt onto the counter, returning to me in a blink.

"I guess I should thank you," he said, the warmth from his body settling against me again.

I grinned, wrapping my arms around his neck as he picked up where he'd left off, smoothing his hands over my thighs, planting my skin with teasing kisses. "You don't have to thank me," I said, nearly sighing the words. He loved to torture me, sometimes for hours. He would tease and play and touch me until I felt like a bottle of champagne ready to pop. "I love making you happy," I admitted, my head spinning from everywhere he touched, teased.

He stilled slightly between my legs and drew his face back to mine. Perched on the counter, he was still taller than me, but his gaze burned. There was such...gratitude and shock and wonder in those eyes. Something I caught in rare instances as if he wasn't used to that kind of affection, that kind of compassion.

"Jansen," I said, my voice softening. "What's that look?"

He pressed his forehead against mine, his eyes closing like an instinct had told him to hide.

"Talk to me," I said, every sensation in my body switching from hungry to hopeful. We'd grown so close this last month, and yet there were still so many pieces of him I didn't understand.

"You do make me happy," he said, eyes still closed. "Are you happy with me, London?" he asked, drawing back enough to look at me again.

"You know I am," I said, not at all frustrated with the question. I would tell him over and over again, I would show him as many times as I needed to until he understood that he was everything.

173

"Then why can't we tell anyone?"

It was my turn to go utterly still. This conversation we'd had just once before. "You know why," I said, blowing out a breath. "Our jobs—"

"If we're honest, we might not get in as much trouble as you think."

"I know," I said, understanding his point. And I wanted to tell everyone. Wanted to be open about the joy Jansen brought to my life. "But I'm just finding my rhythm with my position," I said, and he cocked a brow at me.

"You have excellent rhythm," he said, gripping my hips again to jerk me against him. I hissed at the contact, warmth dancing along my spine.

"And you know Langley and Persephone warned me about dating the players," I continued.

"Which means so much coming from women who *married* players," he said.

I nodded. No argument there.

"Langley has handed me a huge assignment in the New Year's Eve event," I said. "One that will hopefully secure my position for next year instead of Sean."

Sean was a great guy, a good event coordinator, but that spot on the Reapers was *mine*. I knew Langley would give him a good recommendation if the time came where I actually earned the one slot available, so I didn't have time to let myself feel guilty. I would earn my position.

"I'm in charge and it's the biggest event of the year," I continued. "A huge fundraising event packed with fans, pro-athletes, and more. You know all the proceeds go to the

Ronald McDonald House." And we needed to prove to them that we had what it took to bring in the big donations. They had pro-teams nearly going to blows to be their chosen sponsorship of the year. Because not only did they have an incredible organization that provided housing and funds to families in need, but their media coverage was immense. Working together, everybody won. "If I screw it up, not only does the charity suffer—which is the absolute last thing I want—the team's coverage will."

Jansen sighed, his hands settling on my thighs. "And you think being honest about what's going on between us will screw it up?"

I furrowed my brow. "No," I said, almost whimpering when he stepped back enough to lean on the other side of the counter. He folded his arms over his chest. "Jansen," I pled, shaking my head. "That's not what I meant at all. Nothing with you would ever be a negative thing, it's more…" I blew out a breath and hopped down from the counter. "It's me," I said, standing before him so I could catch his gaze. "I need this. To prove myself. To show the Reapers, the *world*, that I am not just Caspian Foster's little sister. That he had nothing to do with my success on the team. That being Jansen Sterling's…being *yours* isn't what's defined my status on the team." I swallowed hard, reaching for the coiled muscle of his forearm. I smoothed my hand over it, sighing when he didn't pull away "Haven't you ever wanted to prove yourself?"

He unlocked his arms, bracing his hands on the counter as he nodded. "I understand better than anyone," he said. "Why do you think I never claimed Sergei Zolotov's last name? Never pulled his connection to me to get on an NHL team?"

A lump formed in my throat. Everything with his biological family was twisted, and with each layer he decided to show me, my heart hurt worse and worse.

"You didn't need his name," I said. "You have an insane talent on the ice, Jansen."

He huffed, nodding.

"What happened?" I asked. "Between you and him?" I held my breath as I waited, patient. I would totally understand if he wasn't ready, but I wanted him to know I *cared*. That I wanted to know all the pieces of him—no matter how dark they may be. Just like he knew mine. "You told me a little bit, but not the full story."

He was quiet so long I thought he'd retreated, building walls to keep me out.

But then he loosed a long breath, and parted his lips. "Sergei met my mother after a game," he said, shaking his head. "One of her friends had dragged her along." He shrugged. "They did one of those meet and greet things you run so well."

I swallowed hard.

"And he…wanted her. Probably for the sheer fact alone that she knew nothing about hockey. It was her friend who loved the game. My mom was just there for her."

I did the mental math, my stomach tightening. "He was married."

Jansen nodded. "Yep," he said. "Not that my mother knew that. All she knew was…" His voice trailed off. "Well, you know how alluring celebrity athletes can be," he tried to joke, but there was too much raw pain in his voice. "Anyway, it lasted a few weeks before she figured it out. She was crushed, naturally. He already had another kid with his wife, and one on the way."

"When she found out she was pregnant with me, Sergei had the audacity to demand a paternity test. My mother didn't want anything, wasn't asking for money. She just felt he had the right to know he had another child on the way." His eyes lilted to the side and cleared his throat. "She did everything he asked. Got the test. Proved he was the father. And, I guess he was banking on her not being faithful to him, or he hoped for it because when she showed him the proof..." His knuckles turned white he gripped the counter so hard. "He turned her away. Tossed her out like she was nothing but trash."

Angry tears bit the backs of my eyes.

"She never went public," he continued. "But Sergei's wife found out, somehow. I think she found a copy of the paternity test or something. Asshole had been dumb enough to hang onto it." He shrugged. "Maxim was born a few weeks before me," he said. "And I didn't even know any of them existed until I was thirteen. When my mother finally felt I was emotionally mature enough to handle the truth and take my own actions, whatever they may be."

My heart clenched. "What did you do?"

He huffed a dark laugh. "I was a thirteen-year-old boy without a father," I said. "I did what any kid would do. I begged to meet him." He shook his head. "I've told you the rest before," he said, and I remembered the moments he'd let me in when we'd been stuck in that amusement park ride.

I shook my head, stepping toward him, but he continued. "Sergei agreed to meet with me, but only in a public place. He sat down with me at some bullshit restaurant, ignoring my mother who lingered just outside. He told me I'd never be his real son. That me simply existing had nearly torn his real family apart. He called me a coward for reaching out, and threatened to stop sending the child support I didn't even know about if I continued to try."

A tear rolled down my cheek. "You were thirteen?"

He nodded. "I walked out of that restaurant a bit older," he said. "My eyes were opened in a way they never had been before. My mother had raised me as both a mother and father, playing two roles and shuffling two jobs to keep us fed. And the money he'd sent? That paid for all the hockey lessons, the gear, the insurance for the inevitable injuries I sustained." He shook his head. "I realized that day that I had to do whatever it took to take care of my mother. To make up for what that asshole put her through. The same asshole who knew I was his son and decided he'd rather treat me like a dirty secret than a human being."

"Jansen," I said, my heart breaking for him. It made sense now, the nerve I struck every time I said I didn't want to go public. But he wasn't something I was ashamed of. I adored him. Craved him. Was a better, stronger woman because of him. "I'm so sorry."

"It's in the past," he said, but it so wasn't. The tension between Maxim and him? The rage and hate? That was still very much current. And everything he'd told me tonight and before? It made so much sense—Maxim was the son allowed in the spotlight, the one worth claiming, and Jansen had been the one tossed in the dark without a second thought.

"I hope you know that I don't want to hide—"

"I know," he cut me off, and I wrapped my arms around his middle. He slid his hand over my hair, holding me to him. "I know it's a different situation, London," he said. "But, I just wanted you to know. To understand...why I get a little cold when that comes up."

I nodded against him. I completely understood—not how a father could do that to his child, but the source of Jansen's pain. His drive to be the best without help. The way Maxim grated on his nerves. And I didn't know if it was simply because Maxim was who he was or if they had a deeper kind of history, but I wasn't about to push that issue now. Not when he was an exposed nerve, raw and vulnerable.

Words and emotions swirled and rose, my heart expanding so much it hurt. But I didn't know how to say what I felt for him—this all-encompassing need to soothe the wound he'd ripped open for me.

So, I showed him instead.

I gently intertwined our fingers and led him out of the kitchen, down the hall, and to my bedroom.

I slowly undressed him, taking care to linger in all my favorite spots, which was practically every inch of his body. He shuddered at the intense silence between us, at my actions that spoke volumes about the worth of the man before me.

Settling him on my bed, I stripped myself bare, smiling at him with genuine compassion, adoration, and just a hint of our usual passionate hunger. I wanted him to see to the heart of me, to know that he was much more than he gave himself credit for.

"Beautiful," he whispered as I pushed him back on my bed, climbing over him to straddle his hips.

"You are, Jansen," I said with all sincerity, running my fingers along the sharp lines of his chest, his abs, and lower. "You're…" I reached between us, gripping what was already hard and aching between us. "You're everything," I said, those tears still coating my eyes.

Realizing another human being meant everything to me was almost enough to overwhelm me, but I held it together.

Held it together for him. Because now wasn't the time to cry and make giant, life-altering confessions.

Now was the time to show him how much he meant to me.

He reached for me like he might flip me over and take the reins, but I shook my head, forcing him gently back to the bed. "Let me take care of you," I said.

I inched backward, kissing down his chest, his abs, and only stopping when I got that glorious length into my mouth. He hissed, throwing his head back as I bobbed up and down on him, devouring him, loving him. And only when his fingers tightened in my hair did I pull back. His growl was short-lived when I settled atop him, sinking onto his slick cock with one fast stroke.

And then I moved on him. Slow, torturous, wild.

I rocked and writhed atop him, relishing his length deep inside me, until we were both peppered with sweat. Until our breaths were one, and he looked up at me with blazing blue eyes that burned every inch of my soul. And I made sure he watched me as I rode him, made sure he saw the depth of what I felt for him.

Because it was endless.

He was endless.

And I was just the lucky woman he'd allowed inside.

I upped my pace when he thrust upward over and over, seeking me as hungrily as I was him. And the words built inside me, almost as strong and fierce as my orgasm, stronger even…but all that escaped my lips was his name as we fell over that blissful edge together.

After we'd cleaned up, I settled him against my chest, slowly smoothing my fingers through his hair, relishing the soothing feeling of his weight next to me. This strong, confident, incredible man. Capable of rendering me speechless with his mouth, and yet he could do so just as easily by just holding me this tenderly.

We held each other the rest of the night, content to lazily touch and tease and soothe. I stared into his eyes, the silent intimacy more than anything I'd every experience before.

And I knew without any further doubt that I wholly belonged to him and him to me.

Everything.

Jansen was *everything*.

I just hoped I could prove it to him.

13

STERLING

I loosened my tie as I rode the elevator to London's floor. It had been three long days without seeing her while we'd played in Vegas, and I wasn't willing to wait another minute.

ME: In the elevator.

LONDON: In the kitchen!

I grinned at her response as a pop star sang that it was lovely weather for a sleigh ride. Christmas would be here in a few weeks, which meant we'd be separated again, seeing that she and Caspian were headed home to their parents' and Mom was coming to visit.

It would have been so much easier to go public, but she still didn't want that. I got it—she felt like she had something to prove, and if it was between Sean and London to get a permanent place on the Reaper staff, then I wanted her to have every advantage...or maybe I just didn't want to be her *disadvantage.*

The elevator dinged, and the doors opened on her floor. The hallway was empty, and I'd heard Caspian make plans with Maxim on the plane, so the coast was clear. It took all of twenty seconds to unlock her door and step inside. Man, that key sure was convenient.

But did it mean something? Did she get the same achy, sweet feeling in her chest that I did right before we saw each other? Had she spent the last three days tying herself into knots because we'd been a thousand miles apart?

I shucked my suit jacket and tossed it over the back of her couch as I made a beeline for the kitchen. She met me halfway, wearing pajama bottoms, a Reaper hoodie, and a huge grin.

No one had ever looked so good.

She flew into my arms, and just like that, I could breathe again. My chest loosened and my dick went hard.

"Fuck, I missed you, baby," I muttered into her hair, holding her off the ground in a tight embrace. It wasn't just the sex with her—though that was pretty damned phenomenal. She had a way of cutting through the bullshit and seeing *me*. I didn't have to fake it with her, and even trying to impress her was pointless. She'd been around it all.

She was completely, openly honest with me, and I couldn't get enough of her.

"I missed you," she murmured in my neck, breathing deep. "I watched the game, though. You had some spectacular saves."

"I hate when you don't travel with us." I adjusted my grip, and she wrapped her legs around my waist. Everywhere she touched warmed, sending a jolt of need sprinting down my spine.

"Me, too, but there are two coordinators for now." She ran her fingers through my hair, eliciting a low groan from me.

"For now. It'll be you. I know it." My stomach…or maybe it was my heart, couldn't even fathom any other result. Not just because I wouldn't see her, but because it was all she wanted.

And it was the entire reason I couldn't so much as touch her in public.

"I think you got better looking while you were gone," she whispered, then kissed me softly.

After being away from her for days, the contact sent me over the edge. I walked forward, bracing her weight on the wall, then kissed exactly how I'd wanted to while I was gone. Deep strokes. Light flicks. I used my tongue like a branding iron to claim her as mine and didn't let up until she was arching against me, her breaths unsteady and her eyes glazed.

"Jansen," she whimpered, tugging my head back to hers.

I leaned into her, grinding my hard cock against her hot center as I lost my head in the kiss. Nothing existed beyond this wall and this woman. Nothing that mattered, anyway.

She tugged at my tie, and I broke our kiss long enough for her to slip it over my head. Her tank top went next. Her bra was pale blue and cupped her breasts like a lover. I had it off with a snap of my fingers behind her back.

Getting my shirt off took a hot minute since I wouldn't stop kissing her long enough to help out. Her lips were so fucking sweet, and I couldn't help but suck her tongue into my mouth.

She moaned, licking the line just behind my teeth as she shoved my shirt off my shoulders. Then her hands were on my skin, stroking my arms, my chest, my back with feather-light touches that felt like little flutters of painless flame.

"I need you," I growled against her mouth, my hands already working at her shorts.

"Good, because I'm going to die if you don't get inside me." She unhooked her legs, and I hit my knees, dragging the little silk shorts and her underwear down the length of her legs at the same time.

She was completely, utterly bare.

My gaze flew to hers as my cock threatened to shred my pants to get at her.

"Surprise," she said with a grin. "I got waxed."

"I see that." Holy fucking shit, I was going to devour all that silky skin. My hands gripped her thighs.

She tugged her lower lip between her teeth. "You like?"

I answered her with my mouth, diving into her pussy like a starving man, spreading her thighs wide with my hands and spearing my tongue into her.

"Jansen!" she shouted, falling back against the wall.

I licked her from opening to clit, then tongue fucked her.

Her knees buckled.

I shifted my grip and supported her, keeping her right where she was as I ate her. She was more succulent than a peach, and I groaned at the taste of her on my tongue, sliding down the back of my throat. Her cries came faster, and I knew she was close, so sucked her clit and dragged my tongue over the bud.

185

She came. Hard.

Was I ever going to tire of hearing my name on her lips? Nope. Never.

"You taste so fucking good, London," I said against her core, going for seconds.

"God…Jansen," she moaned, then tugged at my hair. "I want you inside me."

I would have been content to do nothing but dine on her for the next few hours, but who the fuck was I to deny the woman I lo—

My heart stammered, then thudded even stronger.

Love.

I loved the way she'd listen without judgment. I loved how hard she fought to overcome her fear of small spaces. I loved how driven she was at work, and how effortlessly she kept every ball in the air. I loved the way her eyes lit up just for me, and the way she made me feel like the center of her world.

I just loved *her*.

"Baby, please," she begged, rocking her hips against my mouth.

I got to my feet, then unbuckled my pants and dropped my boxer briefs just low enough for my cock to spring free. The rest could come off later.

She scrambled up me, locking her ankles around my back as I lined up with her entrance. Then I drove home, filling her in one long thrust.

"London," I groaned as her pussy surrounded me, gripping me tight. This woman was made for me. We fit perfectly. Our chemistry was off the charts. This was it. She was *it*, the one.

She gasped, then let out the sweetest moan I'd ever heard. "I love the way you feel inside me." Her hips swiveled, and the friction nearly sent me over the edge.

"I love you," I said, locking my gaze on hers.

Her eyes flared, and her body tensed. Before I could ask if I'd just made a colossal misstep, she grabbed the sides of my face and pulled me into a hard kiss, and damn, I could feel it with every flick of her tongue—she was just as lost for me as I was for her.

She rocked her hips again, and I snapped, pinning her against the wall as I fucked her with long, hard, deep strokes. Later, I'd take it slowly. I'd make love to her with all the care and consideration we both deserved, but I knew how we both needed it this first time.

Our kiss was all tongues and teeth, her nails sharp across my shoulders as I plunged into her again and again, driving us both toward completion. Something fell to the left. We kept going.

Her cries filled my ears, her body locking around mine like a vise as she came again, and the ripples of her muscles pulled me over with her. I emptied into her with one last, deep thrust, locking my knees so I didn't pull us both to the floor.

Our breathing was ragged, our bodies sweat-slick as I rested my head against the wall beside hers, trying to get my body back under some form of control.

"So I guess you like the wax?" she asked, running her fingers through my hair gently.

I couldn't help but laugh. "Yeah, London. I fucking *love* the wax."

* * *

THE NEXT DAY, we were just finishing up practice when I saw London against the wall again, but this time, Maxim was hovering over her.

The hallway was crowded and smelled like sweat as we walked off the ice, heading toward the locker room. I saw Maxim's back first, the Zolotov name standing out against the black jersey like a fucking warning. Then I noted those little black heels with the red bottoms, and spotted London, leaned up against the wall.

I knew it was harmless, that there was at least a good foot of space between them, but it didn't stop the ugly churn of jealousy in my gut.

"We have an extra seat if you want to join us at dinner," he offered, reaching to tuck a loose strand of her hair back.

She got there first, thank God, or I would have had to spend my night burying a body instead of making love to London. She stepped away, putting a little more distance between them, but I was still seeing red as I approached.

"I think I'm busy this weekend," she said, her gaze flickering toward me. The color fell out of her cheeks at whatever she saw on my face, but she quickly recovered and offered Maxim a shaky smile. "It was sweet of you to ask, though."

He nodded and took off with the rest of the team into the locker room, and I slowed so that only London and I were left in the hallway.

I looked both ways, then tugged her into the nearest office, pads and all. "Seriously?"

"He's Caspian's best friend, Jansen. There's nothing going on." She sighed, not that I could blame her. We were both tired of the same damned argument.

"He flirts with you at every possible opportunity, London, which he might not do if he knew we were together," I snapped. Then again, knowing Maxim, he'd just try harder. From what I'd seen, he thrived on a challenge.

"He doesn't flirt. He's just so mean to everyone else that it looks like flirting when he's nice to me." She set her clipboard on the desk and folded her arms under her breasts.

"This is really starting to get to me." I put my helmet under my arm. "I know you love this job, and you think that I'm some kind of—"

"We agreed not to tell anyone," she reminded me, worry consuming her eyes.

"How the hell would you feel if that was another woman out there, asking me to dinner and trying to touch me?"

Her mouth opened and shut a couple of times. "You mean like every single damned meet and greet that I have to coordinate and facilitate? At least you don't have to smile at Maxim and offer to take a fucking picture. Do you know how many phone numbers women shoved into my hands at the last game, just hoping I'd give them to you? Seventeen, Sterling."

I raised my eyebrows. *Sterling.* She was pissed. Good, because so was I. "You're the only woman I call, London. The only woman I sleep with. The only woman I kiss."

"And that goes both ways." She ran her hands over her face. "Why are we fighting about this? We're together. We're committed. We're just not shoving it in everyone's face."

"There's a difference between flaunting a relationship and hiding one, London." I shook my head. "I have to get in there before someone gets suspicious and starts looking for me. Heaven forbid they find us alone together."

I yanked open the door and marched into the hallway.

"Wait, I need to tell you something!" she called after me.

I turned around at the locker room doors. "Tell me tonight. Yours or mine?" The hallway was empty, but anyone could be listening, and I knew it. I just wasn't sure I cared anymore.

"Yours," she whispered.

I nodded and pushed my way into the locker room, leaving her in the hallway. Fuck, I needed to get a grip. Jealousy wasn't going to get us anywhere, and if London lost her position on the Reapers, she'd have to find another job...in another city.

Pull your shit together.

"She didn't want to go?" Caspian asked Maxim, his voice carrying across to me as I sat on my section of the bench.

"Said she had plans." Maxim shrugged, then turned toward me with a calculating gleam in his eyes. "Doesn't mean she won't change her mind. After all, we eat dinner together what? Twice a week?"

"Something like that," Caspian answered, his back turned as he took off his gear, so he didn't see the stare-down going on between Maxim and me.

190

I wasn't about to tell him that I was well-fucking-aware of how many times they ate dinner together every week or that she ended up in my bed every night. Instead of rising to whatever Maxim wanted out of me, I just threw back a bottle of water, then shook my head.

London was mine. The fact that he didn't know that didn't change the fact.

"I'm surprised, though," Maxim said, keeping his eyes narrowed on mine as he unlaced his skates. "She's all about family, so I figured she'd want to meet my dad."

I froze. My heart stopped. My lungs crystalized. My muscles turned to stone.

"Fuck," Briggs muttered at my side.

"After all, she was the one who just handed me his VIP passes for next weekend's game." He lifted his dark brows.

I couldn't fucking breathe. Seeing Sergei Zolotov after a game a couple seasons ago was one thing, but knowing he was coming ahead of time? Impossible. *That's what she wanted to tell you in the hallway*, I told myself. There was no way London knew and had kept it from me on purpose. This wasn't some kind of teen drama. She cared about me more than that.

But does she love you?

"Take a breath," Briggs muttered under his breath. "Sterling. Breathe."

I filled my lungs with air, and it took everything I had not to fly across the room and punch that smug little smirk right off Maxim's face.

As if satisfied with my level of shock, Maxim nodded, then went back to stripping off his gear like he hadn't just shaken up my entire fucking world.

Sergei Zolotov was going to be in my arena, watching *my* game, but we both knew it wasn't for me.

It never was.

14

LONDON

"*A*re you sure I'm ready for this?" I asked, squeezing Jansen's hand as we walked along the sidewalk in downtown Charleston.

"Only you can answer that, London," he said, slowing us to a stop outside the small brick building. An old, giant clock hung above the double glass doors, and I gripped his arm with my other hand. He turned to face me, pulling us out of the way of foot traffic. "I have complete faith in you," he said, planting a quick kiss on my lips. "You've come so far from that night in the elevator."

I nodded. Even my therapist was shocked by the results of our little experiment. She'd conducted a series of her own small tests, pushing boundaries in a safe environment much like we'd been doing, just on a smaller scale. She said I'd made huge advances, quite possibly excelling to as far as humanly possible to manage this fear—but that didn't mean I wasn't nervous now.

"It's your choice," he said, cupping my cheeks. "I'll never force you to do anything you don't want to do, that you aren't comfortable with." A smirk shaped his lips. "But you know I'll give you a little push whenever you need me to."

And he had. He totally, always had. Even when we'd had arguments—like our most recent one about keeping us a secret. And then after, about his biological father coming to a game at Maxim's request. I'd had to hand him those VIP passes and keep my mouth shut. It had stung every inch of my soul to do, but I couldn't lay into Maxim about his father when I wasn't even supposed to know Jansen's side of the story in the first place.

Even with that. Even with all those heated discussions in the beginning of our relationship when we were tiptoeing around our feelings for each other so much it drove us crazy. Even *then*, during those moments, he knew when to push me, ignite me, and when to soothe me.

I melted a little more for the man before me. "How are you so damn amazing?"

Seriously, where the hell did he come from? It had been six weeks of fire and heat and mind-blowing bliss with him, and I *still* couldn't understand why someone like him had chosen someone like me. Not that I was inferior —I loved who I was and how I looked. But I was proudly awkward, inherently flawed, and tragically driven. And him being *him* he could have anyone he wanted.

But he'd somehow, incredibly, he'd chosen me.

Jansen laughed, the smile on his lips real and genuine and enough to shake away the fear digging its claws in me, whispering that I couldn't walk through that door. "I've rented out an escape room for my severely claustrophobic girl-friend, and you say I'm amazing?"

I reached up on my tiptoes, crushing my lips against his. He held me against him, slanting his mouth over mine, groaning as I slid my tongue between his lips. I fisted his shirt, my heart fluttering as he didn't pull away because we were in public, didn't try to tame what was happening between us.

He. Simply. Let. Me. *Be.*

And in his arms?

I was a flame, and he was the oxygen that helped me burn.

"If this is you stalling," he said between kisses. "I can do this all day."

I laughed, breaking our kiss as I smiled up at him. "Okay," I said. "Let's do this."

His brows raised, and he waited a few moments, giving me another chance to say no.

So, I did what I'd become very good at. I grabbed his arm and hauled his sexy ass into the building.

Ten minutes later, we were set up in the escape room Jansen had bought out for just the two of us. The guide explained the rules to us, the objective, but I didn't hear most of it.

Not with the noise in my head—like an old television caught between channels—nothing but crackling white snow. Icy claws crept up my skin, sinking into my lungs.

There were only four walls to the room, the door on the farthest one. No windows. And the guide kept saying *lock.* And even though Jansen had assured me there was a giant green emergency escape button—one I could clearly see right now—I still shivered as the guide exited the room and shut the door behind him.

Jansen remained quiet and calm by my side, and my shoulders tensed. I hated that we weren't like the other normal couples who were booked for the other rooms in the establishment. Wearing happy, excited faces, eager to challenge themselves with a fun, safe game.

But not me.

This was a test to help me heal the old wound that had festered since childhood. And Jansen, he wasn't complaining. Wasn't pushing me to *just have a good time* and *let it go.* No, he stood there, holding me, patient. Standing in support, an island when I was thrashing and stranded in an endless ocean. Because that is how the panic felt—a lonely, cold, vast ocean with no escape. Nothing but the exhaustion of trying to stay afloat, keep your head above the raging water, survive.

But with an island so close to me?

It didn't seem such a lonely place. Such a desolate, terrifying place.

Jansen's support, his willingness to understand and support me felt like he was offering me a life raft. But *I* had to be the one to reach for it. He didn't have the power to heal me. Only I had that capacity, but he was able to help me with the tools I needed to do so.

And slowly, with more strength than I thought possible, I reached internally for the line he'd cast. Mentally gripping it, I grabbed it with both hands, hauling myself closer and closer to the safety of that island until I made it to land and was able to *breathe.*

"Where are we supposed to look first?" I asked, my eyes clearing as I met his blue gaze. I glanced around the room, appreciating it for the first time. It was an Egyptian theme—golden walls covered in hieroglyphics, and a colorfully painted sarcophagus sat in the middle of the room. Other wooden crates were scattered about, some with clay pots and urns on them, others with elaborate puzzle boxes that looked like ancient safes.

Omigod we were locked in a tomb—*that* was the theme of this room.

I waited for that panic to return, to incapacitate me, to knock me off that island and send me right back into that endless, cruel ocean…

But it didn't come.

I felt it, like a phantom sensation, just skating beneath the surface of the new strength I'd mastered, but it wasn't enough to crush me.

The knowledge alone filled me with an almost intoxicating sensation. Or that could be the way Jansen was looking at me, all fire in his eyes mixing with pride. "There should be a concealed scroll that will lead us to the next clue. We just have to find it."

I nodded, dropping his hands and crossing the room. On my own two feet. Without my island. I made it to the other side of the room where a crate with four different clay jars sat. "A scroll could be in here," I said, and Jansen's eyes practically shined as he nodded and came to stand next to me.

"Definitely," he said. We each grabbed a jar and started searching.

Thirty minutes and four clues later, we were stuck, and a cold sweat had crept onto the back of my neck. Nothing debilitating, but enough to make breathing more of a struggle.

"How are you doing?" he asked, smoothing his hand over my back as we took a break from searching for the makeshift key that would open the sarcophagus.

"I'm okay," I said, blowing out a slow breath.

"We can go," he said. "If you need to. The door is just a magnet. All we have to do is push the button, and we're out." He pointed toward the door, and I'm not going to lie, I *thought* about it. For just a split second.

But looking at him, the compassion in his eyes, the understanding...I knew without a shred of doubt that I didn't want that *out*.

Not here.

Not with him.

Not ever.

"No," I said, a rush of adrenaline spiking through my blood. His eyes widened as I smiled up at him, now breathless for an entirely different reason.

God, how had I ever hesitated to give this man my entire heart? To tell him the truth about how I felt about him?

I spanned the small distance between us, reaching up to gently clutch his neck. "I don't want the out, Jansen," I said, and he grinned down at me.

"Okay," he said, his eyes curious.

"I don't want the out...ever."

He cocked a brow at me. "I'm having a hard time following, babe."

I reached up, planting a soft, sensuous kiss on his lips. I drew back, shaking my head at my own absurdity. "If I have to be trapped in an elevator, a room, anywhere…I want it to be with you."

He smoothed his knuckles over my cheek.

"I *love* you, Jansen." The words rushed from me. Before, when he'd said it, I'd been terrified by what I felt for this man. I'd been swept up in a storm of emotion and hadn't been able to say the words back. And there was something to be said about saying them on my own. Without it being an expected obligation.

His eyes guttered as he stilled before me. His gaze fell to my mouth, and he grazed his thumb over my bottom lip. "Say that again," he said, his voice pure gravel.

A warm shudder made my body tremble. "I love you," I said, barely getting the words out before he crushed his mouth on mine. "I love you," I repeated, sighing the words against his kiss.

Heat pooled between my thighs, the hunger I had for him intensifying to almost painful levels. He jerked his head back, sucking in a breath. "You want to finish this?"

"I *can* finish this," I said with absolute confidence.

He smirked, his eyes churning with primal need. "Do you want to?"

I shook my head. "I want you."

He glanced behind us, toward the door, as if he were seriously contemplating fucking me on the first available surface —which was a fake sarcophagus.

I laughed, smacking his perfect ass. "Take me home, caveman."

He growled, showing just the primal male I'd accused him of being.

We were in his home within twenty minutes.

And we didn't make it two steps in the house before I damn near climbed him like a tree.

We left a trail of clothes in our wake, our mouths crashing together as if those three little words had unleashed something starved within us.

"Fuck, you're already drenched for me," Jansen groaned as he stroked his fingers through my slit. I rocked against his hand, digging my nails into the muscles of his shoulders. He hissed, moving his hands to my hips and hauling me up until I locked my ankles around his back.

He took me to the wall, the first available space, and made no preambles of the torture he normally liked to dole out.

No, he plunged inside me with one, sharp stroke that had me throwing my head back. Again and again, he thrust inside me, hitting every deep, aching spot with delicious precision. I clung to him, being able to do nothing but hold on to him as he fucked me against the wall. My mind reeled as my body tangled into a million burning, aching knots.

And Jansen touched every *single* one of them.

And since I was merely a puppet at his mercy in this position, I did the only thing I could do—crushed my mouth to his. I kissed him, devouring his mouth like I would his cock later. Sighed and moaned between his lips, relishing the taste of him as he pounded inside me with such a primal branding I could barely breathe or think straight.

Reduced to nothing but sensation, I succumbed to the glittering pleasure he wrung from my body. He held me like I weighed nothing, drove into me like he wanted to brand himself across my soul. Wanted to ensure that no one would ever be able to follow him.

And no one ever would.

No one *could* ever or would ever compare to him. This incredible, fantastic, brilliant man.

"I love you," I said, flicking my tongue along the edges of his teeth.

He growled, driving into me harder, faster.

Pushing me over that sweet, sharp edge until I shattered around him.

Relentless in his hunger, he kept plunging into me, the heat of him, the rock-hard length of him dragging one orgasm out into another. My thighs trembled as I clenched them around him, my cries likely sounding down the fucking street.

I didn't care.

I couldn't care.

Because all that existed or mattered was him and me and us.

This love that burned and sparkled and consumed. That strengthened and shook me.

"Fuck, baby," he groaned, his fingers digging in tighter where he held me against the wall.

I tangled my fingers in his hair, yanking his head back so I could watch him come. And the *sight* of it—those churning blue eyes that ignited like blue flames, those muscles flexing as he effortlessly held me against that wall, the way he owned every single inch of me in that moment…

It sent me right over the edge with him. Again.

And after? We collapsed to the floor, a mess of tangled limbs and heaved breaths.

I'd never felt happier or more complete than I did in that moment.

I was nearly drunk on the knowledge that Jansen Sterling had claimed me, heart and soul.

15

STERLING

ick. Tick. Tick.

The edge of the desk bit into the back of my thighs as I stared at the clock on the wall in London's office like it was the countdown on a nuclear weapon. Fifteen minutes. That's exactly how long I had to get my ass downstairs and into the locker room to gear up.

"Then you need to get another security screener down there," London said as she walked through the door, her cell phone at her ear. "Because we can't have an hour-long line to get through security, Sean. It's not acc—" Her eyes widened slightly as she saw me, and then her expression softened. "Call Rob and ask him for another screener. I have to go." She hung up and slipped her phone into her back pocket.

"No rest for the wicked, huh?" I asked. "You're supposed to be off today." She'd even come in casual—jeans and a fitted, black Reaper jacket.

"Right?" She took a seat next to me on her desk. "Sean hasn't quite figured out the staffing issues."

"Don't worry, next year there will only be one desk in this room, and it will be yours." I put my arm around her shoulder and tucked her close to my side. Just having her near settled my stomach.

"Speaking of this room…" She nailed me with those glacier-blue eyes. "Are you hiding? Usually you're the first one in the locker room, and I can't help but notice that you're about fifteen minutes from the mandatory check-in time."

I glanced at the clock. "Fourteen minutes."

"I know today has to be hard for you." She stroked her hand down my thigh in a soothing motion.

"I've never played when I knew he was in the stands. He's shown up to a couple of games, but I only knew afterward, and I've sure as hell never been on the ice with Maxim at the same time." Great, the nausea was back in full force.

"What can I do for you?" she asked gently.

I pressed a kiss to the top of her head. "Just love me."

"I do. I love you with my whole heart." She tipped her face up and kissed me. "You are an amazing goalie, Jansen. Sure, maybe he gave you some good genetics when it comes to hand-eye coordination or something, but the rest is you. Your training. Your hard work. Your dedication. He can't touch you out there."

"Still feels like I have something to prove."

"Only to yourself. The rest of us are already well aware of what an incredible player—incredible *man* you are."

The knot in my chest loosened with her words, and I kissed her again before rising to my feet. "I love you, London Foster."

Her smile was bright enough to make me fall all over again. "Good. Now go. I'll see you after."

"You're not going to wish me good luck?" I teased, already backing toward the door.

"You've never needed luck, Jansen. Now go!" She shooed me off with a grin, and I went.

The hallways beneath Reaper arena weren't crowded yet. Security was always tight on game day, and I made my way toward the locker room with minimal interference until I neared the fork in the hallway that intersected the players' entrance and the path to the locker room.

There, two women with passes around their necks waited, both leaning against the wall. One was blonde, and one brunette, but that was all I noticed until one stepped into my path, effectively blocking my way.

"Oh, my God," the brunette whispered. "You're him."

I put on the smile I used for fans. "Depends on who you think I am."

"You're Jansen." She stared at me with wide, blue eyes, the color draining from her face as she gripped the thick strap of her purse with both hands.

She was a beautiful girl, but I wasn't interested. Besides, no one in the world could hold a candle to what London stirred inside me.

"I am." I peered to the left, over her head, and caught Coach McPherson looking at me from where he stood at the entrance to the locker room, tapping his watch. "And I am going to get reamed if I don't get into the locker room."

"Right," she said, shaking her head like she needed to clear it. "It's just that I've heard so much about you that I wanted to meet you." She stepped to the side, making room so I could pass.

"Well, hi," I said, maintaining my fan smile. "I'm Jansen Sterling." There was something oddly familiar about her face, but I couldn't quite put my finger on it. Had I seen her at a game before? "It's nice to meet you."

She swallowed and shifted her feet nervously. "I guess you should probably get to your game."

"They do tend to get mad if the starting goalie doesn't show up," I joked.

She laughed, a smile flashing across her face. "Good luck."

"Thanks." I nodded to her and the quiet blonde who stood just behind her, like she was ready to catch the brunette if she fell. "Enjoy the game…" I waited for her to say her name.

The blonde glanced between her friend and me, then nudged her.

"Mila," the brunette said, her chin rising slightly as she took a shaky breath. "Mila Zolotov. I'm…your little sister."

I blinked once. Twice. Somehow I managed to force some air into my lungs while I looked at her again. Her hair was the same light brown Maxim's was, and there was something about her cheekbones that reminded me of him, too. *Holy shit.*

"From what I know of you, which isn't much"—she scrunched her nose—"you'll probably say something like *I don't have a little sister*. Right?"

My mouth opened to reply, but I shut it because she was right.

"But you do. It's me." There was a vulnerability in her eyes that somehow glued my feet to the fucking floor.

Maxim, I could ignore. He was an absolute asshole who'd shown up with a chip on his shoulder and hatred in his eyes. But this girl? There wasn't any malice in her, at least none that I could see at first glance.

"We have the same eyes," I muttered. "Mine are more gray, but the shape…"

She nodded. "Our grandmother. Maxim and Nikolai have Dad's eyes, but you and I…" She teared up but shook it off. "Well, we get them from our grandmother."

"Sterling!" Coach called out.

I put my forefinger up in his direction, asking for another minute, but I was going to need way more than that to digest this.

"And you?" My gaze jumped to the blonde at Mila's back. Was she another relative?

"Me?" The girl's features were delicate, with big green eyes that reminded me of a Disney princess, and the majority of her body was hidden under an oversized Reaper hoodie. She shook her head, which sent her glasses sliding down her nose. "I'm just Mila's friend." She pushed the glasses back into place.

Mila smiled. "Evie is my *best* friend. We're up at Dartmouth right now, but we've both been accepted to graduate school here in Charleston." The grip on her purse tightened. "I mean, Evie got in at Stanford, but we've been stuck at the-hip since kindergarten, and the University of Charleston has a great MFA program for photography, and you should *see* the pictures she takes. I keep telling her that she can't turn down Stanford, right—"

"Mila," Evie whispered, her cheeks turning pink.

"Right." Mila squeezed her eyes shut and took a breath before opening them again. "Sorry, I babble when I'm nervous, and well, I've been thinking about this moment since forever. I kind of ambushed you, didn't I?"

"Uh…" Words. I needed some words.

"Mila, what the hell?" Maxim came down the hallway from the right—the players' entrance—with his bag over his shoulder.

"Hey!" She waved.

Evie retreated to the wall.

Maxim's eyes narrowed and he stepped between Mila and me. "Don't talk to her."

"Don't be an asshole, Max." Mila side-stepped so she could see me, then shoulder-checked Maxim out of the way. "Anyway, I know you have to get to your game, but I just wanted to introduce myself. Maybe we can have dinner after—"

"You're having dinner with Dad and me," Maxim snapped.

"Sterling! Zolotov! We have a game, just in case you've forgotten," Coach yelled. "Get your asses in here!"

"Right," I said slowly. "Mila, Evie, it was nice to meet you." Those words didn't come close to explaining what had just happened, but it was all I had.

Maxim sucked in a breath, his glare only intensifying until I walked to the locker room.

"Mila, what were you thinking?" he asked gently as I pushed through the locker room doors.

It was game time.

* * *

SHUTOUT.

I played the best game of my life.

Maybe it was knowing I had to narrow my focus to the ice and the ice alone, or maybe it was seeing London's smile during the second intermission as we walked back to the ice, but I was solid.

Fuck that. I wasn't just solid. I was on fire.

I'd taken forty-three shots and blocked every single one.

Axel and Brogan scored two of our goals, and Caspian brought home two of the others, with Maxim putting that fifth one up on the scoreboard. Damn good game.

I was all smiles after fielding a few questions from reporters and was more than ready to get out of there so I could celebrate with London as I walked toward the players' entrance.

"You're actually proud of that performance?"

I knew that accent.

Looking up, I saw Sergei—that's all he was to me—up in Maxim's face at the end of the hallway. My stomach hit the floor. If I turned around now, I could avoid this shitstorm all together, but there wasn't exactly another exit into the players' lot.

And besides, it wasn't like Sergei Zolotov had ever altered his life around *me*.

I gripped my keys in my hand and kept walking.

"I had three points, Dad," Maxim argued as Mila and Evie came out of the hallway just ahead to my right.

"Assists don't count," Sergei snapped, folding his arms across his chest just like Maxim. Shit, the two were so much alike it was uncanny, right down to the way they were glaring at each other.

"Assists don't count to *you*." Maxim shook his head.

"You're slow, your footwork is sloppy, and even worse, you're unfocused," Sergei accused. "Do you know how many players would kill to be at this level? And you're just content to skate by in mediocrity!"

Damn, that was harsh. Was this how he treated Maxim after every game? Sure, he'd come after me twice with those kinds of insults, but I wasn't his son. Not really. Not in the ways that mattered.

Mila's footsteps picked up, Evie keeping pace with her as they hurried toward the pair.

"I don't know what you want from me!" Maxim flung his arms out to his sides.

"I want you to play like you're my *son*!" Sergei jabbed his finger at him. "I flew all the way here to watch you do what—pass a puck you could have scored with if you'd just skated the damn thing up!"

"Daddy." Mila got there and inserted herself between the two.

"This doesn't involve you, Mila," Sergei barked.

"Well, isn't this the little family reunion," I said as I reached the end of the hallway. There was more tension per square foot in this little area than in my entire childhood. Weird.

"Keep walking," Maxim growled, sweeping Mila behind his back in a movement so natural I knew he'd done it countless times before.

A sick, nauseating stone settled in my gut.

Sure, the two Zolotov men were equal in height, but they hadn't always been, and Sergei had at least twenty pounds on Maxim now.

Sergei turned and swept his gaze over me in a quick inspection before pivoting back to Maxim. "You let that no-named bastard show you up in front of your father."

What the fuck is wrong with this guy?

No kid deserved to have a parent ride him that hard when it came to sports, and that's exactly what Maxim was in this moment, Sergei's kid. I'd seen it time and again growing up— the parents who lived vicariously through their children. The parents who screamed at refs and belittled their players after the game—or worse—during it. Mom had always stepped in for those kids, no matter how big or loud the other parents had been.

I blocked out what he'd said about me. That was the only way I was going to make it through this moment.

"You saved my ass in the third," I said to Maxim as I stood behind Sergei. "Not sure I could have stopped that breakaway if you hadn't skated back so quickly to pick up defense during the line change."

Sergei spun back around, rage burning in his eyes. "And as for you—"

"Oh please, like I gave you one fucking thing to pick on tonight, *Dad*." He wasn't anything even resembling that word, but *damn* was it fun to throw it in his face. "I blew even your best performance out of the water, so think twice about coming at me with your bullshit. Or better yet, just stay the fuck away like I told you after the last two games."

Maxim stiffened.

"You're not worth it. You've never been worth it," he said every word slowly as if he wanted to make sure I knew he was speaking his truth, and not from a place of anger like he had been at Maxim.

It fucking hurt, and he knew it.

With a snide little smirk, he spun back to Maxim, and clipped Evie, who had been moving toward Mila's side, sending the blonde careening into the concrete wall.

Maxim moved faster than I'd ever seen him, throwing his hand out and barely catching her head before it had the chance to slam into the stone, then hauling her against him.

Mila gasped.

"For fuck's sake, Dad!" Maxim hissed, his hand cradling Evie's head protectively.

Sergei blanched but quickly schooled his features. "The girl is fine. Mila, bring your friend and meet me in the car. We're done here."

He stormed out, shoving the door open to the parking lot and disappearing.

"Are you okay?" Mila asked Evie as Maxim released her.

"Fine," Evie murmured. "Thank you, Maxim." She looked up at him like he was the answer to every question in the universe, with a yearning so acute it almost hurt *my* heart. Damn, that was…interesting.

Maxim grunted and fished his keys out of his pocket, thrusting them at Mila. "Here. Go to my car. You're not riding with him when he's like this."

"He'll calm down—" she started.

"Not taking that chance. Go. You too, Evangeline." He nodded toward the door.

Mila's lips pursed as she looked over at me. "Jansen—"

"If you have ever loved me, you'll go right now, Mila," Maxim interrupted, his voice dropping.

Mila glanced between us, then gave me an apologetic look. She took Evie's hand and walked out the door, leaving Maxim and me alone. We weren't a family, but that sure as hell didn't stop us from being dysfunctional, and in that moment, I almost felt…bad for him.

"I meant what I said. You saved my ass—"

Maxim whipped his head toward mine, and the fury in his eyes put me right back on guard. "I don't fucking need you to defend me!"

I bristled. "Yeah, you did. Not sure if you noticed, but he was ripping you the fuck apart."

"That was *nothing*." He jabbed his finger at me just like Sergei had done to him a few minutes earlier. "And stay the hell away from Mila. She's the only good thing to come out of my family!"

"What the hell? Like I'd hurt our sister?" I snapped. Wait—

"Our?" He came at me, drawing back his fist. "She's *my* sister, not *ours*. My sister. My brother. My father. My family. None of it belongs to you!"

"Stop it!" London flew between us, putting a hand on each of our chests.

"London!" Caspian roared, sprinting toward us.

"I've got this!" she answered her brother, but her eyes were locked on Maxim. "Go get some air, Maxim."

"Me?" he roared. "Why aren't you yelling at him?"

"Because he's not the one being a flaming asshole!" she retorted.

Maxim scoffed, taking a step back as he did his best to glare me to death.

London pivoted, facing me, but I didn't take my eyes off Maxim. "Jansen," she said softly. "Come on. Let's take a walk." When that didn't work, she laced her fingers with mine and lifted our hands to her heart. "Jansen, please."

The plea in her tone broke through the icy rage, and I looked down into her eyes.

"Come on, baby." She brought my hand to her mouth and pressed a kiss to the back of it.

"Baby? What the fuck?" Caspian asked slowly.

Well, shit.

London sucked in a breath, her eyes widening as her gaze whipped to her brother. "I…uh…just…"

Caspian looked pointedly at our joined hands before arching a brow at his sister. "Want to clue me in here, sis?"

"It's all my fault." I turned to face Caspian.

"I'm in love with him," London blurted, locking her fingers even tighter around mine. "I love Jansen. I have for *months*, but I didn't want you to get mad or for other people to think I was sleeping with a player to secure my job—"

"Sleeping with?" Caspian turned that icy stare on me. "Seriously?"

"I am in love with your sister, man. And I would have told you, but London asked me not to—" I cringed. "You know what? No excuses. I should have told you."

"I know you're pissed at me for falling for one of your team-mates," she rushed.

He put up his hand. "I'm more pissed that you let yourself get into a relationship you're so embarrassed of that you feel like you have to hide, London."

Ouch. He nailed that one right on the head, and he'd known about us for all of thirty seconds.

"You're in love with him?" Maxim roared.

Every head turned toward him.

There wasn't just anger in his eyes and the set of brow but a flash of hurt, too. "You're in *love* with him?" he repeated.

"Yes," she whispered.

"You can't love him because he sure as fuck doesn't love you!" He snapped.

"I'm sorry?" I shouted.

He turned that glare back on me. "You really took that little dare so seriously that you went and made her fall in love with you? Sadistic son of a—"

"You don't know what the hell you're talking about!" Every muscle in my body tensed, but I couldn't lunge at him, not with London between us.

Maxim scoffed. "London, I made some jackass comment in the locker room about dating you because some rookies pissed me off, and this guy"—he pointed at me—"took it as just another way to get under my skin. He doesn't love you. Trust me. He's only doing this because I bet him he couldn't!"

"That's not true!" I was going to fucking kill Maxim. And to think, I'd just felt bad for the asshole. I'd actually stuck up for him.

"You guys had a bet on who could date my sister?" Caspian asked, more incredulous than anything. "You're fucking kidding me, right?"

"Yes!"

"No!"

Maxim and I both shouted at the same time.

London's hand fell away from mine, and she took two steps backward toward Caspian. Her eyes were wide as she glanced between Maxim and me. "Is it true?"

"London. No, it's not true." I shook my head.

"You knew I wanted her, right?" Maxim challenged.

"You what?" Caspian fired off at his best friend.

Maxim ignored him. "You knew it."

"I knew it," I agreed. "It wasn't the reason. It just didn't stop me." I should have let Sergei rip him the hell apart.

London sucked in a breath.

"Baby," I whispered. God, this woman was everything to me. She had to believe me. She had to know the truth.

"That first time you asked me out, was that before or after Maxim made his little comment?" she asked quietly.

Oh, fuck. Oh fuck. Oh. Fuck.

"After," I admitted. "But it had nothing—"

"Is that what this was?" she asked softly, heartbreak lacing her tone. "Was I just some way to get the upper hand on your brother?"

"He's not my brother!"

"He's not my brother!"

Again, we answered at the same time.

"Wow," she said slowly, shaking her head at both of us. "I knew you hated each other, but I never realized just how much."

"No—" I moved forward, but she put her hands up.

"Don't touch me."

She didn't believe me. She chose to believe him. She took *his* side just like our father had when we'd been born.

My heart fucking shattered.

16

LONDON

J took a step away from Sterling, my eyes darting between him, Maxim, and Caz.

"Was that all it was?" I asked again, my voice so low and broken I was shocked Jansen heard me at all. "Everything between us...was to get back at Maxim? To take something *he* wanted?"

"No—"

"You know I didn't even have a *clue* he was pursuing me?" I cut him off, glancing at Maxim, who had no apology in his eyes, just a regretful darkness. "We're friends. He's my brother's best friend. I. Had. No. Idea."

"London," Jansen said my name on a plea.

My mind splintered, racing through each memory I had of us.

The way he'd dodged my calls for an entire month, but then —seemingly out of nowhere—he started talking to me again. Presented me with a bargain to *help* me with my issues—a bargain that ensured we'd see each other on the regular.

That must've been the day Maxim presented him with the bet.

Fuck my life.

My chest *stung.*

"That night in the elevator," I whispered, the pieces coming together as I thought even farther back. "Maxim came to help me..." Tears burned the back of my eyes. Maxim had rushed toward me, going so far as to wrap an arm around my waist to steady me when I had shaky feet. And I'd been so relieved to see him—a *friend.* "God," I sighed. "Is that when it started?" I snapped. "You made your own assumptions and decided to get back at him?"

Jansen's jaw went taut, disappointment and regret churning in his eyes. "No," he said. "You know me. You know that isn't true."

"Fuck that," Caz said. "Both you should've come to me first—"

"She doesn't *belong* to you," Jansen snapped at Caz, his voice low and stone cold. "And neither do I."

My heart ached with his declaration, that I belonged to myself and didn't owe anyone anything. But was it true? Or was he simply telling me what I wanted to hear? Is that what he'd done this entire time? Just to take something that Maxim wanted...for all the times Maxim had taken things from him?

Caspian moved, his brow furrowed, that muscle in his jaw popping—

And I stepped between him and Jansen on instinct. Even Maxim had a hand on Caz's arm, holding him back

"Stop," I demanded, my body trembling with unleashed hurt and anger. I looked up at my brother. "I decide who to be with. And if I decide I want to be with the entire defense roster, then that's *my* fucking choice."

Caz stepped back like I'd struck him.

I moved my gaze to Maxim, softening just a bit. "Maxim, I didn't know. But it wouldn't have made a difference. I value our friendship so much, and I promise I never meant to lead you on…if I did. I honestly didn't have a clue. But I love—" I cut my words short, pain lashing through the center of me. I *thought* what Jansen and I had was love.

I'd been an idiot.

"If it was so real, then why did you hide it?" Maxim asked, fastening his stare on Jansen. "If you weren't playing her, why not take it public?"

I had asked him not to, but I couldn't voice the words. My heart was too busy shattering.

"London," Jansen's voice sounded from behind me, and I felt him reaching for me. I stepped out of his reach.

Backed away from all three of them.

"Sis," Caz pled. "You need to hear me out. Hear Maxim—"

"No," I cut him off, my heart ripping to shreds as I continued backing away from the three most important men in my life. "Fuck you all."

I spun on my heels and didn't look back.

* * *

"You know," I said, my words sizzling with fire. "Maybe I should just act like *them*." I accentuated the word, and Savannah's mouth turned down at the corners. I gripped the drink in my hand a little harder, leaning against the bar at *Scythe*. "Just pursue people, no strings, just sex. No falling in love."

"Oh, honey," Savannah said, smoothing her hand over my back.

Echo, the owner and bartender, whistled and poured me another drink.

I thanked her and threw back the contents, allowing the sweet burn of bourbon to eat away the pain in my chest.

"Do you really believe that he was with you just to take you away from Maxim?" Savannah asked, sipping her own drink.

The chatter and music of the bar filled the background, and combined with the drinks, made my head feel a blissful kind of numb.

"I don't know what to think," I admitted. "I can see it, everything Maxim said. I had no idea he wanted to date me, but let's be real. I've known him for *two* years. If he wanted me, he would've made a move. He saw that Jansen wanted me and then decided to try." I pinched the bridge of my nose. "And I know how deep the pain runs for Jansen regarding his biological family. It's a lifelong wound." I shook my head. "A hatred like that can make people do stupid, hurtful things."

Like choose a girl based solely on revenge purposes, and make her fall head over heels in love with you.

Because even as I wanted to strangle him for what he'd done, it didn't erase the immense love I had for him in my heart. I would always love Jansen. I just didn't like him very much right now.

"What a mess, babe," Savannah said, shaking her head. "Sounds like there is a lot more to it than we know."

I nodded, not able to argue with her about that. But it didn't change the fact that I now had no clue if *any* of it had been real for Jansen.

The searing kisses.

The tender discussions.

The playful banter.

Maybe it was all my fault—I'd asked him to kiss me the first time as a distraction from my own panic. What kind of fucked up start is that? Maybe I deserved this…this crushing feeling sinking onto my chest.

"It's fine," I said, waving off the negative energy. "Like I said, I'll just be like them. Sleep around, no strings, live my life."

Savannah flashed me a pitying look but let me have my anger-fantasy.

"Maybe I'll sleep with the next man who walks through that door," I boldly declared—despite having no real intention of following through—as I glanced at the entrance to *Scythe.*

Savannah followed my line of sight as we waited.

"Oh, for fuck's sake," I grumbled when *Maxim* walked through the door. "Okay, the next guy—"

Caspian.

I resisted the urge to puke and turned back in my seat. "Never mind. I give up."

"Incoming," Savannah muttered under her breath. She raised a brow at me. "Want me to stop him?"

I didn't know which *him* she was referring to, but I knew without a doubt if I told her yes then she'd shut down whichever man was attempting to speak to me.

I loved her so damn much.

"It's okay," I said, spinning on my barstool. Caspian stood there, an apologetic look on his face.

"Can we talk?" he asked, motioning to where Maxim had selected a table across the room.

I blew out a breath. I didn't really want to talk to him, but he was my *brother*, and I knew we needed to have an honest discussion sooner or later. Might as well be after I'd had a bourbon for courage.

"Be right back," I said, and Savannah gave me an encouraging smile. I knew she'd wait for me. Knew she'd have my back in an instant, and that was powerful. It gave me all the strength I needed to face Caz.

I settled into the chair across from Maxim and Caz, my eyes darting between them both.

"London," Caz said, cringing a bit. "I'm sorry that I made you feel like you had to hide your relationship."

I swallowed around the rock lodged in my throat. He'd made the first step, so I wouldn't slam that door in his face. "It wasn't just you," I admitted, sighing. Maxim stared into his drink, his shoulders tense. "I didn't want anyone to know. Not until I'd secured my position with the Reapers. I wanted to stand on my own. To be known for my work, not because I'm your little sister or someone's girlfriend."

"I can't help who I am, sis," he said.

"Not asking you to," I said. "But you have to admit, you've been overprotective of me since that day I got trapped in the storm cellar."

Caspian's eyebrows raised, his eyes widening at my mention of the memory. I usually avoided bringing it up because it used to have the power to send me into a full-blown panic attack.

Not anymore.

Not since Jansen.

My chest felt like it may crack from the pressure.

"I need you to trust me," I said. "As ridiculous as that sounds, it's my choice who I give my heart to. And, apparently, who I allow to break it." Maxim shook his head, but Caspian nodded. "You have to let me breathe, Caz."

"I'll do better," he said, and his voice was sincere. "I don't want you to feel like you have to keep things from me. You've been my best friend since the day you were born. I don't want to push you away. I'll be better, I promise." He visibly swallowed. "But you have to admit, this looks bad. Sterling—"

"Is a selfish asshole," Maxim cut in.

Anger sizzled in those fresh fissures over my heart.

"You don't know the first thing about who he is," I said with a lethal coldness.

Maxim's eyes flared for the briefest of moments before he settled back into his default look—grumbly, determined, cocky. "And *you* do?"

I huffed a dark laugh. Maybe I didn't know him as well as I thought I had, but I knew pieces of his heart. The ones he'd showed me that had scars from Maxim and his father written all over them.

And even if his intentions with me hadn't been in the right place, that pain, the suffering, and the selfless way he'd risen to be the better man *was* real.

"I do," I said, calming my racing heart. "Maybe I'd been blind about the reasons behind us being together, or *his* reasoning behind it, but I know him, Maxim. He isn't whatever you think he is. He doesn't deserve your hatred. He deserves your respect, and quite possibly your acceptance."

A muscle in Maxim's jaw ticked, and Caz let out a low whistle as he hid behind his drink.

I tilted my head, my heart no longer capable of feeling another ounce of pain. "Can you be honest with me for a second?" I asked, and he dipped his chin. "When did you want to ask me out? The first time the thought occurred to you, Maxim?"

He visibly swallowed, and I gave him a small, broken smile.

"When you saw how Jansen was looking at me after the elevator? The way he'd snapped in this very bar after that, way back before the season started? When he thought I'd shown up with you?"

When Maxim didn't answer, I turned to Caz, who cringed.

I reached across the table, laying my hand over Maxim's. He didn't flinch under the touch, just simply held my gaze. "You may be pissed at Jansen, accusing him of using me to make you angry, but you were prepared to do the same thing.

We've been friends for two years, and you never once said anything. Tell me I'm wrong."

He cleared his throat and shook his head. "You're not," he said. "But I still think we would've had fun together."

I choked out a dark laugh, squeezing his hand. "Maybe," I said. "But I wasn't looking for fun. I was looking for something *real*."

Maxim grazed his thumb over the back of my hand, an innocent gesture. "I understand," he said. Then he flashed me a pitiful look. "And I may not know my brother like you do, but I know his hate. Understand it in a way you never will. And his hate? It's strong enough to make him fake it with you."

I thought my heart couldn't shatter any more, but it did.

Completely.

I sucked in a sharp breath, releasing Maxim's hand. I pushed back from the table, nodding to my brother who looked like he wanted to follow me, but knew better than to do so. And there wasn't any maliciousness in Maxim's words—he wanted to help me be smart, to realize the truth behind what Jansen had done—but it still stung like hell.

Savannah met me by the door, a silent show of support as we headed to her car. She drove me back to my apartment and stayed with me the whole night. Distracting me with movies and junk food and drinks until I'd finally been able to ignore what haunted me.

The fact that I'd let Jansen all the way into my life, my heart, my soul, out of a place of pure love and desire.

But him?

He'd come to me out of a place of hatred.

And I didn't have a clue how to recover from that.

17

STERLING

*T*he air had the distinct chill of winter as Mom and I walked through Reaper Village the day after Christmas. One winter in Maine had taught me to never take the milder southern weather for granted ever again.

"Maybe I should've gotten you a puppy," she said, her brow furrowed as she shoved her hands into the pockets of her jacket.

"What?" I nearly laughed but didn't. I wasn't even sure I *could* laugh anymore. The world had taken on a dreary, gray overcast sky for the last two weeks. London hadn't just taken her body from my bed or her heart from my hands—she'd packed up all the joy in life and walked away without a second look.

"You need something to come home to." Mom looped her arm through my elbow. "Your house is beautiful, Jansen." She glanced around us, taking in the quiet suburban neighborhood where the majority of my team lived. "All the houses here are beautiful. But there's no life inside yours."

"I'm gone too much to have a puppy," I said, not even touching the rest of that statement. She knew what had happened between London and me.

"Fine. A Bearded Dragon, maybe?" She hip-checked me and smiled. "Or even a goldfish?"

A smile broke across my face.

"Ah, there it is." She gave my arm a squeeze. "I've been waiting all week to see that smile. I was running out of ideas to get one out of you, but don't worry, I'll still make lasagna tonight. That was my last resort."

"Food?" We crossed the street, and I switched sides with Mom so she didn't walk next to the street. She was in her forties, and more beautiful than ever. I had Greg—my stepfather—to thank for that. Happiness looked good on her.

"It always comes down to food with you, Jansen Sterling." She gave me a pointed look.

My smile slipped. "I'm not sure I can carb-load myself out of this one, Mom."

She tugged on my elbow, stopping us in front of a house I knew all too well. "I've never known you to give up on something you wanted. Grades. Hockey. That Xbox you saved all summer for your sophomore year—you've never walked away from a little hard work."

"Those were all attainable goals." A muscle in my jaw popped as I struggled to breathe through the agony of losing London. It came in waves, some bigger than others, but the pain was always there, waiting to swallow me whole, especially at night. Fuck, I missed her at night, and not just for sex. I missed talking until we fell asleep. I missed hearing about her day and watching her scrunch her nose when something didn't go right. I missed the feel of her body pressed up against mine, her breaths even and steady as she dreamed. I just fucking missed *her*.

"And you don't think getting your girlfriend back is an attainable goal?" Mom cocked her head at me, narrowing her blue-gray eyes in my direction.

"I think there might just be too much damage, Mom." I tugged my beanie hat over my ears. "She didn't listen when I told her the truth. She chose to believe—" I snapped my mouth shut.

"Maxim," Mom said gently. "You can say his name around me, Jansen. I won't break."

My stomach twisted even as my heart softened. There was no venom in her tone when she said his name. None of the animosity I felt toward him. She was so much kinder than I was.

"I hate him," I whispered, even though I wasn't sure that was true anymore, not after seeing Sergei get in his face after that game. Maxim hadn't spoken to me since the incident in the hallway. Then again, neither had London.

Caz had stopped glaring at me last week, though, so there was some improvement.

"I know," Mom said, squeezing my arm and nodding. Her complete and utter acceptance didn't just crack my defenses —it shattered them.

"He took my house!" I motioned to the two-story modern home we stood in front of.

"I know."

"And it's not that I don't like the new one, but I sure as f—" I barely caught myself from swearing and earned an arched eyebrow. "I wouldn't have chosen the one next door if I'd known he was my neighbor. Trust me, there's not a lot of borrowing sugar going on."

"I know, honey." There was so much compassion in her eyes that my chest ached.

"He took my team, and I know it's still my team, but it's like he's this little spot of black mold on a cake, spoiling the rest of it and spreading his…moldiness."

"Hmmm." Mom pressed her lips in a firm line, struggling not to laugh.

"And he's an asshole!" I cringed. "Sorry for swearing, but he is! He's arrogant and calculating, and he stole the woman I love!"

Mom's shoulders fell, and she rubbed her hand up and down my bicep like I was eleven and just lost a game.

"And it's not like they're together or anything." Bile rose in my throat at the thought of it. "But all he had to do was make one stupid comment in the locker room, and it somehow makes me the bad guy. And London believes him! She thinks I pursued her just to piss him off, and I didn't!"

"Did you tell her that?" Mom asked.

"I started to in the hallway, but I was just so pissed, and even I can admit the timing of when I asked her out was suspicious. It's all a complicated…jacked up mess."

Mom nodded. "Do you really love this girl?"

"Yeah."

"Then fight for her, Jansen."

"It's not that simple." I shook my head.

"It really is." She tugged my arm, and we started walking up the sidewalk to my house, where Greg waited. "I never gave you an opportunity to watch me fight for love. I didn't love your father. You know that. And you were out of the house by the time I started seriously dating again, so you didn't see when Greg and I would push past our arguments. But we do. You can push past this, too, Jansen. Just be honest with her. Lay it out on the line, and if she still doesn't listen, then it's on her."

"Her brother is Maxim's best friend. If London and I really, honestly make a go of it, he'll be in my life, Mom. I don't want that for you."

Her grip tightened. "Jansen Marcus Sterling, don't you dare use me as an excuse to hide behind."

"What? I'm not!"

"I love that you want to protect me, honey." She leveled me with the *Mom look*. "But whether or not you want to admit it, he's always been in your life. Maybe not physically, but from the moment you knew about your father, he was there, too. You have two brothers and a sister. That's not going to change, whether you're with London or not. So why not be happy? Don't let your hatred of Maxim steal away your chance with London."

I sighed.

"Also," she continued. "Stop taking him into account for my visits. I'll come and see you whenever I damn well please, and I'm not scared of borrowing a cup of sugar, either. He might be an asshole, but he's just a kid who was born into a situation he couldn't control. Just like you."

I didn't want to admit that she was right, but as usual, she was.

* * *

Mom and Greg left the next day, which also happened to be the day Maxim got back into town. The timer went off, and I pulled the tray of lasagna from the oven, leaving the pan on the granite to cool. Mom had made me six pans in addition to the one we'd devoured last night. Four were in the freezer. I told myself I'd ration them until she came to visit again, but who was I kidding? I'd probably eat every single one of them in the next month.

The doorbell rang, and my heart jumped.

Calm the fuck down, it's not her.

I checked the security camera app and tensed.

It wasn't her.

It was Maxim.

He rang the bell again.

"Impatient asshole," I muttered as I walked to the front door, trying my best to channel Mom's kindness. Trying and failing. I opened the door, anyway.

Maxim looked as uncomfortable as I felt. His jaw was tense, and his hands were in his front pockets. He wasn't wearing a coat.

"Did you need to borrow a cup of sugar?" I asked.

"What?" He gave me a *what the fuck* look.

"My mom," I started, then shook my head. "Never mind. What do you want?"

"Can we talk?" He bit out each word like they were physically painful to say.

He's just a kid who was born into a situation he couldn't control. Mom's words from yesterday rattled around in my brain, softening me like nothing else could. "Yeah. Come on in. It's cold out."

Maxim nodded and walked in, shutting the door behind him. "It's practically tropical from where I just came from."

"Russia?" I guessed, leading him toward the kitchen. Offering him a drink was the appropriate thing to do in this situation, right? I motioned to the barstools that lined one side of the kitchen island.

"No. Saint Paul." He took the seat as his gaze swept over the open-concept kitchen and family room. I got the feeling the guy didn't miss much. "I've only been to Russia a few times, and those were mostly for funerals. Dad played out his contract for Minnesota, and we stayed. He's actually an American citizen now. So is my mother."

"Huh." I took out two bottles of water and slid one across the island to him. "I knew where he played. I guess I just never really thought about where he stayed after his career finished."

Maxim caught it and started to fidget with the lid. "Thanks."

I leaned back against my counter, leaving the island and a metric ton of awkwardness between us.

He looked to my right, where a digital photo frame scrolled through pictures, and his expression changed, two lines appearing between his eyebrows.

"My mom gave it to me for Christmas," I said, twisting the top on my bottle but not drinking it. "What did you want to talk about?" The game tomorrow? Our shared fence line? Our shared genetics? The awkward options were endless around here.

His eyes were still on the frame. Mom had uploaded her favorites, and my stomach tensed as he watched my childhood scroll by. His thumb picked at the label on his water.

"Maxim—"

"You look kind of like Nicolai in that one." He motioned toward the frame. "How old are you there?"

I looked. "Four. Five, maybe. We were hiking up by my grandparents' place."

Maxim nodded absentmindedly, his gaze glued to the frame. "Your mother is beautiful."

My fingers stilled on the bottle in my hands. "So is yours. I looked her up when I found out." Mrs. Zolotov was a tall, striking beauty with thick, brown hair. "Mila looks a lot like her."

"Yeah, she does." Maxim's jaw ticked. "Let's hope her looks are all she got from her."

My eyebrows went up.

He shook his head and sighed. "Weren't you just the lucky one?" His mouth tilted into a wry half-smirk.

My grip tightened on the water bottle, making it crunch. "Lucky one? Between the two of us, you're going to say I was *the lucky one*? I was the secret."

Maxim turned his head slightly to look at me, and the chill in his eyes could have powered my freezer for the next decade. "You honestly think that, don't you? Poor little Jansen had to grow up without a daddy. Let's all pity him."

"You know what—" I pushed off the counter, ready to throw him out.

"You. Were. The. Lucky. One." He meant every word. It was there in his eyes, in the rage so hot it burned ice-cold. "Secret?" The laugh that burst from his chest wasn't remotely happy. It was tortured. "Do you really think you were a secret in my house?"

I settled back against the counter. "I wouldn't know shit about your house. All I knew was I met our...father"—God, the word tasted bitter in my mouth—"when I was thirteen, and he told me to never seek him out again."

"That's Dad for you." Maxim scoffed. "Like I said, lucky one. Trust me, he did you a favor."

"That's easy to say from your side of the story." I'd been a fucking wreck after that little introduction.

"I've known about you since I was eight." He continued to pick at the label on his bottle. "My parents were screaming at each other, and I crept out of my bed to sit at the top of the stairs. Nicolai was already there. My mother told him that she'd leave him and take us all back to Russia if you ever appeared on her doorstep. She knew Dad had a problem keeping it in his pants, but knowing and facing the knowledge aren't the same, and the only thing my mother loves more than her wardrobe is her reputation."

I ran my thumb over the label, considering his words.

"If you think that little show he put on after the game was bad, then you wouldn't have survived my house. I didn't play hockey because I wanted to. I played because he expected it. Did I learn to love it? Sure. But I was also terrified every time I stepped onto the ice because I knew what he would do to me if I performed...poorly. And it wasn't like we spent our weekends at the rink or even five days a week for practices. We had a rink at my fucking house. He made us skate every day. It wasn't just training, it was punishment. Laps. Shots. Drills. All of it. There aren't any cutsie pictures of me grinning in my gear like that one." He pointed to the frame.

I'd been a squirt, ten years old, and my mother had her arms around me as I smiled wide, proudly showing off my championship medal from whatever tournament we'd been at.

"Nicolai was lucky, too. His ACL went out in college, so he never played again." He shook his head. "I would have rather been the secret."

"I wanted a dad."

"You wouldn't have wanted ours."

I thought about the few interactions I'd had with Sergei and couldn't argue with Maxim's point.

"I've hated you since we were eight," Maxim admitted, no shame in his gaze. "You were this intangible threat to my family. I never would have signed with the Reapers if I'd known they were bringing you back."

"Don't hold back on my account." Sarcasm saturated every word.

He smiled. "Never will."

"You took my house."

"I had no idea it had been yours. Guess we have the same taste in architecture." He shrugged.

"And women."

His hands stilled. "She's why I'm here."

"Really? I thought maybe you wanted to walk me through our ancestry."

"Are you ever not sarcastic?" His eyes narrowed on me.

"Nope." I put the bottle on the counter. "You have no right to talk to me about London."

"She's miserable." His shoulders fell. "Her eyes are swollen and red. She looks like she hasn't slept in weeks, and her smile is just…gone."

My chest clenched at the mental picture he presented. "That makes two of us, I guess. But what do you care? You got what you wanted, right? Because it was never about London for you. It was only about taking something else from me."

"The way you put it makes me sound like an asshole, but yeah. I guess." Was that a flash of remorse in his eyes?

"You are an asshole," I countered. "And I loved London. I fell for her in that elevator before I even knew you were on the team. Finding out that you two had a history was…" I shook my head.

"We're just friends."

"I didn't want you to be just *anything*. I've spent the last thirteen years of my life being told I wasn't allowed in your world, so who the fuck are you to waltz in and take over mine?" The injustice of it all was just fucked up.

"Valid point, but in my defense, London has been in my life a hell of a lot longer than yours," he challenged.

We were both right, and we knew it, but that didn't break the tension.

"I called you my brother the other day," he said quietly, dropping his gaze to the water bottle between his hands. He'd picked the label off completely. "It just kind of came out. But I guess we can't really help the fact that biologically, that's what we are. Brothers."

The word hung between us, equal parts explosive and white flag.

Mom was right. We had both been kids, and neither of us had a say in what we'd been born into. And yeah, he was an ass, but maybe I would have been, too, if I'd grown up in that house.

I turned around and grabbed two plates from the cabinet, then dished out a thick slice of cheesy lasagna onto each. Then I put a fork on each plate and slid one over the granite to him.

He caught it and looked at me with raised brows.

"My mom made it yesterday. It'll change your life." I brought my plate and water around the island and took the stool two seats down from his, forking the first bite into my mouth.

"Damn. It's good," Maxim muttered a few bites later. "You said *loved*."

"I'm sorry?"

"When you talked about London, you said *loved*. Not *love*. Do you still love her?" He glanced my way but quickly looked back to his plate.

Maybe it was the lasagna or the weird, landmine-laced, tentative peace between us, but there really wasn't a point lying to him, was there? "I will love London Foster until the day I die. She's the one. She's it, whether or not she ever believes that I didn't go after her because of your jackass bet comment. Even if we're never together again, my soul belongs to that woman." My heart fucking *ached* with how much I loved her.

"Then take some big brother advice and go after her."

"Big brother." I snort-laughed.

"I'm four months older than you." He shrugged. "And if it were me, and I was that far gone for a girl, and it was just a misunderstanding and some wounded pride in the way, I'd fix it."

"Well, you're not me. We're nothing alike." It wasn't just wounded pride. It was...*shit*. Fine, it was slayed pride if I was being honest.

"Yeah. Keep telling yourself that." He motioned to my water bottle.

I'd picked the label off just like he had.

"She believed you."

"Yeah. Well, I thought I was right at the time, and I'm very convincing." He chugged down his water. "Was there any part of you that did it—went after her—just to spite me?"

I shook my head. "No. I didn't want you with her. I was afraid you'd hurt her—emotionally. But I just *wanted* her. Right from the first moment I saw her."

"I'd never hurt London." He bristled. "Not that I'd be good for her, either. Mostly I just wanted to fuck with you. But I believe you, and if I can sit here and say I was wrong, then I think you can probably put on a tux and make her believe she was wrong, too. I'd say go over tonight and beg her to listen to you, but we both know she won't open the door. She's stubborn like that. Besides, a tuxedo is a damn fine weapon against the fairer sex." He smirked.

The New Year's Eve party. It was this weekend.

"Again, just some brotherly advice." For the first time since we'd met on the ice when we were twenty-two, there was no hatred in his eyes.

"She kept me a secret. Just like our father." There it was, the real heart of the matter.

"Yeah. Well, you're just going to have to forgive her for that," he said softly.

"We're not having a moment." I forked in another bite.

"Wouldn't dream of it." He went back to his lasagna, but he was smiling.

He was right. London wasn't going to listen to me unless I caught her in public. She would slam the door in my face before I got a word out.

And even I could admit, I looked pretty damned good in a tux, but what was I going to do if she wanted to take our relationship under whatever was left of the radar?

All or nothing. That had to be the line.

I was done being anyone's dirty little secret.

18

LONDON

I checked myself in the bathroom mirror once again, my stomach fluttering with nerves. The dress I wore was glittering black with an A-line and thin black straps. A side slit exposed one leg all the way up to my hip, and the rest of the dress flowed around me in puddles of silk, stopping just above my ankles. The black pumps I wore strapped around the ankle, and since the dress was elegant enough, I opted for no jewelry and clean makeup.

Tonight was the night I'd worked toward all season.

New Year's Eve.

But that wasn't why my nerves were tangled—it was because I couldn't stop wondering if Jansen would show up.

It had been a little over two weeks since the mess at Reaper Arena, and I *missed* him. I missed him so much it was like someone had carved out a piece of my soul.

The black fabric sparkled in the lights, and I blew out a breath, nodding to myself in the mirror. If he did show, I thought I might catch his eye.

At least I hope.

Because if I'd learned anything from the last two weeks without him, it was the absolute knowledge that I didn't want to *be* without him. Even if he'd started dating me because of a revenge plot, it didn't change how he'd made me feel. How I *knew* he felt about me. Time and space from the situation had forced that clarity into my mind. Jansen wouldn't have done all he did just to irk Maxim. He wouldn't help me conquer my fear, wouldn't go out of his way to truly understand what made me *me*.

And in the end, that's all that mattered. If he showed tonight —to the event I'd stressed was the most important for my career—then it would be a sign he wanted me as badly as I wanted him. If I didn't actually matter to him? If I was just a pawn in a game against his brother? Then he wouldn't show up. Wouldn't be here to support me.

And I'd have to find a way to live with it.

I emerged from the bathroom and was met with the delightful sounds of an event in full swing. My chest swelled with pride as I sashayed through the clusters of the guests, all dressed in their finest. Some sipped champagne, others drank liquor from crystal tumblers, and some nibbled on the delights being served on silver platters. Chatter and laughter and music bounced off the walls, and I couldn't be prouder of the turnout. So many pro-athletes, team owners, and celebrities had shown up at my request, each one of them emptying their deep pockets for such a good cause.

I walked toward the mahogany and marble bar, gazing toward the wall of windows surrounded by brick. Moonlight glittered off the Ashley River just outside, the Historic Rice Mill building providing the absolute perfect space to host this event. Charleston's Ronald McDonald House was less than a mile away, and most of the staff, volunteers, and organizers were already enjoying the event.

Caz chatted with a petite girl with jet-black hair and thick black-rimmed glasses at the opposite end of the bar but waved to me when he saw me. I lifted my champagne flute to him but was content where I was at. I'd mingled earlier, and with how much pressure had been riding on this event, I was ready to relax and enjoy the fruits of my labor.

"That's some dress," a familiar male voice said, and I couldn't help but drop my shoulders just a tad as I turned to face him.

Maxim looked stunning in his all-black tux, but he wasn't the brother I'd been hoping would seek me out. "Thank you," I said. "You look nice too."

"May I?" he asked, motioning to the empty spot next to me at the bar.

I nodded, my heart in my throat. I hated that in the back of my head, I wondered what Jansen would think if he walked in and saw me chatting with Maxim. But, if we were ever going to work things out, he needed to trust me. Plus, it wasn't like I was just going to suddenly stop being friends with Maxim, even if we did have some issues to work through. Also, Jansen may not even show. That thought stung worse than any other.

"I wanted to apologize," he said after ordering a drink. "Properly, this time. That day...I was livid for many reasons. Most of which had nothing to do with you or Sterling."

I arched a brow. "Need to share?"

The line of his jaw hardened, and that familiar darkness swirled in his eyes. Maxim had so many walls up it was a shock he could speak around them at all. "Not today," he said, but I heard the words for what they were—*not with you.*

And I respected that. There were weights only certain people could bear, and I knew I wasn't that person for Maxim. I had been that person for his brother, and I hoped like hell it meant something.

"I understand," I said, and also had hope in my heart for *him.* Hope that he would find someone to bear his scars to, someone to help him see past his hatred, the darkness that clung to him. "And you don't have to apologize again, Maxim," I continued. "You've done so already, several times." And it meant a lot to me that he wanted to save our friendship, especially since he'd become a regular part of my life with his friendship with Caspian. It would've been terribly awkward if we'd hated each other and yet were still forced to see each other on the reg.

"I wanted to, though," he said. "And I needed you to know the truth. A truth I wasn't willing to see before."

I took a sip of my champagne, tilting my head.

"Sterling didn't pursue you because of any plot against me," he said. "And I'm an asshole for even thinking that. Not because I'm a new fan of his—I'm not," he clarified. "But because I *am* a fan of yours. You're smart and funny and understanding. Gorgeous, to say the least, and you can keep up with the guys." Heat flushed my cheeks at his words. "Anyone who goes after you, myself included, can see why you're a catch. I shouldn't have thought there would be any other reason for Sterling wanting you other than you're incredible."

I swallowed around the rock in my throat. "Maxim," I said, and his name sounded like an apology. "I..." What could I say? That I was sorry for not choosing him? For not going out with him when he'd asked? For falling in love with his brother?

"It's okay," he said, waving off my clear struggle for words. "You were right about what you said in the bar a couple of weeks ago. I always knew you were a catch, but I never thought about it that way until I saw how Sterling looked at you." He flashed me an apologetic look. "And you were right about me not wanting anything serious. I'm not the commit-ment guy. I can't be that guy for anyone...but we *would've* had fun," he teased, showing just the tiniest smirk that no doubt would normally melt panties.

Not mine, though. Not when there was only one man I wanted, needed.

"Oh, I have no doubt," I said, laughing as I shook my head. "But Jansen..." I sighed, unable to fully encompass what he meant to me. "He's my island."

Maxim tilted his head, confusion flickering in his gaze before he shrugged. "I get it," he said, straightening his immaculate suit. "Why you fell for him. I mean, my DNA *is* irresistible."

I laughed again and sighed when he slipped his arms around me in a friendly hug.

"I hope everything works out for you," he said, releasing me.

"You too, Maxim," I said, and he dipped his chin before he snagged his drink and headed back into the party.

My chest settled with that little piece of closure, but I couldn't stop myself from scanning the room full of guests.

No sign of Jansen, but...

Oh, fuck, was that Asher Silas heading my direction?

I drank the rest of my champagne in one gulp, my heart racing at the reasoning why Silas would single me out tonight. What if he hated the event? What if we hadn't raised enough money? What if—

"This is a fantastic event," he said by way of greeting, settling into the spot Maxim had just vacated. I released a breath so loud he laughed. "Did you think I was coming over here to reprimand you?"

I chuckled nervously. "Sorry," I said. "I'm nervous. I love the Reapers, and I wanted to make you proud." God, did that sound cheesy? I couldn't help it, it was the truth.

"Well, you've certainly done that," he said, and the bartender set a drink before him. He hadn't even ordered one. The bartender appeared to know who he was and exactly what he liked. Damn, what was it like to be a billionaire with that kind of influence and power? And with how young he still was? His rugged good looks? I couldn't imagine the kind of advances and scandals he dealt with on a daily basis. And here I thought being in the middle of two brother's painful history was bad.

"Thank you," I said, another knot of nerves loosening. "I love this job."

"It shows," he said, taking a sip of his drink. "I hope you plan to stay with us."

"Where else would I ever go?"

Silas grinned. "I have a few owner buddies who've made a game in trying to poach my employees."

"Like Weston Rutherford?" His eyebrows raised, and I waved him off. "My best friend is married to Hendrix Malone."

"Ah," he said. "So you know a few of my friends."

I nodded. "I'm not going anywhere."

"Good."

And now that I had his approval...

"Can I be totally honest with you?" I asked, my heart in my throat. God, I hoped I wasn't about to blow what trust I'd just earned from him.

"I'd prefer it," he said, his tone so business-like I wondered if he always had his owner's hat on or if he ever let loose.

"What are your thoughts on..." I swallowed hard. "Players and staff...fraternizing?" I had no other way to ask, but I couldn't *not* ask. Not if I wanted to continue with my career and hopefully, possibly ever mend things with Jansen.

A small, almost sad smile shaped his lips. He looked down at the amber liquid in his crystal tumbler before his eyes glanced across the room. His sister Harper danced with Nathan Noble, one of his top players. "It's never bothered me before. As long as the job gets done," he said, returning his attention to me. "Who am I to stand in the way of people who are actually capable of finding real love?"

I parted my lips, my heart snagging on the flicker of pain in his hazel eyes. I wondered over his statement, wondered how hard it might be for a billionaire like him to discern real affection from false. But before I could express my gratitude or my concern, he scooped his tumbler from the bar and motioned it toward the party. "Speaking of," he said, then gave me a wink and sauntered into the fray.

My eyes followed where he'd motioned, and my heart stopped before it took off at a gallop.

Jansen Sterling stood at one of the tables near the entryway, chatting with Briggs. He looked good enough to *eat* in a crisp dark tuxedo, those crushing blue eyes striking even from across the room.

He looked so damn wonderful, I thought my knees might *actually* buckle.

19

STERLING

*T*he party was in full swing by the time I got there at eleven p.m. Having spotted an empty seat next to Briggs, I tugged at my bowtie and made my way across the busy ballroom. The fucking suit was tailored to me, and yet I still felt choked, but that could have been nerves, too.

London hadn't been our coordinator for the last two games, which meant I hadn't even seen her since before Christmas, and yet here I was, ready to shoot my shot.

"There you are," Briggs said as I took the chair next to his at one of the tables that lined the dance floor. He rolled a glass of amber liquid between his palms, and I could tell from the bubbles that it was ginger ale.

"Did I miss anything exciting?" I glanced over the dancing couples like I wasn't looking for London, but who was I kidding? I was looking for London.

"If you count Langley hauling off the rookies by their ears after they got trashed out of their minds, then maybe." He laughed and thanked a waitress who put another tumbler of amber liquid on our little table. "It's ginger ale," he said, pushing it toward me.

"I figured. Thanks." I took a sip of the sweet stuff, hoping it would calm the nausea that rose in my gut every time I thought about getting an answer out of London.

"It keeps women from offering to buy me a drink." He shrugged.

"Good point." The band switched songs, playing something a little slower that sounded like it was from the forties. "Hey, I heard you signed a new endorsement yesterday."

He nodded, sipping his drink. "Lusso Men's Wear." He motioned to the tux.

"No shit?" I loved Lusso. It was a little higher priced than what I usually went for, but everything high end was.

"Shocked the hell out of me, but I snapped it up."

"Hi." A blonde in a strapless dress came over and leaned on the table next to Briggs, adjusting her arms so her breasts swelled above her neckline.

"Uh. Hey." Briggs gave her a once-over and smiled.

"You're Cormac Briggs, right?" she asked, looking at him like he was on the damned menu.

"That's me."

I sipped my drink and turned my attention back to the dance floor. This was London's event, so she had to be here somewhere. But instead of London, I saw Brogan Grant making his way toward us.

If I thought I felt uncomfortable in a tux, that guy had to be downright tortured by the way he was tugging at his sleeves.

"I don't want to be here," he said as he took the spot next to me.

"Better than face painting with kids?" I asked.

He grunted.

The girl worked her hand up Briggs's chest, and he moved back suddenly, putting his drink on the table.

"Yeah, I'm going to have to see some ID before you put your hands anywhere near me."

I nearly spit out my drink.

Even Brogan looked over with his brows raised.

"You're fucking kidding me, right?" The girl glared at Briggs.

"Nope. I'm the adult version of Disneyland, and only eighteen and up get to ride." He folded his arms across his chest.

Wow.

"Okay, now I'm glad I came," Brogan muttered.

The girl started to curse Briggs out for assuming she was anything younger than twenty-one as the band finished their song, then played a short-blasted two-tone harmony like an announcement was about to be made.

We all turned to face the stage, and my breath caught.

There she was.

London stood in the center of the stage with Silas, and damn did she look good. Her dress flowed along her curves way that made my mouth water, and her hair was in some twisted updo, leaving her neck bare. My heart launched into a straight gallop.

"Thank you so much for being here tonight," Silas said, pausing while the crowd gave him a round of applause. "Giving back to the community is something that every Reaper takes pride in. We aren't just happy to help out the Ronald McDonald house tonight, we're honored. And for tonight's biggest announcement, let me turn over the mic to the woman who put this all together, London Foster." He handed the microphone to London.

My chest swelled with pride.

"Thank you. I'm so very happy that you guys all showed up!" She laughed, and the crowd did, too. "Together we've raised a half-million dollars for the Ronald McDonald House. And that's just the beginning." She smiled and held out her hand, beckoning to someone off stage. "I'm so proud to announce that with the help of Lusso Design, we've been able to write a one million dollar check to the Ronald McDonald House!"

The crowd exploded in applause, and I was right there with them. Fuck, she was amazing.

A young woman with glossy, black curls in a long black dress walked out onto the stage, wearing a million-watt smile. The woman was gorgeous—though she wasn't close to holding a candle to London—and easily a good five inches taller than my girl.

"You have to be fucking kidding me." Briggs tensed beside me.

"Who is that?" I asked Briggs quietly.

"And we're so lucky to have the brand-new CEO and lead designer, Bristol McClaren, with us here tonight!" London announced, handing the microphone over.

"Thank you so much for having me," Bristol said from the stage.

"*That* is who got me fucking traded." Briggs looked like he'd seen a ghost. "In all fairness, her brother did the trading. She was just the catalyst."

"Good looking catalyst," Brogan muttered next to me.

"Wait…" The gears in my brain turned. "Didn't you say Lusso…"

"Fuck me," Briggs pushed away from the table and walked straight to the bar.

London made her way off stage. This was my chance. "I'll be right back," I said to Brogan, then hauled ass around the dance floor to intercept her.

Shit, this crowd was *massive,* and London wasn't exactly tall. I raced for the entrance to the ballroom. At least I'd be able to catch her if she was leaving.

I wiped my sweaty palms on the fabric of my pants as the crowd parted and London appeared. Her gaze locked with mine and my heart fucking stopped.

Ten feet, that was all that separated us, and we were coming closer with every step she took in my direction. But hey, she wasn't running the other direction, so that had to be a good sign.

Within seconds she was right in front of me, a determined glint in her eyes that could go either way for me.

"You weren't a goddamned bet." It came out as a growl.

"I know," she said softly. "Maxim told me."

Of course, she fucking believes him.

"Which apparently was not the right thing to say," she bit her lower lip and looked left, then tugged me through a door and into…the coat closet. We were in a coat closet.

"Can you give us a second?" London asked the attendant.

The guy took one look between the two of us and walked out.

London locked the door, then leaned back against it, like she needed to block my exit.

"We're in a coat closet." A very small, very confined coat closet.

"I'm okay," she assured me, keeping her eyes locked on mine. "As long as you're in here with me, I'm okay. Jansen, I knew," she rushed. "Before Maxim told me, I knew. The more I thought about it, I knew there was no way you'd do something like that. That's not who you are."

I leaned back against the attendant's counter. "You stole my line." She knew. *She knew.* I didn't know if I wanted to sag in relief or fuck her against the door. "I had a whole speech planned about how I fell for you in that elevator, and now it seems pretty pointless."

Her eyes flared. "Not pointless! I want to hear your speech!" The plea in her eyes was my undoing.

I arched a brow at her as my heart thudded to a steady beat and gravity shifted back to where it belonged. My steps were slow as I closed the distance between us. "I fell for you in the elevator, and no, it wasn't just because you were the most beautiful woman I'd ever seen. I fell for you when we were on the floor, when I saw just how hard you fought to keep calm."

Her hands rose to my chest as I caged her in on one side, flattening my palm against the door next to her head.

"I fell for you on the roller coaster and again when I kissed you for the first time. The fact that Maxim appeared between the elevator and the roller coaster never changed how I felt about you. Was I jealous that he said he was going to date you? Yeah. I'd be jealous of any guy who said he wanted to date you. I'd work my ass off to prove that I'm the right choice." I leaned down and brushed my lips over the shell of her ear, breathing her in. "I will *always* prove that I'm the right choice."

"Jansen." She gripped the lapels of my tux.

"I love you, London." I rested my forehead against hers. "There is so much about life I don't know. I don't know if I'll always get to play for the Reapers. I don't know if I'll get injured in the next game or play until I'm too slow to keep up. I have no clue if Maxim is suddenly becoming more relatable or I'm losing my mind, and I have *no* clue what to do with the voicemail my sister left me this morning. *My sister.*" I palmed her waist. "The only thing I'm certain of is that I love you with every bone in my body, London Foster."

"Oh, Jansen, I love you, too." She brought her mouth to mine and licked her tongue along the seam of my lips.

I groaned and kissed her, tangling our tongues. She tasted like champagne and home, and while I'd gone hard at the damned sight of her, this was a whole new level of need.

My hand slipped through the slit in her dress to find her bare thigh, and she gasped, breaking the kiss.

"Wait."

I froze.

257

"I'm not hiding us anymore…if there's an us. If that's what your speech was saying." Her eyes searched mine, worry creasing her brow. "That there's an us."

"There's an us," I assured her.

A smile flitted across her face. "Good, because I realized that yeah, I really love this job, and I want the position at the end of the year, but not if it comes at the cost of losing you. I don't want to sneak around or hide what you mean to me."

Her words were breathing life back into my soul, but— "I'm not going to be the reason you don't get the job." I refused to be the one standing in her way.

"You won't. That's what I'm saying. I asked Silas, and he's fine with players and staff fraternizing as long as the job gets done." She grinned.

"You…" I smiled slowly, letting this feeling fill me to the brim until it overflowed. "You talked to Silas."

She nodded.

"Because you want us to be public." I needed the words. Too much had gone wrong between us because we hadn't said them in the past.

"So public." She kissed my chin. "So, so, so public." Her hands slid down my chest, my stomach, and then she grasped my dick through my pants. "Like. Right. Now. Public."

Hell yes. I had her legs around my waist before I could even voice the thought. Our mouths collided. Fabric moved. My zipper came undone. I pulled her panties to the side.

She was wet and slick and so fucking hot.

"Please." She tunneled her fingers through my hair.

I slid inside her, and it was everything.

"God. London." I took her hard and deep, kissing her exactly the same way. I couldn't get close enough. Our hearts pounded. The door rocked with every thrust.

She went tight around me, and I angled her hips so I ground against her clit. Fuck, I was close, but I needed her there with me.

"I fucking love you, London."

She came apart in my arms, and I swallowed her cries with a kiss, tumbling right after her.

Finally, we were whole. We were home.

"I love you," she said as our breathing calmed.

"Good." I grinned. "How about I take you home and do this properly? You know, naked. Maybe in a bed?"

Her fingers stroked over my cheeks and the same joy I felt radiated in her eyes. "Oh no. We're dancing, and you're kissing me at midnight. In front of everyone."

"Now that's a plan I can get behind."

We smiled.

When we danced.

And at midnight, I kissed her senseless in front of everyone in that ballroom.

"I didn't think this much stuff could fit in your tiny apartment," Jansen called as he closed the front door behind him. He set the last of my boxes near the stairs, smirking at me.

I walked up to him, wrapping my arms around his neck. "Are you regretting this?" I asked, twirling the diamond around my ring finger.

"Hell no," he said, shaking his head as he snaked his arms around my waist. "I can't wait until you take my name and everyone knows who you belong to."

Warmth flushed my skin, and I trembled as he hauled me against him. "I love you," I said before pressing my lips to his.

He slid his tongue between mine, and I arched into him.

This. Would. Never. Get. Old.

Tasting his kiss, feeling his body, having him to come home to, and vice versa. It didn't matter that we'd had months of bliss between us, I wanted it forever. Which is why it hadn't been even a hesitation when he'd proposed.

"How badly do you want to unpack?" he asked, breaking our kiss long enough to speak.

I shook my head, and hopped up. He caught me without a blink, and I locked my ankles around his back. "Not even a little bit."

He smirked against my mouth. "Where should I make love to you today?"

"Anywhere," I sighed between his lips. "As long as it's *now*."

"Greedy woman," he teased, turning us into the living room just off the entryway. He settled me onto the leather sofa, his weight a delicious thing between my legs.

"Only for you," I said, and that wonderful pride and happiness swelled in his blue eyes. I cupped his cheek, making sure he could see the love shining through in mine.

"Always for you," he said before lowering his mouth to mine.

Always sounded just about this side of perfect, and I would cherish every single second of it.

THE END

Thank you so much for reading! If you love these alphas and want to try something with a little more bite, check out my brand-new, steamy vampire romance, Crimson Covenant!

NEW TO THE REAPERS? The NHL's been at Axel's door since he was eighteen, but he'd never leave the Swedish hockey league while he was raising his little brother. But now he's

SAMANTHA WHISKEY

grown, and the Carolina Reapers are at Axel's door with his greatest weakness: Langley Pierce. The fierce and fiery publicist has sworn off men, but if she wants him to accept her proposed contract, she'll have to accept his...proposal. Read Axel, book one in the Carolina Reapers series here!

WANT MORE HOT HOCKEY ROMANCE? The rink gets steamy when star NHL player Gage McPherson falls for his bff/nanny—click here to read their story and binge the whole Seattle Sharks series today!

CRIMSON COVENANT

Chapter One
Alek

The massive, formal front door of my estate swung open before I could so much as reach for the handle.

"Welcome home, my king." Serge bowed his head and made room for me to pass. The guy was dressed in a suit, which was as casual as he got. He took his job as the head of the talem—our immortal stewards—just as seriously as I took my position as king.

"You know I was only gone for an hour, Serge. Relax a little. Maybe let me get the door every once in a while." The sound of my boots echoed off the vaulted ceiling as I strode through the marble entry and past the sweeping, dual staircases that led to the second floor.

"As soon as I'm dead, sir," Serge called after me.

I shook my head as I made my way into the expansive ballroom that consumed a quarter of the estate's floorplan. We used the hall for celebrations, official court business, and all the other glitzy shit I couldn't stand. Suited talem made their way down the four long tables that ran perpendicular to a raised dais, filling crystal goblets with fresh, crimson blood for the evening repast.

I muttered a curse. It was already ten o'clock, and none of the nobility had risen from their guest rooms yet. Lazy fucks.

Lachlan, my second in command, stood at the foot of the dais, looking as out of place in his leather and tats as I did. He was a hulking brute of a warrior with thick red hair and two Glocks openly holstered beneath his arms. No doubt one was loaded with regular ammunition and the other, silver. His eyes narrowed as I approached. Lesser vampires withered under that stare. I was anything but lesser.

"You look hungry or pissed, and I'm hoping it's the first," he said with a raised brow and a highland burr that even three hundred years on this continent hadn't dulled.

"I just fed." I reached his side, then turned to survey the hall as the first of the nobles trickled in, dressed like they were going to the opera, not just the first meal of the night.

"Pissed it is," the Scotsman noted, turning to one of the talem who was making his way up the steps to the table I was supposed to be sitting at. "Don't bother. He won't drink the canned shite, anyways."

True.

The talem nodded and took his pitcher to the next table.

"Alek, it would make my job protecting you a wee bit easier if you'd feed on the estate." He nodded to the left, where a door led to a sumptuous, velvet upholstered room where willing humans waited eagerly for a set of fangs at their veins.

"I never said I needed your protection." It was the same argument we'd had for the last few hundred years.

"For fuck's sake," Lachlan muttered. "They're right here. They want it. They sign waivers. Though there's something to be said for the days when they didn't." He flashed a grin at me.

"Did he go out to eat again?" Ransom asked with a smirk as he joined us at the foot of the platform. "Can't blame him. The feeders get a little territorial when he's involved. It's like we're back in the good 'ol harem days." He gave a wistful sigh.

"You weren't alive in the harem days, jackass. None of us were. And don't encourage him." Lachlan shook his head and grumbled something about useless nobles as he looked down the tables.

There were half a dozen aristocrats in the hall now, all from the finest families, and they'd all chosen seats at the farthest end from the dais. This court was respected, admired, even emulated...but overall, it was feared.

We were feared.

I liked it that way.

I had no use for the simpering class of nobles who cared more about their proximity to the throne than they did for fighting to keep our species at the top of the immortal food chain. While all vampires were dangerous, those who served in the Order were the most lethal of our kind. We were bigger than average nobility, faster, stronger, and trained to carry out our duty by the Covenant—mete out the king's justice.

My justice.

We were called the Order of the Onyx Assassins, not only for the onyx medallion each of us carried from the day we were initiated, but the death delivered by our hands.

"How long are these festivities, anyway?" Lachlan's gaze moved from one noble to the next, assessing any potential threat as another one of my warriors joined us.

Benedict stood at my left and crossed his arms over his chest.

"Until equinox. Half the nobility aren't even here yet," Ransom answered, clearly enjoying Lachlan's discomfort. "Has Lenora already cornered you? Rumor has it she's looking to get her oldest daughter mated."

"Fuck that." Lachlan flinched.

"He's not lying," Benedict added with a touch of a smile. A quick glance at the unchanged, black tattoos on Benedict's arms confirmed Ransom's honesty. Whenever someone lied around Benedict, the exact words of that lie appeared on the skin of his forearm in a fresh, black tattoo. Most vampires outside our circle kept their mouths shut around him for that exact reason.

Ransom laughed, drawing the attention of the newest nobles. All female, of course. Just because they feared us didn't mean they didn't like to fuck us.

"One day, your mouth is going to get you into trouble, lad," Lachlan muttered.

"Doubt that." Ransom shrugged, his silver screen smile only widening. He was definitely the prettiest in the Order...and as my master of combat, he was also the deadliest.

"Where's Hawke?" I asked, noticing the surly warrior hadn't made an appearance.

"Waiting for us in the bat cave," Ransom answered. "He knows he scares even the purebloods."

We all turned to stare at the combat master.

"What?" he asked with a shrug.

"Stop calling it the bat cave," Lachlan ordered.

A muscle in my jaw ticked as the room filled with more and more nobles. Jeweled wives, mate-seeking mothers, conniving males, ambitious sons, and star-eyed daughters all looked to us—to me. I had no problem leading them. I just didn't want to socialize with them. I preferred the company of vampires who actually *worked* for a living.

"What am I supposed to call it?" Ransom argued.

"Council Chambers?" Benedict offered.

"Come on, it's pretty much a bat cave," Ransom argued. "And I don't see Alek arguing."

I cocked a brow but kept my thoughts to myself. In twenty-four hours, I'd be responsible for one more noble under this roof—one that wouldn't leave at the end of the week's festivities. One I loved more than my throne.

"You honestly think our king should weigh in on whether or not you get to call the war room where our Order meets the bat cave?" Lachlan growled.

Benedict muttered a curse under his breath, then leaned in slightly. "Cassandra Zorin, two o'clock."

My gaze shifted between the third and fourth tables on the right, and sure enough, Cassandra Zorin was breaking from her family to head this way. As purebloods went, she was strikingly beautiful, with long, black hair, high cheekbones, dark eyes, and a lithe figure. She was the logical choice to make, were I to finally choose a queen.

I just didn't want her.

"Fuck," Lachlan mumbled as she came closer.

"My king," she said, whisper-soft, dropping into a curtsy before me with feigned submissiveness. The female would no doubt eat her future young if it meant getting the seat beside me, though the look in her eyes as she glanced over my leather jacket, black T-shirt, and pants said she'd rather eat *me*.

"Good evening, Cassandra," I said in greeting, forcing my manners to the surface. "The hall looks nice. Thank you for seeing to the decorations." I tried to smile. It didn't happen.

Benedict pressed his lips in a firm line and his arms tightened over his chest.

The female practically glowed under the compliment and offered me a coy smile. "Well, as the ranking female of the line of Zorin…" She tilted her head in thought. "The ranking female in *every* house, now that I think of it," she chuckled. "It was not only my duty but my pleasure to prepare the hall for your sister's visit."

"My sister, Avianna, is the ranking female of every house, and she's not visiting. She's returning." I locked down every negative thought in my mind and pictured a vast, empty field. My thoughts had gotten the best of me too many times over the years, and having the strongest compulsion gift in our species—the results had been disastrous. Just because I sarcastically thought someone should fling themselves off the roof didn't mean I actually wanted it to happen.

"Of course she is, and we look forward to her return tomorrow evening." Cassandra's smile slipped. "The court needs a female's touch."

Oh, for fuck's sake.

"And it shall have one in Avianna," Ransom interjected, saving my ass.

"My king, I believe we have a meeting about last night's justice," Lachlan added. "Hawthorne is waiting."

"He is," I agreed. "Cassandra." I nodded my head as custom dictated.

"King Alekxander." Her voice curled around my name in a way that made my stomach sour, and my jaw locked at the flash of color I saw on her forearm as she backed away, then retreated to the loving arms of her father.

"Did you fucking see that?" Ransom's gaze slowly turned toward me.

"Bring our meal to the chamber," Lachlan ordered one of the talem, who carried a tray of bacon and other meats.

Just because I'd fed tonight didn't mean I'd eaten.

"Yes, sir."

I strode from the hall, pushing open the French doors leading to the wide courtyard that separated the Domum— the formal, official rooms of the estate—from the residence, where I lived and trained with my warriors.

"Tell me that wasn't what I think it was," Benedict said once the doors were firmly shut behind us. He inched his way forward to walk in front, his eyes scanning the courtyard for any possible enemy.

"The lass inked herself with your seal, Alek." Lachlan's stride matched my own, just as it always did when we were anywhere outdoors. "At least, I'm assuming she did the inking herself." His eyebrows rose in question.

"If I'd mated, you'd know," I growled. The whole fucking immortal world would know if I'd found the *one* female fated for me. After over four hundred years of wondering if she'd show up, I'd made my peace with the possibility that she never would. Fate was an unforgiving bitch when it came to the losses our species had suffered during my reign.

Not that I'd condemn any female to the torture of living at my side.

"She's getting bolder," Ransom noted with a whistle as we approached the steel door to the residence. The Domum may be every inch a palace, but the *residence* was a fortress by my father's design. I'd simply kept the security updated with modern technology.

"She's a pain in my ass," I snapped as the door opened before us.

"My king, Hawthorne awaits you in the chamber, as well as your meal," Serge announced with a bow of his head.

"Weren't you just in the foyer?" Ransom asked as we swept by.

"I was told you were headed this way," he answered with a slight curve to his lips.

"Fast fucker," Ransom muttered.

Speed was the only gift given to the talem, and Serge had mastered it.

We passed through the entry, and my senses told me there was no one upstairs. Good. Only invited guests and the four warriors in the Order were allowed unescorted entrance here.

"Do we really have to put up with all the nobles until equinox?" Lachlan asked as we made our way to the back of the house, passing my office, the dining room, the sitting room, a commercial-sized kitchen, and the den, which Hawke had outfitted with an eighty-five-inch television and surround sound. He claimed it was for watching football.

Personally, I thought he liked to hear the bones break.

"It's tradition," Benedict said over his shoulder as he descended the stone staircase first, his hand on his hip holster. I didn't bother telling him that Hawke was the only other male in this house—it was good for him to be alert.

Complacency was our number one enemy.

Complacency had killed my parents.

"Don't tell me you aren't enjoying having those sweet, doe-eyed females warm your bed," Ransom shot from behind us.

"I have no problem taking a lass to her bed. I'll be *damned* if one sets a toe in mine. You let a woman sleep in your bed, and you may as well unpack her suitcase into your closet," Lachlan said as we reached the riveted steel door at the bottom of the staircase.

My senses stretched along the tunnels that ran in both directions and found them empty. Given the party, our soldiers weren't training in the compound as usual, giving us a moment of relative quiet.

Benedict placed his palm on the biometric scanner, and a dozen steel bolts unlocked before the heavy door opened.

"It's about fucking time," Hawke snarled.

"There's a party going on, if you hadn't noticed," Benedict countered as we entered the chamber.

The space was cavernous, large enough to fit at least fifty warriors, but tailored only to the five of us. A black, onyx table rested in the center space, accompanied by five heavy chairs. A wall of monitors consumed the right-hand wall, with a few other notable computer stations spaced out along the back. To the left was a well-equipped kitchen, stocked with enough food and blood to last the five of us an unpleasant year in case of emergencies. A bathroom lay beyond that, and in the corner was a collection of couches and bookshelves with a television to keep us occupied if we ever needed that year.

My parents hadn't made it to the safety of this room two hundred years ago.

"So the fuck what?" Hawk fired back at Benedict from where he sat sprawled at the table in one of the massive chairs, flipping one of his daggers end-over-end.

The door shut behind us, and we each took a seat at the table. It wasn't round. I wasn't King Arthur. Fuck that. I was in charge, and everyone in this room knew it.

"Has the wolf been dealt with?" I asked Hawke.

"Justice has been served," he confirmed with a wicked grin and dead eyes. For the rest of us, dispensing the justice of the immortal world was a sworn, sacred duty. For Hawke...well, he got off on it.

"I'll let Luka know." The king of the lycans had agreed with my judgment against his subject, which definitely took the awkwardness out of the impending call.

Death was the penalty for any crime against a female or a child. Period. There was no excuse for the abuse of the fairer sex, and children were far too precious—too rare to ever suffer.

"That leaves the demon issue for tonight if you want this month's sentences carried out before Avianna gets home tomorrow. You also have a request from the Witch Queen for a private audience," Benedict said, filling the monitors with the faces of the lower-level demons who had been sentenced to torture for slander against their king. Sedition was still a punishable offense under their law.

"Xavier can handle his own. We're Assassins, not bounty hunters. Lachlan, check in with him tonight and make sure he's in control of the situation." I leaned back in my chair. "What the fuck does Genevieve want with a private audience? Any business she has can be discussed at the monthly gathering of Conclave, like always."

"So that's a no?" Benedict asked, raising his eyebrows.

"That's a fuck no. Granting private audiences is what leads to everything going to shit. We've worked too hard to keep the Covenant to let it crumble now." Keeping all five species—humans, lycans, witches, demons, and vampires—living in relative peace took a delicate balance of secrecy and transparency within the Conclave. It made human politics look like child's play.

"Okay, then I think all we have is the security detail for Avianna's arrival tomorrow," Lachlan said, leaning forward to brace his forearms on the table at my right.

I slid my phone free of my back pocket with a smile and called my little sister. "I'll just make sure she's on track," I said to the group while it rang.

It…rang.

It didn't beep like it always had, signaling that my sweet, beautiful, kind, honest sister wasn't overseas, tucked away with our aunt like she was supposed to be until tomorrow night.

"Alek?" she answered breathlessly.

"Where the hell are you?" I snapped.

"Oh, Alek, don't be mad!" She gave me a little sigh, and I could almost see her soft, pleading little smile. "I just wanted to see what it was like here, you know? I mean, you talk about it all the time, and I knew as soon as you showed up with your armored car and band of merry men—"

"I'm not Robin Hood, and that armored car is for your safety!" I shouted. "Tell me where you are, Avianna. Right now." I focused on the sounds coming through the phone. Birds. Crickets. Humans speaking English. My heart pounded and my stomach churned at the danger she was in. The borders between boroughs were clearly drawn, and if she'd stumbled into another territory, I couldn't guarantee her safety unless she was wearing an "Alek is my brother so don't fuck with me" T-shirt.

"I'm in the park father mentioned in his journals. Briarwood. The one across from the—"

"Slatemark Opera House," I growled. She was near the heart of the city—where all the territories intersected, but she wasn't in our sector. "Damn it, Avi, you're in Demon territory." I shoved back from the table and stood, my men instantly following.

"I'll get the car." Benedict didn't wait for me to approve. He ran, disappearing from sight before the door closed. Every man in this room was tasked with protecting the royal family. They knew the multitude of powers in my blood. They also knew that Avi didn't possess any beyond her considerable beauty and the compulsion ability all vampires shared.

She couldn't even wend—couldn't shift herself through space, and couldn't stand anyone —even me—controlling her for the moments it took to use our easiest mode of transportation, which meant we needed the car. Too many of Avianna's choices had been taken away. I'd never force wending on her if I could help it.

"I'm on my way. Stay exactly where you are." I pointed at Lachlan and Ransom, who both nodded. Hawke would only scare the shit out of Avianna, so that introduction would have to wait. Besides, there was no one better to leave behind to protect the compound.

"You're overreacting, Alek. I'm fine! We're just enjoying some of this delicious blue fluff the man with the cart sold us—"

"Us?" Cotton candy cart. I knew exactly where she was.

"I have Olivia, of course. I'm not completely naïve."

She had her bodyguard. At least there was that.

"Just stay there." I looked to Hawke. "Call Xavier now. Tell him if a demon puts a finger on my sister, I'll—"

"You're being ridiculous, but I'll wait right here, as ordered." She muttered, "jackass," before the line went dead.

"Fuck!" I shoved the phone in my back pocket, then reached under my leather jacket and unholstered my Glock as I looked at Lachlan and Ransom. "We go now."

I focused on the trees just behind the cotton candy cart in Briarwood Park and wended. My skin embraced the ice of the *between* in the seconds it took to shift places, and then the scent of sticky sugar and a hundred subtle variations of human blood filled my nose.

The park was in the center of Edgemont City, and of the three million humans that lived here, there were less than a few hundred that knew of our existence, all of whom were compelled to keep their mouths shut. The Opera House was at the center of it all, and she was on the wrong side of it.

I took a deep breath, sorting through the scents in an instant. Citrus, iron, cannabis, and apples. Vanilla and cinnamon hit me especially hard. My fangs descended despite having fed only a few hours ago. I pushed past that tantalizing warmth I knew had to be a human and caught the light hint of freesia that was Avianna.

"There." I started down the path at a normal walking pace. The Covenant's first commandment was to never expose the world of immortals that dwelled alongside the humans. Besides, it would have taken precious time to compel any human to forget they'd seen us if we did anything that brought undue attention.

"Son of a bitch." There was a demon just ahead, moving in the same direction as Avi's scent, passing an oblivious human jogger.

I wasn't surprised the jogger looked unbothered by the set of horns that had just blown by. Demons wore permanent glamours. Their supernatural features were invisible to the human eye.

My pulse galloped at the thought of Avi in demon hands, and I increased my pace. We came around the corner of the curved path to see the blue-horned demon shove a human woman out of his path, revealing a dagger in the moonlight.

My heart fucking stopped, as if the scent of vanilla and cinnamon was a physical fist around the blood-pumping organ. The blonde hit the pavement with a sharp cry, a stack of books skittering around her.

Avianna was only a hundred feet away, just beyond the next curve. I could smell her from here, and yet I was powerless against the overwhelming, unbreakable urge to make sure the demon hadn't killed the human. The cleanup was a pain in the ass.

I didn't have time to stop, and in the seconds it took to reach her, I battled the primal, base instinct that called me to the human…and I lost.

I fucking *lost*.

"Go," I ordered Ransom and Lachlan, pointing to the path ahead.

They didn't question the command—they valued their lives more than that. Lachlan would grumble at me privately, but never in front of anyone else.

I stopped suddenly in front of the human woman, dropping to my haunches and running my gaze over her frame in less time than it took my heart to beat. The scent of her blood made my mouth water, and I gritted my teeth against the craving. I ordered my fangs and my cock to stand down.

Damn, I hadn't even seen the woman yet, and I was hard—she smelled that good.

"Asshole!" she shouted down the path where the demon had run.

Obviously, it hadn't been a death blow.

"Are you okay?" I growled, annoyed as fuck at myself for checking on a human when my sister was in danger.

She shoved her mass of blonde hair out of her face and looked up at me with widening green eyes.

Fucking beautiful. I took in a breath reflexively, then wished I hadn't, because all I could smell was *her.*

Oh shit, I was fixating, which was as good as draining the woman right here. A fixated vampire hunted his prey no matter the consequences. The craving was too strong to deny, and it would drive us mad if we didn't satiate it.

Fixation, that's all this was…right? Her blood called to me.

"I'm fine," she said, her gaze flickering down the path again. "He barely got my forearm. But that asshole was chasing two other girls."

Avianna.

I blinked, trying to free myself of the fixation, the craving, but I didn't lunge or pounce on her as fixated vampires did. Instead, I took her wrist, testing her pulse. Quick, but strong, and given the change in her scent, flooded with adrenaline. Fuck, her skin was warm and soft. Perfect in every way.

Gravity shifted.

My chest tightened like a damned vise.

Electricity coursed through my veins.

Every cell in my body screamed one word—*mine*.

Wait. What the actual fuck?

"See? It's not bad." She lifted her arm, showing me the cut, and I bit back a growl. That demon had sliced into her delicate skin and—what if it was laced with poison?

A scream pierced the silence, and we both snapped our heads toward the sound.

Avianna. My heart lurched, worry quickly replaced with icy rage.

"Get out of the park," I ordered the human as I took off. "It's not safe." My sister's cry must have broken the fixation because my body was my own to command again.

"He was wearing a black hoodie and a Halloween mask with blue horns!" she called after me.

I sprinted faster than I should have and turned the corner in time to see four demons— including the one who'd attacked the human woman—advancing on my sister and her bodyguard.

Lachlan shot the first.

Ransom took out the second.

The remaining two stared at me with horror, but not surprise. They knew exactly who Avianna was and one of them had her under his knife.

I saw red, disappearing and wending, materializing in front of a yellow-eyed demon. "You attacked what is mine, and the sentence is death." I wrapped my hands around his neck and twisted, breaking his spine. "Justice served."

The last demon, the blue-horned one who had attacked the human, wended, leaving the three bodies behind.

I was going to fucking kill Xavier for this.

"Alek!" Avi cried, her slim figure racing toward me.

"Avi." I swept her into my arms and clutched her to my chest, cradling the back of her head. I'd lecture this one later. Right now, I just wanted to feel her breathing.

Guilt was heavy and sour in my mouth. How the fuck had I let myself get distracted with that human while Avi was in danger? I'd almost let my parents down. Let our entire species down. The loss of one female was tragic, but the loss of the princess? Unforgivable.

"Are you okay?" I asked her, cupping her cheeks and looking into her eyes. They were pale blue, just like mine. Just like our mother's.

"I'm fine, I promise." She gave me a shaky smile.

"Benedict is almost here with the car," Lachlan told me quietly as Ransom argued with Avi's bodyguard about the safety of the park.

"We need to get out of here before someone reports the gunshot," I told Avi. Humans were a nuisance, not that they could even tell the difference between demons—

The breath froze in my lungs.

She had. Cinnamon and vanilla. Blonde. Green eyes. *Impossible.* But she'd *seen* him. Even told me what he'd looked like.

A human had seen the demon's horns. Horns that by demonic nature, were hidden from human eyes by glamour.

I took a deep breath.

"Fuck." The distance of her scent told me she was long gone.

But I also knew I'd be able to track that scent anywhere in this city.

And I would.

CONNECT WITH ME!

Text SAMANTHA to 77222 to be the first to know about new releases, giveaways, & more!

Text VAMPIRE to 77222 to get all the paranormal news first!

Sign up here for my newsletter for exclusive content and giveaways!

Follow me on Amazon here or BookBub here to stay up to date on all upcoming releases! You can also find me at my website here!

ABOUT THE AUTHOR

Samantha Whiskey is a wife, mom, lover of her dogs and romance novels. No stranger to hockey, hot alpha males, and a high dose of awkwardness, she tucks herself away to write books her PTA will never know about.

ACKNOWLEDGMENTS

Thank you to my incredible husband and my awesome kids without which I would live a super boring life!

Huge thanks must be paid to all the amazing authors who have always offered epic advice and constant support! Not to mention creating insanely hot reads to pass the time with!

Big shout out to A.H. for making this shine. And thank you to each and every single one of you AMAZING readers who love the these books as much as I do!